THE
LAST
CONTRACT

OTHER WORKS BY PHILIP BENTALL

NOVELS

Stray Dog

Wild Flower

POETRY

Where Cows Are Met

THE
LAST
CONTRACT

a novel by

PHILIP BENTALL

RAMSGARD
PRESS

Published in Great Britain in 2023 by Ramsgard Press

ISBN: 979 839037 200 5

'If you want to keep a secret,
            you must also hide it from yourself.'
                        George Orwell, *Nineteen Eighty-Four*

'Memories are killing.'
                        Samuel Beckett, *The Expelled.*

1

'WHERE THE HELL is he?' Sean said, adjusting the van's wing mirror.

They'd been waiting for over an hour for this guy that their boss, Mr Hayes, wanted picking up and Sean was getting fidgety. He started playing with his hair in the mirror, done recently at his girlfriend's salon – shaved round the back and sides, left long on top.

Seeing him, Terry shook his head. 'You are vain, you know that?'

Readjusting the mirror, Sean said, 'I thought you said an hour?'

Terry folded his arms and looked across the car park. 'He'll be here.'

They were parked up in a van outside Hindley Golf Club and they could hear balls being struck on the driving range behind them.

Sean said, 'I wonder who he is.'

'Like I said. It's none of our business.'

'Yeah, I know, but—'

'But – nothing.'

It was the same with every job – no questions. Sean had

been working with Terry long enough to know better. But what with it being his first live cargo assignment, he couldn't help himself. 'He must have done something pretty bad, don't you think?' he said.

Terry turned and glared at him. 'Didn't you hear me?'

'All right,' Sean replied, holding up his hands in defence. He turned and looked out of the window. A silver-haired couple steered battery-powered golf carts across the car park. They stopped beside a BMW 730d, popped the boot, and loaded the clubs in the back. Having once stolen cars for a living, Sean knew the car was worth about twenty grand on the second-hand market – its keyless entry system requiring only a hacked radio to unlock it.

A cloud passed in front of the sun and a shade-line swept briefly across the car park. Watching it pass over, Sean asked, 'Any plans for the weekend?'

Terry shrugged. 'Fishing probably.' Terry was always fishing. Sean figured he didn't have much else.

'Me and Tash are going to that restaurant I told you about,' Sean said. 'With the Michelin star.'

Not looking round, Terry said, 'I wouldn't waste your money.'

'Why not? It's our anniversary. I want to take her somewhere nice.' It was Sean's dream to open his own restaurant one day.

'Her idea, was it?'

Sean looked at Terry, who was nearly twice his age, with his regulation buzz cut, jutting chin, and nicotine-stained fingers, and thought how he didn't want to turn out like him, doing this sort of work, not smiling, for the rest of his life. He had plans – like marrying Tash and setting up his own restaurant. He said, 'You know what your problem is, Terry?'

'What's that?' Terry replied, still not looking at him.

'You need to get a little romance back in your life. Take the missus out.' Sean grinned.

'Let her waste my money, you mean.'

'No. Show her your sensitive side. Open up a bit,' Sean said, still grinning.

Terry shook his head. 'It sounds like Tash has got you where she wants you to be.'

'What? How do you work that out?'

A golf ball pinged against something metallic and Terry glanced across at his wing mirror.

Sean said, 'Tash isn't like that actually.'

Terry replied, 'No?' without looking at him.

'I think you're just jealous, Terry.'

Terry ignored him and looked across the car park.

Sean said, 'You are, aren't you?'

'Give it a rest, Sean.'

'No. I want to know why you think Tash has got me where she wants.'

'We all have our place in the world,' Terry replied, 'nothing wrong with that. A hierarchy helps a species survive.'

'You what?'

Terry gave him a glance. 'You think you're somehow different?'

'Are we still talking about Tash here?'

'In a way.' Terry put his hand in his pocket and removed his tobacco pouch. 'As individuals, we are of almost no consequence. Our genes have potential, but that's about it.'

'What?'

'Our genes,' Terry said, opening his pouch. 'They have

immortality in their grasp, not us. We're just their temporary carriers.'

'Where did you get that from?'

Terry stripped a Rizla paper from its packet. 'Dawkins. *The Selfish Gene.*'

Sean watched, not for the first time, Terry purse his lips with concentration as he separated strands of tobacco and laid them along the trough of the Rizla paper.

'The point is,' Terry said, beginning to roll up the corners of the paper, 'we're here to pass on genes. That's about as significant as any of this gets. Think about it. In a hundred years' time, do you think anyone will remember any of us?'

'Yeah, right, Terry – whatever.'

'Like I said, it's our—' Terry stopped mid-sentence and looked across the car park.

'What is it?'

'It's him.'

Sean scanned the car park but couldn't see anyone. 'Where?'

'The clubhouse.' Terry licked along the gum of the Rizla.

'Are you sure?' Sean leant forward in his seat. 'I can't see him.'

Terry checked the photo lying on the dashboard of a man in his mid-thirties, slim, six-one – the man Sean now saw coming out of the clubhouse.

'Shit,' Sean said, sitting back in his seat again. 'It is him, isn't it?'

Terry, calmly removing loose strands of tobacco from the end of his rollie, said, 'Keep still.'

Sean realised he was juddering his leg and stopped.

Terry stuck the cigarette in his mouth and put on his cap.

'Are you ready?'

'Yeah, of course.' Sean felt his heart rate go up several notches. He let out a deep breath and ran his hands through his hair.

Terry asked, 'You remember what you've got to do?'

'Yeah. Drive round. Then pick you up.'

Terry reached for the door handle. 'Remember. Just take it slowly. Okay?'

'Yeah, sure.'

Terry got out of the van, closed his door and nodded at Sean through the window.

Sean nodded back at him, then pulled up the hood of his hoodie and started the van. His arms shook as he gripped the steering wheel and watched Terry head in the direction of the clubhouse. About halfway across the car park, Terry stopped and lit his cigarette; whether that was part of the plan, Sean couldn't remember.

The cargo came down the clubhouse steps, looking just like he did in the photo, Sean thought, dressed in beige chinos, polo shirt, and boat shoes. Only everything felt a lot realer than it had five minutes ago.

Sean looked back at Terry, puffing on his cigarette, and got ready to pull out. He knew he mustn't rush it – that he had to make it look like he was just driving round until Terry had the cargo. Releasing the handbrake, he was about to pull out when he saw the cargo stop and take out his phone. 'Shit!' he muttered, stopping the van.

He glanced across at Terry, who was now pretending to examine a large electric meter box. He felt his leg tremble as he held down the clutch, the engine idling. Then he glanced at the cargo speaking on his phone and thought how he looked like the sort of guy you'd expect to see at a golf club – mid-thirties, well-dressed, in good shape. Not the sort of guy about to be forced into the back of a van. But it was one thing looking at someone's photo and quite another seeing them in the flesh, Sean thought. He hadn't expected to feel so nervous. His pulse was racing like he'd taken a hit of amphetamines; his mouth was dry.

It had all seemed so easy when Terry explained it to him in the pub on the Sussex coast six months ago. How they just had to pick up this guy and take him to some farmhouse so someone could come and speak to him. Sean remembered thinking about the money at the time, how it was nearly three times more than he normally got for a job. With that much, he'd thought, he wouldn't have to put off tying the knot with Tash, or setting up his restaurant.

'You sure you're up to this?' Terry had asked him at the time. 'Yeah, of course,' he'd replied. Why wouldn't he be? And Terry had given him that *can-I-trust-you?* look. Well, sod him, Sean had thought, he could handle it. Besides, he wasn't going to be doing this forever.

Watching the cargo speak on the phone, Sean felt his hearing go weird for a second, like on a plane during take-off.

The cargo ended his call and pocketed his phone. Then sweeping his hand through his hair, he continued down the steps into the car park. Directly after, Sean saw Terry emerge from behind the meter box, taking a puff on his rollie, and start to follow him. It was like the pause button had been released; the film on play again, the sound back. The scene unfolding before Sean's eyes like it'd been explained to him in the pub on the Sussex coast that night.

And here they were. No going back now.

Sean released the clutch and pulled forward, the loose gravel crunching under the tyres of the two-tonne transit. He headed up the nearest row of parked cars towards the clubhouse, his hands shaking on the steering wheel.

He saw the cargo stop to let a woman pass in a golf buggy. The woman, in three-quarter length tartan trousers and tight roll-neck, waved to him as she went past. They seemed to know each other. Terry hung back, with his head turned to the ground.

Sean observed the woman in the buggy stop outside the golf course's pro shop and go inside, wondering what she'd remember about this moment when asked about it later. Would she recall Terry? The van?

Dust hung in the air where the buggy had gone past. The cargo crossed the road and walked down a row of cars. Terry followed him.

Sean, watching them, drove slowly along the top of the car park. He saw the cargo stop briefly, taking out a set of keys and pressing a fob.

Scanning the row of cars, Sean looked for the winking tail lights. And there it was, an Audi A3.

Sean noticed Terry had spotted it as well.

The cargo then took out his phone again. Had it buzzed with a message? He checked the screen as he walked along, Terry closing in on him, lifting his hand from his jacket, gloves on now.

Sean changed up to second, checking his wing mirror, and accelerated down the lane of cars towards them. This was it. About thirty metres ahead of him, he saw Terry draw up behind the cargo.

Terry must have said something because the cargo looked

round. But before he could work out what was going on Terry had him round the neck, doubled up.

Sean drew up alongside them, got out and opened the sliding side door. Terry dragged the cargo into the back where he began to strap his hands with a cable-tie.

Sean got back in the van and kept an eye on his wing mirror as he waited for Terry. A moment later, he saw Terry getting out of the back of the van and slide the door shut. The cargo's phone was lying on the gravel. Noticing it, Terry picked it up and, opening the Audi's boot, chucked it inside. Scanning the car park, he closed the boot and approached the van.

'Okay. Let's go,' he said, climbing inside.

Sean pulled away, his heart going like the clappers, and headed down the driveway. Glancing at Terry along the way, he asked, 'Do you think anyone saw us?'

Texting on his phone, Terry said, 'Just drive.'

2

Parked up in a lay-by alongside a wood, Graham Hayes was sat in a silver Kia Caren, yawning hard, when his phone buzzed with a message.

I'm getting too old for this, he thought.

The message was from Terry: they had the cargo. Hayes then opened a photo on his phone of a woman – early-thirties, blonde, five-six. The cargo's wife, Amanda.

Hayes had a greying goatee and shaved head and scratched at both now as he checked his rear-view mirror. The road was an unmarked country lane. Only three cars had passed in the last ten minutes. Through a line of trees, he could see down to a large detached house, surrounded by sloping lawns and flowering rhododendrons.

Noting the time on his watch, Hayes shook out a mint gum onto the palm of his hand and put it in his mouth. Poxy things, he thought. Six months after giving up smoking and he was still chewing the damn things. He'd be fifty-three next month. Fifty-three, on his second marriage and a father again. His kids from his first marriage were all grown up now – Chloe, 24, studying ceramics at Royal Holloway; Jamie, 20, trying to make it as a rock star. Pam, his new wife, was fourteen years his junior and Malaysian. He'd initially employed her to help out in the house after he'd split up with his wife. Well, one thing had led to another…

Hayes sat there, chewing the gum as he pictured Terry and Sean leaving the golf club with the cargo. From there, he'd instructed them to head to a derelict farmhouse in the West Country, where they'd wait for his call. Meanwhile, he was at the cargo's house to take photos of the wife. You didn't ask the contact employing you on a job why. He'd give Terry another few more minutes before doing what he had to do.

Working as a freelancer in the intelligence and security sector, Hayes was used to the jobs no one else wanted to touch. Nowadays, government agencies were so hamstrung with bureaucracy they couldn't fart without having to file a report. That was where he came in. Apparently, his employer was going to make this whole thing look like the cargo had just disappeared and was having some kind of a mid-life crisis or something. What a luxury they were, Hayes thought. Why couldn't he disappear somewhere? His whole adult life had felt a bit like a mid-life crisis. He deserved a break.

Hayes checked his watch and saw it was time. He got out of the Kia, putting on a grey flat cap and crossed the road. On the other side, he disappeared up a track through the wood.

The sun was shining. He moved quickly through the trees and soon came to the end of the wood where he stopped beside a hunting gate and looked across the adjacent field. Two horses stood in the far corner, heads down, eating grass and swishing their tails. Hayes listened out for the sound of people, but all he could hear was birdsong, so he climbed over the gate and started round the edge of the field.

Coming to a water trough, he stopped and looked through a gap in the hedge. The ground sloped down towards the house, which was situated at the end of a long rhododendron-lined driveway. At the front of the house was a turning-circle of loose stones, while at the rear a two-tied lawn, divided by a low stone wall, led to a tennis court and the shade of pine trees. All round, a secluded and pleasant spot.

Hayes unzipped his jacket to uncover a camera hanging round his neck. A Nikon digital SLR with 50x optical zoom range, he lifted it and focused in on the house.

He tracked across the downstairs windows – pictures on walls, a leather top desk, a computer, framed photos on window sills. Then he came to the front door, where there was a cluster of balloons tied to the door's brass knocker. He scanned the front of the house, noticing coloured streamers from party poppers lying on the gravel. It was then he heard a vehicle approach in the distance.

Hayes lowered the camera and saw a car coming down the driveway. He lifted the camera again and zoomed in on it. A woman was driving, short highlighted brown hair, mid-thirties, with a kid in the back.

Through the camera, Hayes followed the car's progress.

It stopped at the front of the house, and the woman got out. She was wearing Lycra shorts and trainers – on her way to or from the gym it looked like. She helped a young girl, seven or eight, out of the back. The girl was holding a present, done up with a red ribbon.

Hayes moved the camera to the front door as it opened. Another kid came out, wearing a polka-dot dress and sparkling headband, and went to say hello to the new arrival. A woman followed her, blonde, skinny jeans, UGG boots.

It was the cargo's wife, Amanda.

Hayes zoomed in on her, could see her pearl earrings, the blusher on her cheeks. She curled some hair behind one ear, bending down to say hello to the kid. Her long grey cardigan touched the ground as she did so.

Hayes held his finger down on the shutter-release button – click, click, click – then looked up from the camera, chewing the gum a little quicker than before.

The two kids ran off inside while the women stood and chatted for a moment. Hayes zoomed in again, taking pictures of Amanda as she spoke. He could see the outline of a phone in her back pocket, a silver bracelet round her wrist…

Click, click, click.

The gym woman drove away. Amanda waved goodbye from the doorway, then turning to go inside, she paused to check her mobile.

Hayes zoomed in. He saw her tapping the screen, her lips pursed in concentration. It looked like she'd just received a message.

Click, click, click.

She went inside and Hayes followed her with the camera as she walked through the downstairs of the house.

Click, click, click.

She disappeared out of sight, then a moment later, there was the sound of kids screaming before a group of them ran across the lawn at the back of the house.

Hayes moved along the hedge for a better view. He saw a large patio area and wisteria-covered arbour. He zoomed in on a trestle table laid up with paper plates, cups and napkins for a kid's party. Hayes saw the cargo's wife appear through the French doors carrying a tray of sausages on cocktail sticks; then another woman, Southeast Asian – probably Thai, Hayes thought – carrying jugs of squash.

Hayes lifted the camera again, got Amanda in his sights, and released the shutter once more. She was leaning over the table, placing the tray in the middle; she had a pair of sunglasses on her head now.

Click, click, click.

For a moment, the two women stood and watched the children running round the garden. Hayes noticed Amanda smile lovingly in a way that only mothers can when observing children. Hayes took a photo of her like this – hands on her hips, sunglasses on her head. Then, lowering the camera, he looked at the picture on the display screen. She was certainly an attractive lady, and probably didn't deserve any of this. But then they never did.

As the two women walked back through the French doors, Hayes heard the swishing of horses' tails, and looking round, he saw he was being watched. The two horses had wandered over to say hello.

It was time to go.

He climbed over the gate and followed the track through the wood again, sunlight splintering through trees, pigeons cooing.

He came to the roadside and crossed the road. Getting into the Kia, he removed his cap and reviewed some of the photos on the display screen, still chewing the same piece of gum, and scratching his goatee occasionally. Then he turned the ignition, pulled a U-turn in the narrow lane and drove off in the opposite direction.

After a mile or so, he rejoined the main road and followed

the signs for the next service station. Before long, he pulled into a car park, bought a coffee and went to use one of the payphones.

'You have the photos?' his contact asked down the line.

Hayes, phone in hand, looked across the service station car park, the sound of cars zipping along a dual carriageway in the distance. 'Yup,' he said, slurping his coffee.

The line cut out for a second. When it came back, his contact said, 'Drop site: East Chaldon Bridge. Seven o'clock.'

Hayes checked his watch: he had two hours. 'And the handover?' he said. He'd told Terry to expect to stay at least a night at the farmhouse. But nothing was certain.

His contact said, 'We'll let you know.'

The line went dead.

Hayes was used to the uncertainty. In his business, no one trusted anyone for more than a few hours, let alone days, which meant instructions often got delayed to the last minute.

He walked back to the Kia, connected the camera to a laptop and began uploading the photos. He viewed them on the laptop, thinking how photos made people look part of the past, whether they were still alive or not, and how eventually everyone would end up as just a face in a photo somewhere that few people, if any, could put a name to, and that would happen sooner than people thought.

Hayes remembered his father had had all these retirement plans, including how he was going to get a boat, work on it at the weekends and then take it out fishing. Then one Sunday evening, just after the six o'clock news, cup of tea in hand, he'd had a massive coronary, at fifty-three. Not very old by today's standards. But what could you do?

With his fifty-third birthday creeping up on him, Hayes had told his doctor about his father's heart attack, and he'd advised him to quit smoking for starters. In this bloody job? Hayes had thought. The doctor also told him to reduce his alcohol consumption and start eating a more balanced diet. Pam had been a good influence in that respect, cooking a lot of Asian food, low in fat; even had him on that low-cholesterol margarine – for what it was worth. Then the baby came along and he quit smoking and cut down on the booze as well.

But still, he couldn't get the number out of his head.

Fifty-three.

Hayes removed the gum from his mouth, which was probably something else he should consider cutting out. He'd switched to the sugar-free variety recently only to read somewhere that the sweetener they used was linked to abdominal pain and cancer. You couldn't win nowadays.

Hayes hooked up a printer he had stashed under the passenger seat and printed off copies of the photos. Then collecting them up, he put them into an envelope, sealed it, and put it in a bag along with the USB. Why they wanted hard copies as well he didn't know and he didn't ask. Then he unfolded a map on his lap and located East Chaldon, tracing his finger along the railway line to where a B road crossed the line over a bridge, the drop site.

Hayes then turned the ignition, lowering his visor to cut out the sun, and headed along the slip road to rejoin the dual carriageway.

3

Sean heard banging coming from the back of the van and looked across at Terry.

Terry said, 'Okay. Pull over.'

Sean, checking his wing mirrors, pulled into a field gateway.

Friesian cows filled the field, heads down eating the grass. An electric fence divided the field. Some of them lifted their heads at the sound of the van

Sean turned the van in the gateway so it was parallel to the road, the sliding door facing the field, and turned off the ignition.

Terry said, 'Okay, cover up. We'd better have a look.'

Sean got out the balaclava Terry had given him on one of their reconnaissance trips –chucking it at him at the time, saying, 'Try this on,' and Sean had checked himself out in the car's rear-view with it on, giggling, all a bit of a joke back then. Well, there was nothing funny about it now.

Terry said, 'Okay, just remember. No talking. No names.' Together they pulled down their balaclavas and got out of the van. Sean watched Terry open the side door.

The cargo was curled up in a corner. His trousers were

covered in dust from rolling about on the floor. He looked pale and sweaty; his mouth was taped and hands tied.

Terry climbed into the back of the van with him. The cargo squirmed on the floor. Terry grabbed him by the shoulder and pulled him up, and he groaned.

Terry said, 'Shut it.'

All charm.

Sean heard a car in the distance and peeked round the side of the van. Inside he could hear Terry ordering the cargo to 'Keep still,' followed by a scuffle and slipping of feet. The sound of the car faded away as it headed off in another direction.

Returning to the side door, Sean saw Terry holding the cargo down with his foot, the man struggling. Terry dug in his pocket and pulled out a packet containing a syringe. He stripped off the wrapping and took off the needle cap.

Sean looked at the cargo's sweaty face, his messed up hair and untucked shirt, feeling sorry for him now, thinking how things had changed for him. One moment about to get into an Audi A3, and now this.

Sean noticed the cargo desperately trying to turn his head to see what Terry was doing. His eyes widening as Terry stabbed the needle into his upper arm and injected him.

Removing his foot, Terry stepped back. The cargo tried moving, but didn't get far. He slumped in the corner and just lay there, breathing hard.

Terry got out of the van, slid the door closed, and removed his balaclava. He let out a deep breath and wiped his face with his hand. Sweat glistened on his forehead and scalp; his cheeks were red.

'Okay,' he said. 'Let's go.'

Sean got in behind the wheel and started the engine. Terry, urinating in the hedge first, got in after him. Sean pulled out onto the lane and accelerated up through the gears.

After about a mile or so, they joined the dual carriageway. Sean stayed in the left-hand lane and kept to the speed limit. Neither of them spoke for a while. Then Sean turned to Terry, and said, 'What did you tell Karen by the way?'

Karen was Terry's wife; and although Sean knew he preferred not to talk about anything personal, he would still ask him stuff from time to time. It was only after months of working together, for example, that he even found out Terry was married, then a while longer before he discovered what her name was.

Terry was rolling a cigarette on his lap. 'About what?'

'About this.'

Terry didn't look up. 'What about this?'

'About the cargo and stuff.'

Terry licked along the gum of the Rizla, saying nothing.

Sean said, 'I mean – doesn't she ask questions?'

'Sean, have you been talking to someone?'

'What?'

'You heard me.'

'No.'

Terry grabbed him by the neck and squeezed.

'No, I swear!'

'You said something, didn't you?'

'No!' he said, feeling Terry's thumb on his throat.

'You sure?'

'Yeah. For fuck's sake, Terry! Let go.' Sean swerved out of his lane.

Terry released him.

Sean rubbed his neck, and said, 'Jesus! What's wrong with you, man?'

Terry lowered his window and lit his rollie. 'Just drive.'

Sean looked at him in disbelief. 'You don't have to fly off the handle like that.'

Exhaling smoke through his nose, Terry said, 'You don't tell anyone our business, you understand? No one. That includes your girlfriend.'

'Yeah, I know.'

'No one, you understand.' He gave him a look.

'I know. Jesus!' Sean looked at the road ahead, remembering how he'd said to Tash in bed last night after sex that this job was going to be different. Tash, propped up on an elbow, smoking a cigarette, one breast showing above the duvet, saying, 'How exactly?' And Sean wanting to tell her the truth, thinking it'd do no harm, that he could trust her...

Terry said, 'Sean, look at me.'

'What?' He didn't look.

'You didn't say anything, did you?'

'No, I didn't!' Sean could hear the crackle of tobacco as Terry sucked on his rollie. Although he hadn't given Tash any of the details, he'd let slip about the pay cheque being triple what he normally got.

Terry said, 'I hope so, for your sake.'

Glancing at him, trying to play it cool, Sean replied, 'How long have we been working together?'

'I wonder sometimes.'

'I'm not an idiot, you know. I was just wondering what you told your wife, that was all.' Sean knew he was a hopeless liar.

Terry dragged on his rollie, flicking ash through the gap in the window, and said, 'When it comes to work, you can tell your girlfriend whatever you want, but not the truth. It's as simple as that.' He stuck the rollie back in his mouth.

Sean said, 'All right. There's no need to go on about it.'

Looking straight ahead, Terry replied, 'You want to be careful, Sean. You start opening your mouth – you'll find yourself in all sorts of trouble.'

'I told you I haven't said anything, all right?'

'Well, just keep it that way.'

Neither of them said another word for a while. Terry took out the map, checked road signs, and smoked. Sean watched him out the corner of his eye as he traced his finger across the page, lips moving as he read place names. Terry and his lectures, he thought, he'd had enough. As soon as he got his money, he was out of here.

After about ten minutes of silence, Terry said, 'You'll need to come off this road soon.'

Sean, still feeling pissed off with him, didn't say anything right away. He looked straight ahead, the road undulating across open countryside, the sun setting through a line of pylons.

Terry said, 'Sean. Did you hear me?'

'Yeah,' he replied, eventually.

'We're getting near. You need to concentrate.'

4

Hayes flicked on his headlights as it grew dark. He passed through the village of East Chaldon, which consisted of a cluster of houses, a village green, a shop, and a church.

He left the village north of the downs and pulled up on the side of the road, with fields either side. He looked at the road map he had folded open on the passenger seat.

Hayes estimated he was about three-quarters of a mile away from the drop site. He studied the map then looked out of the window to get his bearings. At the end of the road, he saw the T-junction where he needed to turn left. After that, he just had to follow the road for half a mile to the hump back bridge, the drop site.

Hayes looked at the dashboard clock, then checked his wristwatch. He had fifteen minutes.

He lowered the window and rested his arm on the sill. A cool breeze blew against his face and it felt good. Although originally from London, Hayes felt a close affinity to the English countryside now. 'It feels like home to me,' he'd told his daughter, Chloe, when she'd stayed last. His daughter, smiling, had said, 'You're just getting old, Dad.' They'd lived as a family in South-West London, the kids going to local schools, and the only time they went to the countryside was to visit his wife's parents, just outside Dorking. He often remembered in the car on the way down, the kids complaining, 'There's nothing to do there.' Hayes had never imagined then he'd move out to the countryside himself one day. But move out he did. Soon after the divorce, he bought a converted barn, middle of nowhere, with an orchard. He hadn't looked back since.

Hayes heard the bleating of sheep in the dark. He breathed in deeply through his nose and smelt what he thought was manure. He checked his watch again; thirteen minutes to go. Chewing gum for most of the day, he felt his jaw muscles beginning to tire.

A car turned at the end of the road. He checked his rear-view mirror. The car disappeared in the opposite direction. He looked at his watch again. Twelve minutes.

His stomach rumbled. He was getting hungry. Leaving this morning, he'd told Pam, 'I won't be back until late.' Pam feeding Adam on the sofa, one large, veined breast protruding from her unbuttoned top, had said, 'What about supper?' Hayes, admiring her breasts, as he had from the start of their relationship, had told her not to worry, that he would get something on his way home, but he knew she'd leave him something anyway. She always did.

He guessed it was an Asian thing. He imagined families out there still sat down and ate together. But the truth was he didn't really know. Pam's culture was largely a mystery to him. He'd only been to Malaysia once and that was to meet her parents. The whole thing had been a bit of a strain, what with the language barrier, meeting all those aunts and uncles, and having to smile the whole time. His face had ached by the end of it. Hayes knew his limits. Foreign travel just wasn't for him.

Both Chloe and Jamie thought he was mad having another kid. Just as they did when he announced he was getting married again. 'Look what happened the first time,' his son Jamie had said. Even Chloe, usually the more forgiving of the two, had her doubts. 'Isn't she a bit young?' she'd asked, referring to Pam being fourteen years his junior. To this day, neither of them was that comfortable around Pam. Her English was still far from perfect, limiting her ability to partake in conversations, and the fact that she was so different to their mother seemed to irk them. Jamie again: 'Dad, she behaves like your housekeeper still. It's embarrassing.' Maybe Pam did give him an easy ride of things, Hayes thought, and that somehow made it seem like he had got away with something. Maybe they were right and he had got away with something and he deserved a hard time. He'd certainly sat in hundreds of lay-bys over the years, like now, and missed countless birthday parties and parent nights at school. He couldn't blame them if this was how they felt. There was a price to pay for everything in life, he thought.

Hayes noticed the hairs on his forearm stand up with goose bumps in the breeze. He heard the sheep bleat in the dark again and tried to stop thinking so much – it didn't do any good in the long run. He looked down and saw the dashboard clock change from 18:59 to 19:00. It was time. He turned the ignition and pulled out onto the road.

Approaching the humpback bridge, he saw the headlights of a car judder round the corner. He glanced up to his rear-view and, seeing the road was clear behind him, pulled up to the verge.

Holding the carrier bag with the photos and USB in it at the ready, he watched the car approach. Heading towards him at speed, the car swayed across the road to avoid potholes. The car was a black Lexus saloon, with new plates. It dipped its headlights and, braking hard, swung in beside him.

Seeing its back window open, Hayes chucked the bag through it, and no sooner had he done so, the car was on its way.

On his way home, Hayes opened a fresh packet of gum and put a stick in his mouth as he re-joined the dual carriageway. Periodically, he checked his rear-view mirror for anyone following him. The radio was on Magic.

After an hour or so, Hayes came off at a junction. Turning down a private drive, he drove the Kia into a breaker's yard. Getting out, he locked the car with the key fob and exited through a hole in the chain link fence and walked along a footpath – backs of houses, graffiti on walls, a dumped shopping trolley. Then round a corner, he activated the central locking of another car. The lights of a VW Golf blinked in a line of park cars. He checked around himself before crossing the road, got into the VW and drove off.

It was 22:38 on the dashboard clock when Hayes pulled into the driveway of his converted barn. He stepped out onto the loose gravel. A full moon shone above the poplars at the end of the orchard. He crossed over to the house, an outside light clicking on.

Pam had gone to bed. She'd left the downstairs light on. Coming into the house, Hayes wondered what she'd left him by way of supper. He was starving. True to form, she hadn't let him down. Going to the fridge, he found a cling-film wrapped bowl of risotto.

He poured himself a glass of wine and microwaved the food. As he waited, he jabbed the remote of the small TV he kept in the kitchen. It came onto the BBC News channel. There'd been an outbreak of fighting in the West Bank. Hayes watched the coverage – plaster dust, building rubble, bloody-headed youths on stretchers. Just terrible. The microwave pinged. He sat down and used a spoon to shovel the risotto into his mouth, stopping every few mouthfuls to take a gulp of wine and look up at the TV.

He enjoyed the house to himself like this. It felt peaceful, despite all that was going on in the world. Hayes knew, however, he didn't want it like this all the time. He'd learnt over the years, too much of your own company wasn't a good thing. He used to come in some nights, have a bottle of wine with a takeaway, and just fall asleep in the chair. His body couldn't take it after a while. He started to suffer from Irritable Bowel Syndrome, his stomach bloated up like a balloon; he got headaches, felt tired all the time. 'You look terrible, Dad,' Chloe had told him once. 'Are you all right?' He'd put on an exaggerated smile and said, 'Of course. Absolutely fine. Fit as a fiddle.' He wasn't though; he felt like shit. Pam never mentioned his drinking, the takeaways, late nights, that wasn't her style. In the early days, she often found him asleep on the sofa in the morning. Bringing him a coffee, saying, 'You work too hard. You must be so tired,' always giving him the benefit of the doubt. But he soon started feeling guilty and undeserving of Pam's attention until, finally, when Pam was three months pregnant with Adam, he realised enough was enough. Something had to change. That was when he went for his check-up with his GP and started thinking about his dad and turning fifty-three soon.

After finishing the risotto, Hayes put the bowl in the sink, sat on the sofa and finished his glass of wine. The camera crew were still in the West Bank. What a world, he thought. It was then that his phone buzzed. It was Terry. Standing up and lowering the volume on the TV remote, he said, 'What's going on?'

Terry said, 'We're just coming to the farmhouse now.'

Hayes pushed the door to, thinking of Pam upstairs. 'Any problems?'

'None.'

'The cargo?'

'He's fine.'

'Good. If he starts bothering you, just tell him someone wants to speak to him, that's all. And that it's nothing to worry about.'

'Yes, boss.'

Hayes hesitated, then said, 'I'm still waiting to hear when the handover is.' He knew the longer they had to wait the riskier it became for all of them. 'How's the boy doing?' He'd been a little nervous when he heard Terry was taking Sean along, since he hadn't done anything like this before.

Terry said, 'All right.'

'Keep your eye on him, won't you?'

'Yes, boss.'

'I'll speak to you tomorrow.' When he hung up he held onto the phone for a moment, looking across the kitchen and picking out certain objects – a bottle of olive oil, a pepper mill, a knife block, a radio. Familiar objects that reminded him of his home life, making him forget work, and soon the conversation with Terry felt like it had never happened.

After washing up his bowl and glass, Hayes locked the

downstairs doors, set the house alarm and came upstairs. He looked in Adam's room. Pam was asleep on the sofa bed alongside his cot, her highlighted dark hair covering her cheek. She was turned towards the wall, her knees pulled to her chest, her hands under her head. She had taken to sleeping in Adam's room the last few days, as Adam wasn't settling so well, saying, 'I don't want to disturb you.'

Hayes pulled the door to and went into the master bedroom opposite. He'd never told Pam what he really did for a living. In the early days, he mentioned he ran a courier service. 'I think it must be a good job,' she'd replied, smiling. They were in the kitchen sharing a glass of wine, at the dating stage. Hayes had shrugged. 'It pays the bills, I guess,' he'd said, expecting at least a few follow-up questions, but that was it. In the two years they'd been together, Pam had never asked for more details.

His ex-wife, however, had always been on at him. Asking him where he'd been, why he was so late. And he'd been forced to share more details with her than was comfortable. But he doubted it had helped their relationship. A problem shared was, in Hayes's experience, often a problem multiplied.

Pam asked him about food and mealtimes. That was her greatest concern – whether he was eating properly. They talked about food, Adam, and the weather. When they had exhausted these subjects, they said nothing. They sat in front of the TV, Pam on the sofa, looking at a magazine or doing something on her iPad; Hayes in his armchair with a glass of wine, changing channels from the remote. Some nights, after a few glasses, Hayes would sit next to her, she'd rest her head on his shoulder and he'd stroke her hair. Some nights, when Adam was asleep, they'd go to bed early and make love.

Hayes lay on his bed with the light off. For a while, he couldn't stop thinking about the job, his day coming back to him in a series of mental images: sitting in the lay-by outside the cargo's house, taking photos of the wife, then the drop-off at the bridge… As was the case with every job, Hayes had no idea what was really going on. He knew nothing about the cargo or why they wanted to question him. The information Hayes received was deliberately restricted to his requirements for the job. The bigger picture, if there was one, was never shared, which was probably for the best, he often thought. If he knew too much about these people and what it was they'd done, he'd probably never get any sleep.

Hayes intentionally left a top window open and a gap in the curtains. That way, he could hear the breeze in the poplar trees alongside the orchard. No matter how slight the breeze was you could still hear the sound of the leaves. He found it restful at night. In years gone by, he'd have a cigarette as he lay in bed like this. Not anymore. Now he just listened to the sound of the wind in the trees until he fell asleep. Which was what he did tonight.

5

THE ROAD SURFACE had changed, he felt sure of that, to some kind of unmade track. They'd slowed right down, the vehicle bouncing about; then a metallic rattle of what must have been a cattle grid.

Lawrence's heart raced, as he struggled to breathe through his nose, his mouth taped, hands tied.

He must have passed out again, he thought.

The van stopped for a second, then brushed against some kind of bush as it set off again. Were they getting near to where they were meant to be going?

Lawrence was slumped in the back. Perhaps he should try standing up, he thought, but nothing seemed to happen. He wasn't sure if this was because he hadn't tried or because he just couldn't move. It was like the messages from his brain weren't reaching his body. For a second, he couldn't remember how he'd got like this. Then things started coming back to him, snapshots of memory: the meeting with clients at the golf club; shaking hands with people round a table; a guy with a beard and red cheeks asking him, 'How's the family, Lawrence? You've got two, haven't you?' Him saying, 'Yes a boy and a girl. It's her birthday today in fact.' Then walking through the clubhouse; the sunshine outside; the call from Amanda; the woman in the buggy waving to him; then walking across the car park, checking messages from the office, and seeing the thickset man behind him.

Lawrence felt the van come to a stop, heard the sound of the passenger door opening, and one of the men getting out, then the clink of something metallic. A gate perhaps. They had arrived, he realised. But where?

The van then pulled forward into an enclosed space, a garage of some kind, the engine echoing for a moment in its surroundings before being turned off. There was the sound of the driver's door opening and closing, then footsteps passed the side of the van. A moment later, he heard the voices of the two men – one older, one younger.

Sweating, he tried to wipe his face only to be reminded his hands were tied behind his back. He tilted his head to one side and rubbed his face on his shoulder.

The voices died away. There was no traffic noise. He imagined they were somewhere remote, visualising the long, unmade track that had bought them here. A farmhouse perhaps?

He listened out for the sound of footsteps once more. He heard something plastic flapping in the wind outside the garage. Perhaps he should try to get away now, he thought, while he still had the chance. He yanked his arms about, trying to get them free, but the cable-ties were so tight he could barely separate his hands. The plastic cut into his skin.

Breathing heavily, Lawrence looked round for something to use. He couldn't see anything. There were dents in the side of the van, which he hadn't noticed before, and he told himself to make a mental note of them in case he needed to describe it later. Then he heard footsteps coming back in his direction and he tried sitting up.

The footsteps stopped by the side of the van. Lawrence heard the rattle of keys and the sound of the central locking. The sliding door came open and the two balaclava-clad men stood there, looking at him.

'Come on,' the older one said. 'Time to get you inside.' He stepped inside the van, put a hood over Lawrence's head and everything went black.

He felt the two men hold him upright under the arms. 'That's it, slowly does it,' the older one said. They walked him outside. He felt the nip of the cold air through the fabric of the hood. The ground was rough and potholed. After a while, they stopped. He heard one of the men open a door and they went inside what must have been a house. The two men escorted him up a narrow staircase, brushing against the walls, the older one saying, 'Keep going. Nearly there.' Both of them were breathing heavily; the older one reeked of cigarettes. Then they stopped again, and another door was opened. They went in. Once inside, the men let go of his arms and he fell to the floor. He heard footsteps cross the room, then come back towards him again. There was a brief pause. He wondered what was going to happen next. *Were they going to kill him?* The older man pulled the hood off his head. Then, without saying anything, both men walked out of the room, shutting the door.

It was dark and cold. Looking about himself, Lawrence could just make out wallpaper hanging off the walls and cracks in the plaster. The flex hanging from the ceiling was missing a bulb. The only window had been boarded up. There was a bed against the wall and a table and chair opposite.

The place smelt of damp and mould. It was clear no one had lived here for years.

Lawrence looked towards the door and listened out for the two men, but with the tape still over his mouth he couldn't hear much beyond the sound of his own breathing. He wondered where the two men had gone. Were they even still here?

He thought about standing up and looked down at his feet, trying to move them. Although he couldn't feel anything, he saw his feet move. Next, he concentrated on his legs and bent up his knees. But when he tried moving his arms, he got no response. They must still be tied, he thought. He tried standing up by rolling over onto his side and getting up like that. But it didn't work. Then he rolled onto his front and, with his face pushed against the floor, managed to lift himself up onto his knees.

Once upright, he felt a rush of blood, as if the floor had been tipped up at an angle. Standing up, he lurched across the room and crashed into the wall. He steadied himself for a moment, wondering if anyone had heard him downstairs. Then, leaning against the wall for support, he crept across the room to the door.

He put his ear against it and listened out for any sound, wondering what was going on down there. He presumed the men were still around as he hadn't heard the van leave. He imagined them speaking to someone else, someone in charge maybe. Perhaps they were deciding what to do with him next, he thought.

But he couldn't hear anything. He stood there for a while, a draught blowing under the door. Then he walked across to the window and looked up and down the sheet of plywood bolted to the frame. The wood didn't look that old, he thought, unlike the rest of the room.

He leant against the board and gave it a nudge with his shoulder. It was solid. With his back to the window, he felt along the lower edge for something to get hold of. But the gap was too small.

Looking round the room again, he noticed the bed was made up with blankets and it suddenly occurred to him that maybe he was here for the night and that the men weren't coming back any time soon. He felt his pulse quicken at the thought.

Had they really just left him here?

He tried to think how far away they'd parked the van, wondering if it was too far for him to hear anything. He remembered the walk from the van across to the house, the cold air, the sound of the flapping plastic, and reckoned it was no more than fifty metres.

Surely, he would have heard them drive off?

Lawrence's eyes focused on the bed again, noticing there was a pillow without a cover, when suddenly he felt jogged awake from a trance. He wondered how long he'd been standing there, looking at the bed. It felt like it could have been anywhere between a few seconds to several minutes. He felt disorientated, confused and not in full control of himself. What had they drugged him with? he wondered.

He started back towards the door again, and for a moment, it seemed to move in the opposite direction from him. Then he was standing at the door, as if he'd been there all along. He had a sense of déjà-vu, like he had been in this room a long time, repeating the same movements. He tried moving his arms, forgetting they were still tied. He couldn't believe what was happening – that this was really him locked in this room.

Lawrence sat down against the wall and felt his breathing quicken, as he struggled to get enough air. He tried getting his hands free, so he could rip the tape off his mouth, but the activity made his breathing worse. Snorting through his nostrils, he felt his chest tighten, and starting to panic, he tried making a fist and banging against the wall, but he barely had the strength to lift his arm.

6

IT WAS JUST after midnight. The wind was getting up. Terry lifted his head, hearing the sound of something flapping outside. He was sitting in the kitchen, rolling a cigarette, a saucepan of water just coming to the boil on his portable gas stove that he kept for when he went fishing.

He stood up, lifted the pan off the stove and, turning off the gas, poured the water into a mug with a teabag in. For a moment, he just stood and looked at the water change colour; then, using his fingers to grip a corner of the teabag, he started dunking it. Squeezing it on the side, he dropped it into a black bin bag he'd hung on a cupboard handle.

The flapping sound continued outside. Terry parted the curtains covering the window by the back door and, cupping his hands, stared across the courtyard. A full moon lit up the night. He saw a strip of black polythene caught round a post in what must have been an old silage press.

He stood there for a moment, looking round the courtyard. Rusty five gallon drums and old tractor tyres lay about the place while corrugated iron sheets hung precariously off buildings; weeds had sprouted up through the concrete. The farm, he knew from the map, lay in a valley surrounded by open fields. There wasn't a house for miles.

Terry came away from the door and sat down again to finish rolling his cigarette – taking his time, picking out loose strands of tobacco, and inserting a roach. Sean used to offer him his tailor-mades – Marlboros usually – back when he still smoked. 'Go on, have a proper one,' he'd say. 'Save all that messing around.' It was all the messing around that made rollies worthwhile in Terry's opinion. But such an explanation was wasted on Sean.

Terry took a sip of tea and lit the cigarette. Then taking out his glasses case, he removed a pair of black-rimmed specs, and put them on. With the cigarette in his mouth, he picked up a book, a biography of Field Marshal Montgomery, and opened it to a bookmark. He was about a third of the way in. He was a keen reader, particularly of military history and biographies.

Sean was asleep on the sofa in the sitting room next door. They had agreed: Terry would do the night-shift and Sean would take over in the morning. Terry couldn't trust Sean to stay awake through the night.

As Terry read, the polythene sheet continued to flap outside. A draught swirled through the house. After a while, he heard Sean start snoring next door. He stopped reading for a moment and listened. He worried about Sean like a parent might. Could he really rely on him not to open his mouth about this? He was such a kid still, Terry thought, recalling their conversation earlier about what he might or might not have told his girlfriend about this. Had he said something? Terry suspected he might have. Why else would he have asked him about his wife and what he told her otherwise?

As it happened, Terry told his wife nothing, other than that he'd be away. In the past, he'd invented all sorts of stories – a delivery to Antwerp, a pick-up in Brussels, a transfer in Le Havre. Telling her he worked for a company called 'Hayes Distribution', back in the day when they still thought they might have kids together. Karen, his ex-wife, wasn't stupid of course. She'd soon sussed out he wasn't your regular van driver. But by then their marriage had taken a turn for the worse. It was discovered Terry had a low sperm count, so they dropped the act, and came to an arrangement. So long as he paid for her gym subscription, her shopping trips and overpriced haircuts, he got an alibi when he needed it. Who said love was dead?

But he wasn't going to tell Sean all that.

He stretched his arms above his head and yawned, replacing the bookmark and getting up. He was about to carry his cup to the sink when he remembered the water was turned off. He set the cup down on the sideboard instead as he wasn't going to waste their bottled water rinsing it. That's when he heard a noise from upstairs, an unmistakeable banging.

He grabbed a torch off the table and went into the hallway. He stood and listened for a second, resisting the urge to call out. He couldn't hear anything and flashed the torch up the stairs. Something told him he should go and have a look, so he went up and knocked on the cargo's door.

'What's going on in there?' he said. With the window boarded up, the door bolted, and his hands tied, the guy's options were limited, Terry thought.

There was no answer. Terry realised he was going to have to take a look and, holding the torch under his arm, slipped on his balaclava and unlocked the door.

The cargo was curled up on the floor. When Terry shone the torch at him, he sat up and squinted in the light.

Terry pointed the torch in his face. 'What are you doing down there?'

The cargo moaned through the tape.

'You weren't trying to escape, were you?' Terry said, sarcastically.

The cargo shook his head. He looked deathly pale and his hair was wet with sweat. Terry wondered if he had given him too much tranquilizer.

'Come on, get up,' Terry said, flashing the torch round the room and checking everything was in order. 'You've got a bed to lie on.' Nothing looked out of place. The guy had probably been having a nightmare, Terry thought, and who could blame him? He shone the torch in the cargo's face again. 'Did you hear me? Get up.'

The cargo tried moving but soon flopped on the floor again. Dust snowed through the beam of the torchlight. Terry walked over to where he was lying, checked the cable tie round his wrists and prodded him with his foot. 'Come on, up we get.' But he didn't move. Terry reached down and grabbed his upper arm. He felt hot and sweaty. The guy came round again, flinching. 'That's it,' Terry said, and he helped him up and onto the bed. The cargo lay there.

The guy looked like shit, Terry thought. Maybe he was bluffing, but Terry didn't want to risk it. The last thing he wanted was the guy dying on him, so he left the room to get some water.

Grabbing a bottle from the kitchen along with a roll of tape, Terry hurried back upstairs and removed the tape covering the cargo's mouth. He gasped in air. Terry took the lid off the bottle and held it up to the cargo's lips. He attempted to take a drink, but started coughing and spilt most of it down his shirt. Terry tried again, this time with more success. Nodding when he'd had enough, the cargo said, 'Thank you.'

'That's alright. Now listen to me. I don't want to hear another peep out of you. Understand?'

'I'm sorry. I didn't mean to—'

'Not a thing.'

The cargo looked at him in a way that made Terry feel as if he didn't have his balaclava on – like he could see his face. 'Just get some rest,' Terry said, less certainly.

'What's going to happen?' the cargo said.

Terry paused. 'Nothing.' He didn't know if this was true or not. He somehow doubted it. Then he remembered what Mr Hayes had said to him on the phone, even though he knew it could mean anything. 'Someone wants to speak to you,' he said. 'That's all.'

Sitting up, the cargo said, 'Who?'

'Just someone,' Terry replied, wishing he hadn't said anything now. He shone the torch round the room, double-checking. 'It's nothing to worry about.' He knew the opposite was probably the case.

The cargo said, 'Where are we?'

Terry shone the torch in his face again. 'Just shut it, all right?' Holding the torch under his arm, he ripped off another length of tape.

Seeing what he was doing, the cargo begged, 'Please, no more tape. I won't say another word.'

'No, you won't,' Terry said, slapping the tape over his mouth.

7

LAWRENCE LAY THERE in the dark and listened to the man locking the door and his footsteps going back downstairs. Then all went quiet. The wind whistled outside. He got the impression they were far away from anywhere. He couldn't hear any cars, voices, or barking dogs. Judging by the sound of the wind, it didn't sound like there were any trees nearby either, just open space.

He rolled over on the bed, trying to find a comfortable position to lie in. His arms ached from being tied behind his back. Part of him was surprised he wasn't more disturbed by what was happening. He didn't know why. Was it shock? Adrenaline? The injection? The two men didn't seem particularly unreasonable, he thought. Besides, they probably knew as little as he did about what was going on here. They were just doing their job. He guessed whoever was in charge would soon realise they'd made a mistake locking him up and all would be resolved. Then he thought about Amanda at home with the kids, and wondered if she'd called the police yet. She would have tried ringing his mobile first, he thought. He imagined hundreds of missed calls and texts on it. Then what? Would she try the golf club? His office? Clients?

He knew Amanda wouldn't panic; she'd look at this logically. Maybe his phone was down. It had happened before. Or he was busy with clients. Again, not out of the ordinary. Amanda was level-headed in these situations. But it was getting late. Would she call a friend first, get advice, and then the police?

Lawrence wondered what the time was. There was no light round the window boards, making it difficult to tell. He thought back to his game of golf. Pictured himself talking to clients, then getting up, shaking hands, saying he had to get home, it was his daughter's birthday. It was mid-afternoon, three-ish. The woman in the buggy, the walk to his car, then the man forcing him into the van. He tried to calculate how long they had driven for. Two, three hours. Maybe more. He remembered it was dark when they'd arrived here, so it had to be after seven. Then add a couple of hours onto that for the time he'd spent in this room. That made it around nine o'clock now, he thought, possibly later.

He wondered what the men were doing downstairs, and who it was who wanted to speak to him.

He lay on the bed feeling cold. He could hear the sound of the wind outside, and for a moment, he thought he heard the rustling of a hedgerow. At a certain point, he realised he was dropping off to sleep.

He tried keeping his eyes open, telling himself he mustn't sleep, that someone might come. Trying to focus, he went over what had happened to him that day again, thinking there must be clues to explain this, seeing himself standing on the steps of the clubhouse, answering his phone. It was his wife, Amanda: 'Hiya. Have you finished?'

'Yup. Just now.' He could hear the sound of excited

children at her end. 'How's the party going?'

'Yeah, all right. Pretty much chaos.'

'It sounds like it's livening up.'

'Yeah, something like that.'

Then Amanda calling out, 'Guys, do you think you could all go outside, please... Samantha, where's William?' A girl's voice in the background, saying, 'He's here.' Amanda again: 'What are you doing, William?' Then to Lawrence: 'Did the meeting go okay?'

'Yeah. They want me to find a property in France.'

Amanda to one of the children now: 'Oh, dear. Well, give it a rub.' Then back to him: 'You couldn't get some bread on your way back, could you?'

'Sure. Anything else?'

'I don't think so. I'll text you if there is.'

Then his daughter's voice: 'Is that Daddy?'

'Yes. Do you want to say hello?'

His daughter now: 'Hello Daddy. William took my wand and won't give it back.'

'Oh, dear. I'm sure he will if you ask him nicely.'

'No, he says it's his now.'

'Well, I'm sure he didn't mean it.'

A pause; then: 'Daddy, when are you coming home?'

'In a little while. I've just finished.'

'Okay. See you "in a little while"!'

Amanda again: 'See you later, then. Don't forget the bread.'

Lawrence had met Amanda at university. He was always telling the story to friends about how they'd ended up together. After graduating, they lost contact for a while, then ran into each other at a restaurant completely by chance a few years later, finding out they were living on neighbouring streets in Putney. They were married not long afterwards. Kids. House in the countryside. Having lost both his parents when he was young, Lawrence was unashamedly proud of his family and never got tired of telling this story. As far as he was concerned, that was when his life really began.

He kept thinking about what had happened to him that day, looking for clues that might explain how he came to be here, and wondering if the police had enough information yet to find out where he was. Surely, with all the CCTV cameras about nowadays, he reasoned, it wouldn't take them long. Maybe they were already on their way.

Like this, the hours passed.

He wasn't sure if he'd been asleep or not when he heard a crow caw outside, then other birds joining in. He realised it must be getting light. As he lay there listening to the birdsong he felt reassured to know it was the morning and wondered if someone was coming to talk to him today. Then he heard what he thought was the sound of an engine.

Though it was a long way off, there was no mistaking it. He got off the bed, trying to be quiet, so as not to disturb the two men – if they were still here, that was – and went over to the boarded-up window.

With his ear to the board, he heard an engine. Not a car, more like a bike, he thought.

He stepped back from the window, wondering what he should do. It was then he noticed a slither of light coming through a crack in the board just above his head.

He stood up on tiptoes to see if he could see anything, but the crack was just out of reach. He'd need the chair, he thought, and checking at the door first to make sure no one was coming, he went over and picked up the chair behind his back and walked to the window with it.

Taking several deep breaths to settle himself, he got up on the chair. It was the thinnest of cracks. He put his eye to it. The first thing he noticed were distant treetops, then a vast, sloping field, the wind gusting across it, rippling green shoots of corn.

He pressed closer to the crack, his eye beginning to water. He saw two pigeons cross the valley, twisting in flight and banking on the wind.

He wiped his eye, then put his eye to the crack again.

For a second he couldn't hear the engine. Then the sound returned. Straining his eye to see what it was, Lawrence spotted something flash between the trees. A second or two later, a red quad bike appeared over the slope, its driver standing up on the footrests.

Lawrence felt his heart in his throat as he watched the bike come closer.

8

'Who do you think it is?' Sean said, standing by the window and parting the curtains. He'd just woken up and saw it was already light outside.

'Don't know,' Terry replied. 'Come away from there.'

'Probably some farmer,' Sean said. 'Don't you think?' He saw the guy had a dog on the back of the bike with him.

'Yeah, something like that.' Terry stood by the door, listening out for the cargo.

Sean said, 'What if he comes this way?'

'We ignore him.'

'What if he sees the van?'

Terry glared at Sean. 'Just come away from that window, will you.'

Sean said, 'He's heading up the slope now.'

Terry joined Sean at the window. They saw the red quad bike cutting across the field, about half a mile away, where the track joined up with the road. The guy riding the bike was standing up on the footrests.

Terry took out a pair of binoculars and zoomed in.

Sean said, 'Where did you get those from?'

Terry, ignoring him, continued tracking the guy through

the binoculars.

Sean said, 'He's just a farmer, isn't he?'

'More likely a gamekeeper.'

'What's that?'

Terry, lowering the binoculars, said, 'Don't you know anything?'

'Why should I know that?'

Terry looked back through the binoculars again. Sean observed the guy stopping and opening a gate. It was then they heard a loud bang come from upstairs. Terry lowered the binoculars and looked round.

Sean said, 'What the fuck was that?'

'Cover up. We'd better see what he's up to.'

Sean followed Terry out of the sitting room. Putting on their balaclavas, they headed upstairs.

Outside the cargo's room, Terry bent down, removed the strip of tape covering the keyhole, and called out, 'What's going on in there?'

Sean noticed Terry had put on his balaclava inside out because the seams were showing.

Through the keyhole, Terry said, 'Walk backwards towards the wall.'

Sean heard the sound of footsteps inside the room.

Terry said, 'Now, turn round.'

He unlocked the door and went in. The cargo turned his head when they came in, and Terry told him, 'Don't move. Just face the wall.' Terry checked his hands, the cable tie, then removed the tape from his mouth, and said, 'What was that noise?'

The cargo, gasping for breath, said, 'Nothing. I just fell over.'

'Are you having a fucking laugh?'

'No.'

Terry looked round the room, saw the chair lying on its side by the window, and said, 'What's the chair doing there?'

'I just fell over. I told you. I was half asleep.'

Terry signalled to Sean to pick it up. Then he motioned to the bed and Sean got down and looked underneath it, but couldn't see anything. He shrugged at Terry.

Terry checked his watch, then said to the cargo, 'All right. It's time for you to eat anyway.' He indicated to Sean to go downstairs.

Sean remembered how they'd bought extra sandwiches for the cargo when they'd gone shopping the day before. He had wondered at the time what fillings he might like, still feeling like it was all a bit of a laugh... How things had changed.

He went downstairs and fetched the sandwiches. When he reappeared, Terry signalled for him to put them on the table, which he did.

The cargo, seeing what was going on, said, 'I'm sorry,' and half-turned his head.

Terry said, 'Just shut it. You understand? Not another word.'

The cargo nodded.

Terry led him to the table. 'I just want you to sit there and eat. You think you can manage that?'

The cargo said, 'Please – how much longer am I going to be here? I have a wife and kids… they'll be worried.'

Sean glanced at Terry, feeling sorry for the guy, and wanting to say something.

Terry gestured for him to leave the room. Sean mouthed

Why? in his balaclava. But Terry gritted his teeth and waved him away.

Sean knew better than to argue. Coming down the stairs, he heard a loud bang on the floor, then Terry's muffled voice through the wall.

Sean went into the sitting room and checked through the window, using Terry's binoculars, to see if he could see the guy on the quad bike. But he wasn't there.

A moment later, Terry came in, pulling off his balaclava; he was sweating.

Sean said, 'What did you do to him?'

Terry walked to the window, parted the curtain, and checked through the binoculars.

'There's no one there. I checked already.'

Terry scanned through the binoculars anyway.

Sean looked at him, and said, 'What happened up there? I heard a bang.'

Terry said, 'Nothing,' and lowering the binoculars, he wiped his face with his hand. Then Sean watched him take a swig from a bottle of water that was on the table.

Sean asked, 'He is all right, isn't he?'

'He's fine.' Terry wiped his mouth and screwed the lid back on the bottle. 'He's having something to eat.'

Sean, still feeling bad, said, 'I feel sorry for him. Don't you?'

Terry said, 'No.'

'A wife and kids. He seems like a nice guy.'

'Seems... yeah.'

Sean said, 'Nicer than you, anyway.'

Terry took out his Nokia, held down a button and waited for it to turn on, saying, 'It's the nice ones you've got to worry about.'

Sean shook his head. 'What about his wife and kids?'

'What about them?' Terry said, looking at his phone, the screen lighting up.

Sean said, 'You must feel a bit sorry for them?'

'Not really. For all we know the guy's a paedo, doesn't have kids.'

'I don't think so.'

'No?' Terry pressed keys on his phone.

Sean said, 'He doesn't seem the type.'

'And you would know, would you?'

'No, just saying.'

Sean looked at Terry reading what must have been a text message, his lips moving. He waited for him to say something.

Terry then put his phone in his pocket, and said, 'Wait here, all right?'

'Why, where are you going?'

'Outside. To phone Mr Hayes.'

Sean followed him into the kitchen, not wanting to be left alone. 'What about the guy on the bike?' he said.

Terry went over to the window by the backdoor, lifted the curtain and checked outside. 'Just wait here, all right?' And he opened the door and went outside, closing the door behind him.

Sean went over to the window and watched Terry walk across the courtyard towards the barn, a crow flying off from its roof. Then thinking he heard a noise upstairs, Sean glanced over his shoulder, freaked out at being left alone in the house with the cargo.

He looked round at Terry again, who was standing outside

the barn now, phone in hand. He'd probably want to tell Mr Hayes about the guy on the bike, Sean thought, knowing Terry felt the need to report everything. Sean had once asked him, 'When do I get to meet Mr Hayes?' This was early on, sitting in a rented Vauxhall Astra outside one of those new luxury high-rises on the South Bank, waiting to take pictures of someone. 'You don't,' Terry had said. 'That's my job.' Sean, wondering if Terry had maybe invented Mr Hayes for effect, then asked, 'Okay. What does he look like then?' After a long pause, Terry replied, 'He has a beard.' Sean shook his head, still suspicious: 'What kind of beard?' Terry then turned on him, and said, 'This is very simple, Sean. Mr Hayes tells me what to do. Then I tell you want to do. That's as far as this goes.' Sean didn't ask again.

He watched Terry pressing keys on his phone, the sun flashing across the courtyard, and noticed how the outbuildings around him had become overgrown with brambles, their roofs collapsed inwards, whole buildings slanted. The place needed levelling, he thought.

Coming away from the door, Sean took out his own phone and looked at the blank screen, wanting more than anything to turn it on and check his messages. But Terry had insisted his phone remained off at all times while they were here, for security reasons. Sean didn't dare risk turning it on and getting caught. Terry would literally kill him.

Sean could still remember meeting him for the first time. Terry's first words to him: 'Your past doesn't have to decide your future, you know.' Sean was trying to steal a car at the time, threading a coat hanger between a door frame, when Terry pitched up – hands in coat pockets, cigarette smoking in his mouth, like he thought he was Clint Eastwood or something. 'You're free to choose,' he'd said, removing his fag. Sean had told him to fuck off, sixteen at the time and not knowing any better. Terry didn't, of course, and it was the start of their partnership. Sean hadn't stolen anything since. What with meeting Tash, and dreaming about opening a restaurant, he was on a different path now. He hadn't expected still to be working with Terry, five years later, mind you. But going straight had made saving money for the restaurant a little harder. He needed at least twenty grand, he reckoned. But once he had that, he was good to go.

Sean got up, parted the curtain and looked across the courtyard. Terry still appeared to be speaking on the phone, looking down at his feet as he toed at something on the ground.

Sean came away from the door. Looking towards the stairs, he wondered if the cargo had finished his food, or if he'd even started it. With Terry pushing him around, he probably didn't feel much like eating, he thought.

Sean walked out into the hallway and listened for any sound coming from the cargo's room, but couldn't hear anything. As he was standing there, he noticed a mirror on the wall and went over to have a glance. Looking at his reflection, he played with his hair for a moment, thinking it needed a wash and some conditioning. A picture was hanging on the opposite wall. He turned round and looked at it. In the picture, geese were flying over a river. Someone must have left it here. Then he noticed some letters lying on the floor, next to what must have been the old front door, boarded up now. He went over and picked a couple of them up – junk mail from what he could tell; the envelopes were damp. It creeped him out to think how long they'd been lying there and he put them back down again and started towards the kitchen when he heard the cargo's voice: 'Hello? Is someone there?'

Sean hesitated, wondering if he should just ignore it, or say something.

The cargo tried again. 'Hello? Is anyone—'

Sean called up, 'What do you want?'

'I'm sorry. I need the loo.'

Sean hesitated, looking over his shoulder towards the kitchen door, worried about Terry hearing them. 'You'll have to wait,' he said.

The cargo went quiet for a second, then said, 'You're the other guy, aren't you?'

Sean didn't know what he meant by that. 'What?'

'It's usually your colleague I speak to.'

It took Sean a second to realise who he was referring to. He'd never thought of Terry as his 'colleague' before.

'Well, he's busy,' he said.

Another silence, then: 'Is something going on?'

'No. Just keep it down, all right.' Sean felt like he'd said too much already.

The cargo said, 'Please. Can't you just tell me what this is about?'

Sean looked over his shoulder again. If Terry was to come in now he'd go fucking ballistic. 'Listen,' he said. 'I don't know anything about this. All right?'

The cargo said, 'Please, can't you tell me anything?'

'I told you. I don't know.' Sean started back towards the kitchen.

The cargo said, 'At least, can you phone my wife? Let her know I'm all right.'

Sean stopped in his tracks. So he really did have a wife and kids, he thought.

'Please. That's all I ask.'

'I'll have to speak to my colleague,' Sean said, still feeling strange about that word. He just wanted to get the guy off his back now.

'Thank you.'

'I'll speak to him, I said. That's all.'

The cargo said, 'I'll give you her number.'

'What?' Sean couldn't believe he'd let the conversation get this far.

'You know, just in case. If you can't ring her, well, that's fine.'

Sean felt panicked and didn't know what to say.

The cargo said, 'If you could just let her know I'm all right.'

Sean bit the dry skin off one of his knuckles.

'Are you still there?' the cargo said.

'Yeah.'

'Please. I've done nothing wrong. This is a mistake.'

Sean glanced over his shoulder, worried Terry might have crept back in without him noticing. 'That's not my concern,' he said, trying to sound tough like Terry, but it felt unnatural.

'I understand. You're just doing your job. But please. Let me give you her number.'

Sean hesitated. 'How come you can remember her number?' he said, thinking no one remembered phone numbers anymore and hoping this might distract him.

'I had my children memorise it in case of emergencies,' he said.

Sean was silent. It was just a number, he thought. What

harm could it do? He wasn't actually going to ring it.

The cargo said, 'You must understand. You have a family, don't you?'

Sean didn't answer that.

'Please. I won't say another word.'

Sean thought he must be mad for doing this. He looked round for a pen when he noticed Terry's rucksack on the table. Knowing Terry usually kept a pen for doing crosswords, he had a look inside. He was feeling around in the rucksack when he felt something metallic. Closing his hand around the object, he soon realised it was a gun. Pulling it out, he held it in the palm of his hand. Some of the coating on the barrel had worn away. It wasn't very big, he thought, like one of those starter pistols. Still… it was a fucking gun!

Upstairs, he heard the cargo say. 'Hello? Are you still there?'

Sean wanted to shout back, *Shut the fuck up*. He dropped the gun in the rucksack, took out a biro and checked on Terry through the window by the back door. He was still there, but off the phone now and looking through his binoculars. Shutting the kitchen door behind him, Sean came back into the hallway, wondering why Terry had a gun. What wasn't he telling him?

The cargo said, 'Hello? Is that you?'

Sean shouted up the stairs, 'I thought I told you to keep quiet.' He really meant it now.

'I'm sorry. I thought maybe it was your colleague.'

'Just tell me what the number is.' Sean realised he'd lost control of the situation and wanted to get this over with as quickly as possible now.

The cargo said, 'Can't you just tell me what this is about?'

Sean was losing whatever cool he had left. 'Do you want me to write this number down or not?' he said.

'I'm sorry. Please.' The cargo read out the number and Sean jotted it down on the back of a receipt he'd found in his pocket, with no intention of ever ringing it, but just to get the guy off his back.

The cargo said, 'Thank you.'

Sean said, 'Forget it,' stuffing the receipt in his pocket and thinking he'd bin it as soon as he got the chance. Then he went back into the kitchen, wanting to get away from the cargo as quickly as possible. That was when he saw Terry coming in through the back door.

Feeling his heart in his throat, Sean waited until he'd come in and closed the door, then said, 'Everything all right?'

Terry stared back at him. 'What's going on?'

9

Mark Haddon stopped the quad bike against his small semi-detached farm cottage. His terrier jumped off the back of the quad and ran to the door. His two other dogs, spaniels, whined in the kennel next to the cottage. Mark removed the .22 LR Anschutz from the quad's gun case, telling the spaniels to 'shut up' and followed the terrier to the back door. He removed his boots on the doorstep and came inside. His wife, Clare, was feeding their two year old, Ollie, in the high chair at the kitchen table. Mark learnt his .22 against the wall and took off his jacket, which was flecked with mud from riding the quad. Ollie stopped eating and kicked his legs with excitement when he saw his dad. Mark pulled a face at him.

Clare said, 'Mark, can you not leave your gun there, please? Ollie's old enough to pull it over.'

Mark replied, 'I wasn't going to,' still pulling faces at his son. He was. He picked up his rifle, removed the magazine and bolt, and put the gun in the cabinet under the stairs.

Clare called out from the kitchen, 'And be careful not leave bullets lying around. I found one in the fruit bowl the other day.'

Mark chuckled to himself, came back into the kitchen, and kissed his wife on the neck as she carried Ollie's bowl to the sink.

'I'm serious,' she said, rinsing it out. 'He nearly put one in his mouth yesterday.'

Mark, still smiling, said, 'He likes the taste of them. Don't you, buddy?'

'It's not funny,' she said, drying her hands.

Mark took out a bowl, shook some cereal into it and poured in the milk. He'd been up since six but hadn't eaten yet.

He sat down and began eating, managing to slop milk on the table.

Clare tutted, 'You're worse than Ollie.'

Mark said, 'You love it really,' his mouth half full.

'Do I?'

Mark, shovelling in spoonfuls of cereal, said, 'You haven't spoken to Kate, recently, have you?' Kate was Simon's wife, the tenant farmer who farmed most of the Sudley Estate where Mark was the gamekeeper. Kate was the local gossip and Clare was her closest confidant. Mark and Simon referred to them as the 'Sudley Witches'.

'No. Why?' Clare said.

'Just wondering.'

'I haven't seen her since the weekend.'

'She didn't say anything about Hillards Farm, did she?'

'Hillards?'

'You know, the derelict place on Sudley Down.'

'No. Why?'

'I was down there this morning. It looks like someone's been there.'

'So?'

'Just curious.'

Clare said, 'Maybe someone bought it.'

'Maybe.'

Clare wiped Ollie's mouth with a cloth, and said, 'There you go.' Then she lifted him out of the high chair and put him on the floor. Ollie came round the table to Mark and tried climbing up on his knee.

'How are you doing, buddy?' Mark said, lifting him up and bouncing him up and down.

'Careful,' Clare said, clearing the table. 'He's just eaten.'

'You're all right, aren't you, buddy?' Mark said, putting him down again.

Clare threw an empty yoghurt pot in the bin and wiped the floor round Ollie's high chair.

'When you see her,' Mark said, 'can you mention it?'

'Yeah, sure,' Clare replied, rinsing the cloth under the tap. 'But what makes you think someone's been in there?'

'Vehicle tracks.'

'Probably Simon, no?'

'He doesn't usually come in at Hillards. Uses the entrance at the Grange.'

'Someone from the estate office then,' she said.

'Maybe.

'Or dog walkers,' Clare suggested, turning off the tap and drying her hands. Her hair was tied up in a ponytail but strands hung loose round the sides. She got out her phone to check her messages. 'You worry too much,' she said, tapping the screen.

'Do I?' Mark took a sip of tea. 'They had trouble at Leeson's a few months back. A gang of them just drove straight in and helped themselves.'

'Oh,' Clare said, distracted on her phone now.

'They took everything. Even a tractor.'

Typing a message, she replied, 'You think it's the same lot?'

'Don't know.'

Clare's phone buzzed and she smiled.

Mark said, 'Who's that? Your boyfriend?'

'Yeah, right. Like I've got time.' Typing a reply, she said, 'It's Noah's mum.'

Mark said, 'You couldn't put a bit of toast in for me, could you?'

'No! Do it yourself.' Clare put down her phone and started loading the washing machine. As she bent over, Mark could see her leopard print knickers under her leggings along with a spare roll of fat pinched in the elastic. Having Ollie was her excuse. Mark still fancied her rotten and was all up for having another kid as soon as possible. Getting up to put the toast in, Mark gave her arse a gentle smack.

'Oi!' she said.

Mark chuckled.

Clare finished loading the machine, then called out to Ollie, who was rummaging around next door. 'Come on, sweetie,' she said. 'What are you doing? We've got to go.' Clare opened her bag and took out a compact. Checking herself in the mirror, she put on some lipstick and blusher. She said to Mark, 'What are you up to today?'

Mark, flicking through a local paper whilst waiting for the toaster to pop, said, 'Back at Sudley. Coppicing. You?'

'Ollie's going to Noah's.' She flipped closed the lid of the compact, zipped it up in her bag, and said, 'Are you out later?'

'Don't know. May go lamping. Not sure yet.'

'Could you do Ollie's bath?'

'Sure.' The toast popped. Mark buttered it, spread on some marmalade.

Clare called Ollie again, 'Come on, sweetie. It's time to go.'

Mark sat down with his toast, tea and paper.

Clare helped Ollie on with his jacket. As she was doing this, Ollie squatted down and picked up some dried mud off the floor. Clare said, 'Leave it, sweetie. Daddy will do it later,' giving Mark a sarcastic smile. 'Won't you?' Mark blew her a kiss.

With Ollie all ready, Clare put on a quilted coat and grabbed her keys off the table. 'See you later,' she said as she led Ollie out by the hand.

Mark heard Clare talking to Ollie outside as she got him into the car, then the sound of the closing doors, the engine starting, and Clare driving off down the lane. The house fell quiet without them. Mark finished his toast, drank his tea and came to the end of the newspaper; then he got out his phone and considered phoning Simon. But Clare was probably right. The vehicle tracks were probably either dog walkers or someone from the estate office. Could even be teenagers looking for some privacy; wouldn't be the first time Mark had caught some kids, parked up in their mum's car, music on, smoking a spliff, or getting it on. He understood how it was.

Mark put his phone away and took his breakfast things to the sink. He'd drive out to Hillards Farm later on, he thought, and have a look then. He was working that way anyway. He rinsed his plate. Through the window, he saw a pair of crows sweep low across the neighbouring field, then land on a fence post. Turning off the tap, Mark thought about getting his .22.

10

Terry glanced round the kitchen, sensing something was different to when he'd left ten minutes ago to speak to Mr Hayes.

'I'm not using my phone if that's what you think,' Sean said, holding up his hands to indicate he didn't have it on him.

Terry said, 'What were you doing through there?'

'I just went to check on everything.'

'I heard you talking.'

Sean shook his head. 'No.'

'Don't lie to me, Sean.'

'I'm not. I was just in the hall.'

'Yeah, and what were you doing there?'

'Just checking on things.'

Terry grabbed Sean by his hoodie and yanked him across the table. The chair tipped up behind him.

'I heard you talking, Sean. What's going on?'

'He wanted the toilet, that's all. But I said he had to wait for you. Jesus, man!' Sean tried to push Terry away.

'Don't bullshit me, Sean.' Terry tightened his grip, squeezing down on Sean's windpipe. 'What's going on?'

Sean knew whatever happened he couldn't mention the

phone number or Terry would go ape. 'Nothing. I swear.'

'I don't believe you.'

'It's the truth. Go and ask him.' Straight away, Sean knew this was the wrong thing to say. What if the cargo did tell him?

'Why didn't you come and get me?'

'What for?' Sean broke free from Terry's grasp and rubbed his neck. 'That hurt, you know.'

Terry said, 'What else did you talk about, Sean?'

'Nothing, I told you. Why do you always have to be so violent?'

'What else?'

Sean rubbed his neck, trying to stall for time, but Terry kept pressing him.

'Sean, *what else*?'

'Nothing. Just that he thinks this is a mistake. He's innocent. Shit like that.'

Terry reached forward to grab Sean again, but this time Sean was ready for him and batted his hand away.

'Leave me alone, man. Jesus!' He felt bad for lying to Terry, but knew he didn't have a choice. Anyway, he didn't really see it as lying, because he wasn't actually going to ring the number, and in his mind that somehow made it okay.

They heard banging from upstairs. The cargo called out, 'Excuse me. I need the loo.'

Terry looked towards the door.

Sean said, 'You see! I told you.'

Terry said, 'Where's that bucket?'

'Outside his door.'

'Wait here.' Terry left the room.

As soon as he'd gone, Sean glanced at Terry's rucksack

on the table and remembered the gun inside. Could he really trust Terry? He heard him upstairs, unlocking the cargo's door and giving him the bucket, then coming back down again. When he came back through the kitchen door and glared at him, Sean knew he wasn't finished with him yet.

'We're going outside,' Terry said, and walked over to the back door.

Sean said, 'What for?'

'You heard me.'

'Why? What happened?' Sean wondered if the cargo had said something.

'This won't take long.'

Sean said, 'Come on. This is crazy.'

Terry said, 'Outside,' holding the door open.

Sean stepped outside. Terry followed him out, closing the door behind him.

The breeze swirled, kicking up dust off the concrete. Sean wiped his eyes.

Terry said, 'What happened, Sean?' but sounding more reasonable now.

'What do you mean?' Sean asked, knowing he wasn't out of the woods yet.

'Have you promised him something?'

'No! Of course not. I told you. He wanted the toilet. I told him to wait. Then he complained about this being a mistake and stuff like that.'

'What stuff?'

'All this – being locked up here.' Sean gestured across to the farmhouse.

'You believe him?'

'No, I felt sorry for him. That's all. He's got a wife and

kids.'

Terry said, 'So you let him talk?'

'Come on, Terry. The guy doesn't know what's going on. Give him a break.'

'Haven't you listened to a word I've said?'

Sean realised he'd said the wrong thing again. 'Listen, Terry, I promise, I didn't say anything.' He held up his hands.

'So he didn't ask you to do anything?'

'No. Like what?'

'You tell me.'

Sean wondered if Terry knew exactly what had happened and was just trying to get him to confess. 'He wanted to speak to his wife,' he said. 'That's all. You heard what he said.'

'So he asked you to ring her?'

Sean shrugged. 'Sort of.'

'And what did you say?'

'Nothing.'

Terry stared at him, expecting more.

Sean said, 'What? Jesus! *Nothing!*'

Terry said, 'So you didn't say you'd help him?'

'No. Of course not.' Sean put his hands in his pockets where he felt the receipt with the phone number on.

'Are you sure?'

'Yeah. I felt sorry for him, that's all.'

Terry said, 'It's not our business to feel sorry for him. You understand?'

'Yeah, I know.'

'This is not a joke, Sean. We're at the bottom of a very long chain here. If we mess up, people above us in the chain won't hesitate to sever the links below. You understand what I'm saying?'

'Yeah. I'm sorry, Terry.'

'Right. Let's go inside.'

As they turned to go, Sean noticed Terry stop and turn his head, like a dog that had caught a scent.

Sean said, 'What is it?'

Terry put up his hand to stop him from saying anymore.

Sean then heard the distinct sound of the quad bike.

Terry motioned to the garden wall and they squatted down behind it.

Sean said, 'Is he coming this way?'

Looking round the wall, Terry said, 'No.'

Sean peeked over Terry's head and saw the quad bike passing along the ridgeway about a mile away, the rider hunched up over the handle bars, dust hanging in the air. 'What's he doing?' he said.

Terry replied, 'Going back to work probably. Come on. Let's go inside.'

'Aren't you worried?'

'He's not doing us any harm.'

'Do you think he knows we're here?'

Terry shrugged. 'Doubt it.'

'What if he comes over?'

'As I said, we ignore him.'

They went back inside. Terry locked the back door and made sure the curtains were covering the windows. Then, after putting on their balaclavas, they went upstairs to check on the cargo. They found him sitting on the bed.

Terry said, 'Finished?' as he glanced at the bucket of piss.

The cargo nodded.

Sean just stood there, trying not to look at him in case they made eye contact.

Terry said, 'Okay, stand against the wall. Hands behind your back.' The cargo did as he was instructed, and Terry tied his hands and taped up his mouth again.

Afterwards, they went back downstairs and Sean watched Terry fill a pan of water for tea. 'Do you want one?' Terry said, lighting the stove.

Sean hesitated. He didn't really drink tea, but thought it would be friendlier to say yes. 'Okay,' he said. With his hands in his pockets, he was clutching the receipt and wondering if he should say something to Terry now. Get it out in the open, now that things had calmed down a bit. He didn't like keeping things secret from him.

Terry walked over to his rucksack and took out his rolling tobacco. For a second, Sean thought he'd noticed something.

Terry said, 'You going to stand there all day?' and started to roll.

Sean sat down, wondering how to begin.

Looking up from his rollie-making, Terry said, 'What?'

'I was just thinking.'

'Yeah?' Terry raised his eyebrows, in a better mood now.

Sean said, 'Yeah, I mean, who's going to look after this guy after we're gone?'

'That's not our concern.'

'I know. But…'

Terry licked along the gum of the Rizla. 'But what?'

Sean was about to put his feet up on the table when Terry gave him a look. He was always telling him off for that. Like he was his bloody mother – or what he imagined a mother to be like if he'd had one. 'No, I'm just saying,' Sean said, watching Terry with the rollie in his mouth feel his pockets for his lighter. 'Are they going to just leave him here or what?'

'Not our concern,' Terry said, producing the lighter. 'Do you want me to write that down for you?'

Sean shook his head.

Terry lit the rollie.

Sean asked him, 'Do you know when we're leaving yet?'

'Mr Hayes will let us know.'

Sean said, 'I can't wait to get home. What about you?'

Terry shrugged, exhaling smoke from his nose. 'Not bothered.' He checked the pan of water. It was just beginning to bubble. He held the handle, saying, 'A job's a job.'

No, Sean thought, it wasn't. This was not like any other job he'd done before. He was fine with delivering packages or snooping through people's rubbish, but live cargo – forget it. He couldn't wait to get home and start looking for a site for his restaurant. Perhaps this was what he needed to get him going, he thought. He'd feel bad for leaving Terry of course. But it couldn't be helped. Besides, as Terry himself once said, 'Your past doesn't have to decide your future.'

Sean asked him, 'Do you ever think about doing anything different?'

'How do you mean?' Terry said, still holding the handle of the pan.

Sean shrugged. 'Just something different, you know. Not this.'

Looking into the pan, Terry said, 'As I said, a job's a job. Be grateful for what you've got.'

Sean said, 'Yeah, I know,' thinking how he didn't want to work for Mr Hayes forever but not wanting to say this to Terry.

The water came to the boil and Terry lifted the pan, fag in mouth, and started pouring the water into the two cups,

Trying to lighten the mood, Sean said, 'You can come and work for me when I set up my restaurant.'

Terry dunked the teabags, like he hadn't heard him. Sean realised he'd made him feel uneasy and felt bad, but couldn't think of anything to say to change the subject. He watched Terry squeeze the teabags then toss them into the bin bag.

'Milk?' Terry said.

Sean said, 'Yeah,' though he wasn't really bothered. He only drank tea when he was with Terry, preferring lattes or cappuccinos the rest of the time.

Terry handed him his tea.

Sean said, 'Thanks,' and took the mug and wrapped his hands around it for warmth.

Terry relit his rollie, went to the back door and lifted the curtain over the window. He puffed on his cigarette, blowing smoke against the glass, and sipped his tea.

Sean said, 'What are we going to do now?'

'Drink our tea. And wait for Mr Hayes' word.'

11

HAYES DROPPED THE bag of shopping on the kitchen table along with Pam's car keys. He took the milk out of the bag and put it in the fridge. As he did so, he recalled his conversation with Terry earlier in the day, in which Terry had mentioned seeing this guy on a quad bike. He knew Terry was just being thorough by mentioning it, but he didn't like it. The sooner he could get them out of there the better, he thought.

Hayes called out, 'Pam? Are you there?'

There was no answer. The washing machine was running in the utility room, going into its spin cycle.

'Pam?' he said, thinking she must be outside in the garden, hanging washing. He looked from the window but couldn't see her. In the next moment, he heard Adam gurgling upstairs and then Pam talking to him. Not wanting to disturb them, he returned to the kitchen, filled the kettle and got out a mug with *DAD* written on the side (a birthday present from Adam that Pam had ordered), then put two heaped spoonfuls of Colombian Supremo into a cafetière. Once the kettle had boiled, he waited a moment for it to cool (ninety-four degrees being the optimum brewing temperature), then added the water. He carried the cafetière and cup, along with some biscuits, into his office next door.

Closing the door behind him, he put the biscuits, mug and cafetière on the desk and opened the room's window, adjusting the blind to let in more light, then sat down at the desk and turned on his laptop. As he was waiting for it to load up, he pressed down the plunger on his cafetière and poured his coffee. He thought of himself as a serious coffee drinker and had endless amounts of coffee-making accessories. For a while now, coffee-related presents had become a standard fall-back for his family at Christmas.

Hayes wafted the cup under his nose and took in the aroma. It was one hundred percent Arabica beans – strong, with a hint of caramel. In the old days, he would have had an accompanying cigarette; now he was stuck with biscuits and gum.

The laptop loaded. Hayes hammered in a password, typing with two fingers, and was taken to a secure page where he entered another. The page took a while to load; Hayes leaning back in his chair, an orthopaedic high-back that had cost him a small fortune and would 'change his life,' he had been told. The chair was certainly wonderfully comfortable, no denying that – but change his life...?

A gentle breeze reached him through the window. The sun was shining and he could hear birds singing. He took a sip of coffee, then the page cleared, and he started flicking through the photos of the cargo and his wife.

There was something about this case, about these two, he thought.

He stopped on a photo of the cargo's wife, standing in the doorway to the house, speaking to the woman in Lycra;

then moved to the next one, of her waving goodbye; the next, her looking at her phone, then opening the door and going inside.

She was certainly an attractive woman, he thought, with a lovely home. The question was: how well did she know her husband?

Hayes nibbled at a biscuit, then moved forward through the folder of photos: the cargo's wife laying the table outside, her hair falling forward; then standing back, hands on hips, stroking back her hair and folding her arms. As he clicked through the pictures, stopping to look at some for longer than others, he found himself gazing into the eyes of the cargo's wife and wondering what thoughts were going through her head at that moment. He knew from experience you could waste hours like this…Other people, other lives.

Hayes heard Pam's voice outside, turned round and looked though the slats of the blind. He saw her walk out onto the patio with a basket of washing with Adam in a sling. Humming to herself, she started pegging clothes up on the line. Hayes often thought how you could drop Pam anywhere in the world, in any situation, be it a war zone or a tsunami-battered coastline, and she would be much the same and just getting on with life, humming to herself, hanging washing.

The breeze flapped the laundry on the line.

Hayes turned round again, drank his coffee, and broke up another biscuit. He came to a photo of the cargo. He was approaching his car, talking on his mobile. From his appearance, he looked like any well-to-do professional, with looks and luck on his side; the sort of person, it often got reported, you'd least suspect of doing wrong. But in Hayes's world, they were just the sort you had to look out for.

Hayes took one last look at the cargo's photo and then closed the folder. It was 11:08. He refilled his cup from the cafetière. Just the money now to check: half now, half on transfer.

Using a series of passwords, he logged into a bank account, clinked on recent transactions, and noted the first half of the payment was sitting in the account, as agreed.

So far so good.

Hayes logged out of the account and went onto Google and searched for any mention of the events of yesterday. Perhaps there had been some kind of press release. When your employer's identity wasn't even known to you, such operational details weren't going to get shared out. What would be the point of using Hayes's services if they were? An employer had to be sure that nothing would connect them to a job, so contractors like Hayes were deliberately kept in the dark. Hayes had several trusted contacts who fed him work. This job had come through one of them. All his contacts had links with government security and intelligence agencies, but that was a wide net. At the very least, Hayes presumed his employer on this particular job had enough operational control to be working the strings from behind the scenes, so information could be fed to the media if and when it was deemed necessary. Some 250,000 people went missing each year in the UK alone, so this was hardly headline news. The fact was, if someone wanted to disappear they had every right to. Hayes imagined his employer would be working from the same assumptions and spinning them to their advantage.

Hayes couldn't find anything on the internet, which made things easier as far as he was concerned. The last thing he needed was CCTV images and e-fits out there in the public domain. He couldn't afford for anything to go wrong, not at his stage in life. He had Pam and Adam to think about now. He knew if anything did go wrong the agency would drop him in it in a heartbeat. It was the main reason why they used people like him in the first place.

As soon as he had a hand over time, he would get Terry and Sean out of there, then there would be a deep clean – computers, surveillance photos, SIM cards, vehicles. There would be no trace of them once he was through. What happened to the cargo afterwards wasn't his concern. It didn't bear thinking about of course. Not if you wanted to sleep again.

Hayes knew how it worked. He'd been here before on other jobs. Compartmentalise. Wipe the slate clean. Reboot. Just don't dwell on it – that was the worst thing to do. Like picking at a scab, the thing was only going to bleed. There were bills to pay, mouths to feed, the grass to cut. Just move on.

Hayes shut down the laptop, and leaning back in his orthopaedic chair, he drained his cup of coffee. For a moment, he just sat there, listening to the cooing of a wood pigeon and the breeze in the poplars, not thinking about anything in particular. Then he checked his phone, just in case he'd missed anything – he hadn't – before picking up his cafetière and cup and leaving his office.

Pam was putting one of her breasts away having just finished feeding Adam when he came into the kitchen. She put Adam on her shoulder to burp him. Seeing him, she smiled. Her dark, silky hair gleamed in the light. He tried to smile back but imagined he'd only managed a grimace. Somehow, it didn't put Pam off.

'Hello,' she said. 'How's work going?'

Hayes went and stood by the French doors. 'Fine.'

'Not going out today?'

'No,' he said, looking across the garden.

Adam burped. Pam said, 'That's it. There's a good boy.'

Hayes turned round and watched them for a moment. As he did so, he wondered if he was going to see Adam grow up and get married. Somehow he couldn't imagine living that long, the number fifty-three coming into his head again.

Pam said, 'Say hello to Daddy,' lifting one of Adam's arms and waving it for him.

Adam gurgled and smiled.

'I think I'll mow the lawn this afternoon,' Hayes said, coming over and stroking his son's head.

'Okay,' Pam replied. 'Do you want lunch before?'

He wasn't that hungry and probably could have managed without, but felt he should for form's sake. 'Maybe a sandwich or something.'

Pam smiled. 'Okay.' She stood up. Hayes wanted her to stay a bit longer and just sit. He didn't know why. He didn't care about lunch really.

Hayes stroked his son's head again and Pam smiled as he did so. Hayes knew they'd both be all right if he wasn't around. Pam could survive just about anything, he reckoned, and Adam would be fine, kids just got on with it. Of course, Hayes couldn't say anything to Pam about how he felt. Where would they be if he did that? He knew the deal between them. He provided the house and income; she looked after him and Adam. It was an old-fashioned set-up. In such an arrangement, the man didn't start banging on about dying.

Sometimes he wondered whether he should say something

about it to Chloe and Jamie. But where would he start? *'You know I'm going to die one day. Well, about that…'* Jamie would just laugh at him and who could blame him. He wasn't ready to hear his dad talking like that. *'Get a grip, Dad. Jesus!'* he would say, or words to that effect. Maybe that was why his own father had never said anything to him, Hayes thought, because he knew he wouldn't have been listened to. And so it went round.

As Pam started getting lunch ready, Hayes wondered what Jamie might be up to. They didn't see much of each other anymore. They exchanged texts once in a while; Christmas cards. Maybe he would give Jamie a ring and see what he's doing, he thought. Once this job was done, he had some free time coming his way.

The idea of seeing Jamie cheered him up. They could go out for a curry together. Pam wouldn't object. On the contrary, she was always encouraging him to contact his two other children, despite their frosty treatment of her.

'I'm just going to give Jamie a call,' he said. 'See what he's up to.'

'All right,' Pam said.

Hayes picked up the cordless from its bracket and walked through the house with it, selecting Jamie's number from the phone's contacts list.

It started to ring. Hayes sat down on the sofa and put his feet up on the table, getting comfortable. But after about ten rings the phone clicked over to a recorded message. Hayes hesitated for a moment, deliberating whether to hang up or not; then came the bleep for his message.

He said, 'Hello Jamie. It's… er… Dad.' Calling himself 'Dad' felt awkward. He cleared his throat. 'I was wondering if you'd like to meet up. I'm coming into town soon. We could go for a curry or something … Anyway, I'll try you again… Okay, speak later.'

Hayes hung up and felt a wave of disappointment. What was he thinking? Jamie had his own life now. He didn't owe him anything. He should just be grateful they still exchanged Christmas cards. Hayes thought about ringing Chloe instead. Things had always been easier with his daughter. Jamie, he could feel, still resented him. And who could blame him? Whenever Hayes tried to bring up the past, Jamie's usually response was, 'Please, Dad, do you have to?' Maybe it was just his age.

Occasionally, Hayes asked after his ex-wife. 'How's your mother?' he'd say. The usual response was, 'Yeah, fine.' And that was it. No elaboration. Long ago, Jamie had compartmentalised his two lives with his Mum and Dad, and they couldn't be bridged. The past was the last thing he wanted to talk about. No doubt it was a reminder of how things had gone wrong. Somehow, Hayes couldn't get the balance right.

Hayes sat on the sofa, holding the phone, but decided not to ring Chloe. He looked out of the window at the lawn again and thought about mowing it later. That was pretty much all he looked forward to now, he thought. That was his future. He would try his best, of course, for Adam's sake. Take him for rides on the tractor, read him stories, take him to the pub when he was older. But Hayes couldn't help feeling the years closing in on him. That mowing the lawn was the best he could hope for, and when he couldn't do that, there was always the sound of the wind in the trees to listen to.

Hayes heard Pam behind him and looked round.

She was carrying a pile of clean washing towards the stairs. 'Lunch is ready,' she said.

'I'm just coming.'

'No hurry.' She smiled, balancing the clothes in her arms. 'How's Jamie?'

Hayes hesitated. 'No reply.'

Pam smiled again. 'He's probably busy rehearsing with the band.'

'Probably.' He watched Pam head up the stairs with the pile of washing. Nothing seemed to trouble her.

Noticing he was still there, she called down, 'There's some salad in the fridge as well if you want. Help yourself.'

Hayes nodded. 'Thanks.' Though, for some reason, he wasn't hungry. He just wanted to mow the lawn now. Then his phone buzzed.

Thinking it might be Jamie, he felt a rush of anticipation as he went to pick it up. But it was his contact. 'Hello?' he said, walking back towards his office, so Pam wouldn't hear him.

'We're ready for the handover. Can you confirm the cargo's status?'

'He's at the farmhouse,' Hayes said, pushing the door to. 'In the back bedroom, as agreed.'

'We need your men out of there by six tonight.'

'I'll let them know.' And the line went dead.

Leaving his office, Hayes sat down at the kitchen table where Pam had left his sandwich on a plate and started texted Terry the news.

12

'What do you think he's doing up there?' Sean said, picking up a dusty vase off the mantelpiece and having a look at it. He was that bored.

Terry was sitting in a chair reading his book. 'Leave that,' he said, looking up over his reading glasses.

Sean put the vase back. 'He must be wondering what's going on.'

'I thought I told you to put him out of your mind.'

'Yeah. I'm just saying. I'm not going to do anything. Anyway, what's the time?'

Terry sighed and glanced at his watch. 'It's nearly twelve o'clock, okay?'

'All right. Calm down.'

Terry shook his head and looked at his book again.

Sean said, 'I don't know how you can just sit there reading all the time.'

Head down, Terry replied, 'You should try it someday.'

'I read. Anyway, I can find out everything I want on the internet. I don't need to read a—'

Terry's phone buzzed. Sean watched Terry set down his book, take out his phone, read the text message, then send a short reply.

'What's going on?' he asked. 'Is that Mr Hayes?'

Terry pocketed his phone and picked up his book again. 'Yeah.'

'What did he say?'

'He wants us out by six.'

'Excellent! I can't wait to get out of here. What about you?'

Terry looked up, and said, 'Sean – I'm trying to read.'

Sean knew when not to push it. He walked over to the window, parted the curtains and looked outside. It was the only window that wasn't boarded up. He followed the tractor tracks across the sloping field to the wood at the far end of the valley about three-quarters of a mile away. He wondered where the guy on the quad bike had gone.

Behind him, Terry said, 'Come away from the window.'

'There's no one there.'

'I don't care.'

Sean let go of the curtain. Then he asked, 'Can I go outside?' He needed to do something. He couldn't just stand around doing nothing until six o'clock. He knew he was pissing Terry off but he couldn't just switch off like him.

Terry didn't say anything.

Sean said, 'This place is doing my head in. Seriously man, I'm not like you. I need to do something.'

Terry put down his book now and removed his glasses.

Sean backed off, scared Terry was going to grab him or something. 'What are you doing?' he said.

Terry said, 'What's it look like?'

'Why have you stopped reading?'

'What – with you jabbering away?'

'Sorry, man. I can't relax.'

'I can see that.' Terry folded up his glasses and put them in their case. Sean noticed one of his thumb nails was black with a bruise. He also noticed greying stubble was beginning to show on Terry's chin. It made him look older, Sean thought, and somehow less threatening.

Terry looked at his watch again.

Sean said, 'I'm beginning to feel like we're the ones imprisoned here. Do you know what I mean?'

Terry said, 'Sean, just shut your mouth for a minute, will you?'

'Sorry.'

Terry got up, went to the window and peered outside, then walked across to the door.

Sean said, 'Where are you going?'

'To the kitchen. To make some tea.'

Sean followed him out of the room, noticing Terry glance up the stairs on his way. When they were safely in the kitchen with the door shut, Sean said, 'It's very quiet up there. Do you think we should go and check on him?'

Terry said, 'I'm going to throttle you in a minute.' He filled the pan with water.

Sean said, 'I'm sorry,' puffing loudly and running his hand through his head. 'I just need to get out for a bit ... Please, Terry. If I see anyone I'll come straight back in.'

'What are you going to do out there?'

'Nothing. Just get some fresh air.'

'Why are you so keen on fresh air all of a sudden?'

'I told you. I just need to get out of this house for a bit.'

Terry lit the gas stove and set the pan on top. He held the handle of the pan for a moment. Sean wondered what he was thinking about.

The truth was Sean had very little idea what Terry thought about most of the time. Terry never really opened up about anything. He talked about books and stuff he'd watched on TV, but never about anything personal. Sean struggled to imagine what Terry might talk about with his wife over dinner. Perhaps they didn't talk about anything. Perhaps they ate separately. Sean knew very little about Terry. Like, if he had any siblings or what his father did. Sean, on the other hand, told Terry everything, even what dreams he'd had the night before. Perhaps he talked too much. Terry certainly thought he did, telling him once, 'If you want to get on in this world you've got to learn to keep your mouth shut sometimes.' But he didn't listen to everything Terry told him. Although he respected Terry and was grateful for what he'd done for him, Sean didn't want to turn out like him. In Sean's eyes, Terry took too much shit from people, especially Mr Hayes. He needed to stand up and say more about what he thought, Sean reckoned. Give his opinion more. But if you ever said anything like that to Terry he just lost it. So Sean had given up trying. Terry was Terry. You couldn't change him.

'Ten minutes,' Terry said. 'All right?'

'Serious?' Sean grinned, wanting to hug him.

'Go on. I'll be out in a minute.'

Sean opened the back door and stepped outside. He stood for a moment, putting his hand up to his head as the wind whipped through his hair. He saw an old washing line snagged up in the bushes of the garden. He picked up a stone and threw it across the courtyard, brushing his hands together afterwards to remove the dust from handling the stone. He sat on a wall and looked up at the sky. Layers of grey cloud spanned the horizon. He stared into the distance, thinking about nothing in particular. A minute or two passed. When he heard Terry coming out of the house he jumped up. Terry was carrying his cup of tea and the wind blew the rising steam from the cup.

They walked over to the barn together. One half of the barn was open-ended for tractors to be able to come in and out. Just inside, Terry put his cup on a breeze block and began rolling a cigarette. Sean kicked at patches of dried manure stuck to the concrete floor. Out the back there was a pile of rusty five gallon drums and rolls of stock netting half-buried in clump of brambles. Sean stood and looked at it for a moment.

The sound of Terry sparking up his rollie made him turn round again. He watched Terry puffing away. The rollie's tip glowed in the gloom of the barn. Terry looked through the wooden slats out across the courtyard. He took a slurp of tea. Sean walked back towards him, saying, 'See anything?'

Terry said, 'Nope,' not looking round.

Sean picked up another stone and, turning round, threw it towards the back of the barn, intending for it to fly out the back, but the stone clattered into the barn's side.

Terry turned round and glared at him.

Sean said, 'Sorry,' holding up his hands. He came over and stood beside Terry and looked outside. 'What's the time now?' he said.

Terry didn't look at his watch. 'About one o'clock.' He took another sip of tea, then relit his rollie.

Sean said, 'I can't wait to get back home.' He looked across at the house. For a second, he'd forgotten about the cargo locked upstairs. Sean felt unsettled, and said, 'We're just going to leave him here, aren't we?'

Terry dragged on his rollie. 'That's right.' The burning tobacco crackled.

Sean said, 'What if Mr Hayes's client doesn't show up?'

A small ember fluttered from the end of Terry's rollie and Terry caught it in his large hand. 'Not our problem,' he said.

Sean said, 'Of course – I know – but…'

Terry said, 'We give him some food. Pack up. Then go.'

'So we'll be home tonight. Yeah?'

Terry exhaled smoke through his nose. 'Unless you've got other plans.'

'No. I was just wondering.'

Terry knocked the ash off through a crack in the concrete, then rotated the tip of the rollie on the breeze block, as if he was sharpening it.

Sean said, 'What about tomorrow?'

'What about it?'

'What are we doing?'

Taking another drag, Terry shrugged.

Sean said, 'Has Mr Hayes not said anything yet?'

'Not yet.'

'Maybe we've got the day off.'

'Maybe.' Terry spat out a loose strand of tobacco that had got between his teeth.

Sean said, 'It seems like we've been away for ages. What day is it today?'

'Thursday.'

'Cool. Nearly the weekend. You're fishing, aren't you?'

'Yeah.' Terry sipped his tea and looked off into the distance.

Sean looked in the same direction, across fields and treetops, and thought how empty this place was, with no one about, no houses, nothing, and reckoned he couldn't live here, it would drive him mad. He said, 'I'll be at that restaurant with Tash I told you about. I can't fucking wait!

Terry turned to him, and said, 'Have you had enough fresh air yet?'

Sean shrugged. 'Yeah.'

They set off across the courtyard when Terry stopped and stuck out his arm. 'What was that?' he said.

Sean paused beside him. 'What was what?'

Terry scanned the horizon; the wind gusting.

Sean said, 'What is it?'

'Shh!'

It was the sound of the quad bike again, but coming their way this time.

13

LAWRENCE LIFTED HIS head when he heard the sound of the bike. He was sitting on the floor near the window. He sat up, turned his head to the door and listened for the two men, having heard them go outside earlier. He couldn't hear anything.

He got up, pushing off the wall to balance himself and put his ear to the window board. The quad bike was getting closer all the time.

Lawrence pulled the chair over to the window, climbed up, and looked through the crack in the plywood. To begin with, he couldn't see the bike. He saw the field and treetops in the distance. His heart was racing, his breathing getting heavier. Then he saw the bike pass through a gap in the hedgerow and head towards them.

Just then, he heard a door bang downstairs and the voices of the two men. He got down off the chair and carried it back to the table. Then he heard footsteps coming up the stairs.

He wondered what he should do if the bike came over to the house. With the tape on his mouth, he couldn't call out. Perhaps he could kick at the window board. This might be his only chance to let someone know he was here, he thought.

He heard the door being unlocked. The bike was nearing the house and he wondered if he should start banging on the window now.

He backed off towards the wall as the door flew open. It was the younger guy, clad in his balaclava. The older guy must have stayed downstairs to deal with the guy on the bike, he thought.

The younger guy closed the door behind him. His balaclava, obviously put on in a hurry, wasn't on straight. He was clutching a length of wood, and shaking. He put his finger up to his lips.

Lawrence heard the bike right outside the house now. The sound of the engine reverberated against the walls. The young guy glanced round, breathing heavily, then tugged at his balaclava trying to align the mouth and eye holes better.

Lawrence shifted his weight from one foot to the other, the floorboards creaking.

The young guy looked round, and hissed, 'Keep still.'

Lawrence then heard the bike stop and the engine switch off, thinking the guy must be coming to the door. This could be his chance.

Lawrence noticed the young guy's eyes flick from side to side as he tried to hear what was going on downstairs.

Breathing in deeply through his nose, Lawrence got himself ready.

The young guy leant towards the door, clearly desperate to know what was going on.

Someone started knocking on the door downstairs. The guy on the bike, Lawrence thought, it had to be.

The young guy turned to him and put his finger to his

lips again.

Lawrence nodded.

There was a moment's silence, both of them breathing heavily.

Then another knock came from downstairs, harder this time, and Lawrence watched the guy's chest rise and fall with each breath as he stared at the door.

More silence.

Then came a man's voice. 'Hello? Is anyone in?'

Hearing the voice made Lawrence realise what was happening to him was real. Not a dream or happening to someone else. This was him locked up in here. It gave him hope that this situation was going to end.

There was another moment's silence.

Lawrence looked at the young guy – six foot and skinny – and thought about charging at him. There was about three metres distance between them. If he could get to him before he had a chance to react, and knock him over, then he might get a chance to run downstairs and be seen.

His heart was beating hard as he had these thoughts, his muscles stiffening in anticipation. He moved his feet apart.

The young guy had his head turned towards the door, still trying to hear what was going on. Lawrence knew this was his chance. That he wouldn't get a better opportunity than this. He took a deep breath, lowered his shoulders and lunged at him.

He caught the young guy around the waist. The guy groaned, having the wind taken out of him, and they came crashing to the floor. The length of wood fell out of his hand.

Lawrence rolled over and stood up, using the wall for

support. But the young guy grabbed his legs and pulled him over. They struggled on the floor. Lawrence kicked out with his legs, knowing he didn't stand much chance with his hands tied. But he kept hoping the man on the quad bike would hear something and either try breaking down the door or get on the phone to the police.

As he tried getting up again, Lawrence looked up and saw the older guy come into the room. Closing the door behind him, he walked straight over, fist clenched, arm raised.

Lawrence tried to sway out of his way. But the incoming fist was too quick. It hit him on the side of his head and Lawrence felt a jarring sensation, as if his brain had come loose. For a second, he saw bursting balls of light drift across his vision, then he passed out.

14

AFTER KNOCKING ON the door, Mark climbed back onto his quad bike and pressed the ignition button. Revving the engine, he looked up at the farmhouse. The windows were all boarded up, so he couldn't see much. The tyre tracks grew fainter as they came into the farmyard and didn't appear to lead anywhere. Maybe someone had bought the place, as Clare suggested, and was just having a look round. In which case, it was none of his business.

Mark drove out of the farmyard, thinking that he could come back after dark and have another look then. If someone was about there would be a light of some kind. He crossed over the cattle grid in the gateway and headed down the pot-holed track, splashing through puddles.

At the end of the driveway, he stopped and glanced back at the house again. It looked a sorry sight with its missing roof tiles and rotten window frames. He'd heard the old boy who used to live here had died alone and penniless. He'd farmed it with his brother apparently. But when the brother died, the old boy couldn't keep the farm going. Neither of them had married. Their mother had lived with them up until her death. Apparently, she'd run the place before them, her husband having died in the war. So the story went anyway. No doubt, some banker from London had bought it now, Mark thought, and would throw some money at it, convert the barns into offices or rent them out as a wedding venue, and come here at weekends, probably with two chocolate Labradors, and cause him more headaches than he had already.

For a second, looking at the house, Mark thought he saw movement behind one of the only un-boarded windows. But the more he looked, the more he talked himself out of it, the sun appearing from behind clouds and flashing across the courtyard. Just a trick of the light, he thought.

He turned the bike and accelerated off. There was no doubt, though, someone had been up here recently, what with the fresh tyre tracks. He wasn't imagining that. Maybe someone sussing the place out. He'd heard of several instances of squatters taking over abandoned farms at night.

Mark followed the track over the downs and headed towards the village, wanting to get something from the shop. He joined up with the road and rode past the church before coming into the village.

Pulling up outside the shop, he got off the bike and went inside. A radio was playing in the background.

Mark bought a loaf of bread, milk and some chocolate Hobnobs. As he was leaving, he saw Simon's pickup truck coming along the road. He gave him a wave and Simon pulled over.

Simon was pretty much Mark's only friend in the area. Although Mark had been here five years now, the opportunities to socialise were limited in his job.

Leaning out of his truck's window, Simon said, 'Aren't

you supposed to be on holiday?'

'Yeah, this is it – the wonders of Sudley village shop.'

Simon grinned. 'I know how you feel.'

'What about you? How's life in the fast lane?'

'Oh, don't.' Simon shook his head. 'We're so behind – Carl's off bloody sick again.'

'Get someone else.'

'I wish I could. Not that easy, mate.'

A 4x4 went passed beeping its horn and Simon waved; Mark didn't recognise who it was, and Simon said, 'Chris from Marshalls.'

Mark said, 'I was going to ask. You know Hillards Farm?'

'What, Coleman's old place?'

'Yeah. What's going on up there?'

'Nothing. As far as I know. Why?'

'It looks like someone's been up there recently.'

Simon said, 'I know it was sold a while back. Someone came in and boarded up the windows and what not.'

'I saw that.'

'Ring Jill at the estate office, see if she knows. Or better still – speak to my wife. She seems to know everything.'

'Yeah. Was going to get Clare on to it.'

Simon said, 'I expect someone's going to do it up when the time comes. Probably some builders having a look round.'

'Yeah. That's what I thought.'

Simon glanced up to his rear-view mirror, then said, 'I know they had some trouble at Chalding recently. If that's what you're thinking.'

'Yeah, I heard about that. There was also some trouble on the Ashford estate.'

'Was there?'

'Yeah. Some quad bikes went missing.'

Simon shook his head.

Mark said, 'I'm going to have a look round after dark. See if I can see anything.'

'Well, you be careful, young man,' Simon said, glancing up to his rear-view again, and getting ready to pull out. 'I don't want to have to come and get you out of a ditch. I can't spare the manpower at the moment. See you later.'

Mark waved him off, then headed home, thinking about what Simon had said about someone buying the cottage, boarding up the windows and builders coming in to have a look. It sounded like the most plausible explanation. He'd still drive out there later, though, to have a look, he thought. Just to be sure.

15

'HELP ME GET him over to the bed,' Terry said, putting his hands under the cargo's arms and attempting to drag him. Terry knew he had panicked and hit the cargo too hard, worried the guy on the quad bike might hear something if he hadn't.

Sean was just standing there, staring. Couldn't believe Terry had just knocked the guy out cold. Blood was running down the cargo's face.

'Sean!' Terry said. 'Snap out of it.'

Sean looked up at Terry, his eyes bulging through the holes in his balaclava.

'Help me,' Terry said.

Doing as he was instructed, Sean took hold of the cargo's legs and together they lifted him over to the bed. Blood smeared the pillow.

Sean watched Terry remove the tape from the cargo's mouth. 'Is he going to be all right?' he asked. The cargo's shirt was covered in dust and blood; he looked like he didn't deserve any of this. Sean felt bad he hadn't phoned his wife now. What harm could it have done?

The cargo started coughing, coming round.

Terry said, 'Get me the water.'

Sean handed him the bottle.

Terry helped the cargo to a drink. Water ran down his chin and soaked his shirt. He coughed again. He looked wide-eyed, round the room, then at Terry. 'What's going on?' he said.

'Nothing,' Terry said. 'Just don't try that again. All right?' He tore off another strip of tape.

The cargo said, 'Please. Wait—' But Terry stuck the tape over his mouth and signalled to Sean they were leaving. Terry followed him out.

Downstairs, Terry shut the kitchen door, ripped off his balaclava and checked his watch.

Sean stood the other side of the table from him, feeling a little afraid of what Terry might do next.

Terry went to the window, lifted the curtain and looked outside, saying, 'Whoever that nosy fucker is – he's gone now.'

Sean glanced at Terry's rucksack, seeing it had moved. Had Terry taken the gun out – just in case? 'Do you think he heard anything?' he asked.

'I don't know.' Terry moved away from the window, checking his watch again.

Sean said, 'I'm sorry.'

'What for?'

'For fucking up.'

Terry shrugged. 'It's not your fault,'

Sean said, 'He just ran at me.'

'Forget it. It's happened now.' He took out his phone and checked his messages.

'He took me by surprise, you know.'

'It doesn't matter.'

Sean looked at his hands; they were shaking.

Putting his phone away, Terry said, 'I shouldn't have left you with him.' He walked to the door.

Watching him, Sean said, 'What is it?'

'I reckon we give him his dinner early and get out of here before that guy comes back sniffing around again.'

Sean said, 'What time is it?'

'Four.'

'I thought you said we're leaving at six.'

'I did. But by the time we've given him his food, got our stuff together, it won't be far off that.' Terry picked up the carrier bag of food and emptied it on the table.

Sean was about to offer to help when he noticed blood on his arm from the cargo. He tried rubbing it to get the blood off, but it didn't work, so he went to the sink and poured water from the bottle over it.

Terry, seeing what he was doing, said, 'Don't waste the water.'

Although they were leaving soon, Sean didn't argue. The blood looked to have gone anyway.

Terry put a packet of sandwiches to one side.

Sean said, 'Are you going up?'

'We both are.'

'What if he tries it again?'

'He won't.'

'Are you going to tell him we're leaving?'

'No.'

Sean remembered taking down the wife's phone number. What if the cargo was to mention it now, in front of Terry? Wouldn't it be better if Terry heard it from him first? Sean said, 'What if he starts asking questions again?'

'You just ignore him.'

Sean puffed out a deep breath, not wanting to go back upstairs, feeling shaky.

Terry said, 'We give him his food. Wait for him to finish. Then get out of here. Okay?'

'What, and say nothing?'

'And say nothing.'

16

AFTER EATING HIS sandwich, Hayes went outside and started mowing the lawn. It was one of the few times he really got to switch off.

On his last visit to his GP (a routine cholesterol check-up), Hayes had mentioned he wasn't feeling quite himself and his doctor suggested he might be depressed, asking him, 'Are you sleeping okay?' Hayes had been prescribed sleeping pills in the past but found they affected his appetite and ability to concentrate, so gave up on them. 'I'm fine,' he told his doctor, not wanting any more pills. His doctor then said, 'I can put you in touch with someone to talk to, if you like.' Hayes wished he hadn't said anything.

He'd been to a counsellor once with his ex-wife when the wheels were coming off their marriage (his ex's idea). What a waste of time that was. His ex had a field day, of course, off-loading all her baggage about him, like she'd been rehearsing this moment all her life, the councillor occasionally turning to him, and saying, 'And how does that make you feel, Graham?' Not since his parents had died had anyone called him Graham.

Hayes chewed on a piece of gum as he went up and

down the lawn, taking great care to keep the lines straight. Done properly, it took nearly two hours. When he was nearly finished, and without thinking about anything in particular, he felt tears come to his eyes. Just like that, no warning. It had only started happening recently. Crying for no reason. He let out a deep breath, not wanting to let himself go, and finished up the lawn. Then he drove back towards the orchard, stopping to empty the grass box in a gap between some fir trees on the way. In the orchard, he parked the tractor up in a lean-to shed, removed the ignition keys, and padlocked the door on his way out.

He walked out into the late afternoon sunshine and stopped for a moment to collect himself. Although the urge to cry had passed, he felt shaken by it. He thought of Terry and Sean getting ready to leave the cottage about now and it made Hayes realise how much his attitude towards work had changed. Five years ago, he would have been demanding a running commentary. Now, he was quite happy to leave most of it to Terry and keep communication down to a minimum. He didn't know whether this was good thing or not. For most of his first marriage, his ex had accused him of being a workaholic, wondering why it was always him who put in the extra hours and went out in the middle of the night. 'Can't someone else do it?' she'd always say. How times had changed.

The sun was going down behind the line of oak trees in the neighbouring field; an orange tinge lay on their upper branches. A wood pigeon climbed in the sky, making a clapping sound with its wings before gliding in a downward arc. Hayes watched the progress of the pigeon for a moment. Before now, he hadn't paid much attention to the birds or trees. But now, like the mowing, he found it all very soothing. He didn't know quite why this was. He only knew his younger self would have scoffed at him for feeling like this, and dismissed him as having gone soft in the head, or worse, showing signs of cracking up. Well, maybe he was… cracking up, that was. Either way – he wasn't sure he really cared.

The wood pigeon glided towards a line of Scots pines, and slowing up with a tilt of its wings, it landed on an upper branch. Hayes continued across the lawn, and coming to the patio round the house, he heard Pam's voice speaking on the phone. It was Jamie.

When Pam saw him, her eyes lit up and she waved him over. 'He's here. Just hold on,' she said.

Hayes took the phone off her and went into the sitting room with it.

'Hi Jamie,' he said. 'Thanks for ringing back.'

There was a pause. 'What is it, Dad?'

'Nothing.'

'You left a message.'

'Yeah. I was just wondering how you were.' Hayes was shocked things had got this bad between them.

'Dad, I haven't got long. I've got to go out in a minute. I've got a gig. You're not dying or anything?'

Hayes said, 'No. I'm not dying.'

'Right. So what's wrong then?'

'Nothing's wrong.'

'What is it then?'

Hayes felt his heart rate increase, like his father must have done after the six o'clock news that Sunday night, years ago. He said, 'I was just wondering if you wanted to meet for a curry.'

'What for?'

'Give us a break, Jamie. I'm your dad!'

'I can't tonight.'

'I didn't mean tonight. What about the weekend?'

'Maybe. You sure this is not about anything?'

'No. Like what?'

'You haven't spoken to Mum, have you?'

'No. Should I?'

There was a pause. 'It's just odd you want to meet like this.'

'Is it? I don't think so.'

Then sarcastically, Jamie said, 'No, Dad, you wouldn't.'

Hayes recognised the pattern of the conversation and tried to change it. 'So how's the band going?' he said. 'Where's your gig tonight?'

'Listen, Dad, if you want to meet for a curry, that's fine. But let's not pretend we're best buddies all of a sudden. All right?'

'All right.'

17

'I'M NOT REALLY hungry,' the cargo said.

'Just eat,' Terry said, ripping open the sandwich packet and putting it down on the table in front of him.

The cargo said, 'Is everything all right?'

Terry said, 'No questions. Just eat.' He nodded at Sean. Sean cut the cable tie round the cargo's wrists.

The cargo rubbed his wrists as his hands were released. Terry pushed him in the back. 'Didn't you hear me?'

The cargo picked up a sandwich and took a bite.

They stood and watched him. He chewed slowly and drank from the water bottle between mouthfuls; his mouth clearly dry. When he finished Terry told him to stand up, turn round and face the wall. He did as he was told. Terry said, 'Hands behind your back.'

The cargo obliged, saying, 'Is someone coming to see me?'

Terry cable tied his hands; the cargo saying, 'Please. What's going on?'

'Shut it.' Terry tore off another strip of tape and slapped it over his mouth.

Back in the kitchen, Sean said, 'He's going to be all right, isn't he?'

Cupping his hands, Terry relit a rollie he had saved and looked out of the back door window.

'I can't help feeling something bad is going to happen to him,' Sean said, remembering how the guy had just sat there, not saying a word, as he ate the sandwiches.

Terry pocketed his lighter, puffing on the cigarette, and came away from the door. 'I'm telling you, Sean. Put him out of your head.' Smoke poured from his nostrils. 'We're out of here in ten minutes.'

'Isn't he going to wonder where we've gone?' Sean said.

'I don't know. And I don't really care.'

'Shouldn't we hang around and make sure this geezer coming to see him actually turns up?' Sean felt somehow responsible for the cargo after he'd got him to write down his wife's telephone number.

Terry looked at him through a cloud of smoke and said, 'I thought you couldn't wait to get out of here.'

'I can't. But what if this guy doesn't come and the cargo dude is just left here.'

'I told you. That's not our problem.'

'Terry – he'll fucking die up there, man!'

Terry shrugged as he sucked on his rollie.

Sean said, 'I don't want that on my conscience.'

'That's a big word for you,' Terry said.

'Fuck off.'

Terry listened at the door. There was a creaking sound upstairs; then it went quiet.

Sean said, 'This is crazy, you know that.'

'Come on – get your shit together,' Terry said. He checked his phone then picked up his rucksack.

Watching him, Sean remembered the gun inside. Sean had no doubt Terry would be capable of using it. He'd seen him do some pretty questionable things in his time. Plus, he knew Terry would do anything Mr Hayes told him.

Terry stopped and looked at him. 'Did you hear me?'

Sean said, 'What?'

'Get your arse in gear. Where's your bag?'

'It's in the sitting room.'

'Well, go and get it.'

Sean went next door and picked up his gym bag, pulling on its drawstrings and slinging it over his shoulder. As he came out into the hall, he noticed the picture of the geese on the wall; then glancing up the stairs to the cargo's room, he wondered if the cargo realised they were leaving and that was why he had been so quiet when they gave him his food. Sean contemplated what he should do with his wife's phone number. Maybe he should leave it for a day or two, and give the guy coming time to question him, then phone anonymously from a pay phone. That way Sean would know the cargo wasn't just going to be abandoned here.

Terry was checking his phone again when he came into the kitchen. He looked up. 'Okay,' he said. 'Have you got everything?'

'Yup.'

'Right,' he said. 'I'll meet you in the van.'

'What are you going to do?'

'Just do it, Sean. I won't be long.'

Sean stepped outside and felt a chill in the air now, the sun setting across the valley, the breeze picking up. He huddled up in his hoodie, pulling up the hood, and walked across the courtyard to the shed where they'd left the van. When he got there, he glanced back over his shoulder at the house but couldn't see Terry yet. Then he unlocked the shed door, propping it open with a brick, and got into the van.

Out of the breeze, it was quiet and he felt a moment of peace. As he sat there, he looked at a can of Red Bull in the footwell from the journey over and remembered feeling very different to how he did now. He took out his phone and held it in his hand. He would soon be able to use it again, he thought. He looked at the van's digital clock and saw it turn to 17:48. He wondered what Terry was doing inside. He half-expected to hear a gunshot. What would he do then?

Without really thinking, he took out the receipt with the phone number on. He wondered what he was going to do with it. He wished he hadn't written it down – that way, he wouldn't have to be thinking about it now. He thought again about telling Terry, but knew he'd go ballistic on him. Then he thought about telling Tash, but reckoned she'd make him phone the police, and he knew he couldn't do that. He felt on his own with this. What if this guy never went home, but was found dead a few weeks later?

Sean saw Terry leave the house, carrying his rucksack over his shoulder.

Sean stuffed the phone number back in his pocket and watched Terry approach the van, noticing him glance across the fields towards the track where they'd last seen the guy on the quad bike.

Terry got into the van and closed the door. Sean watched him relight a half-smoked rollie and waited for him to say something but soon gave up and asked him, 'Did you speak to him?'

Terry, sucking on the rollie, wound down the window.

Sean said, 'It's none of my business, right?'

Terry exhaled through a gap in the window.

Sean stared off into the distance for a second, the sky streaked with sunset and getting darker; then looked at the house and thought of the cargo up there in his room. 'I can't believe we've only been here for a night. Can you?' he said.

Terry had his mobile out and was typing a message. 'No,' he replied. 'Come on. Let's go.'

Sean turned the ignition keys.

Terry said, 'Keep the lights off until we're at the road.'

Sean pulled out of the barn in the half-light, glancing up at the boarded windows of the house and wondering if the cargo could hear them.

As they neared the cattle grid at the gateway to the track, Terry instructed, 'Take it slowly.'

Sean slowed right down, the van rocking from side to side over the uneven metal rails. Sean then headed down the rough track, changing up to second gear, as he snaked about to avoid the potholes.

When he came to the road he stopped. Car headlights flickered in the distance. He waited, lights off, engine idling, until the car zipped past. Then he pulled out, flicking on the van's lights, and changed up through the gears, the distance growing between them and the farmhouse, at last.

18

WHEN THE OLDER man came into the room Lawrence had
been lying on the bed. He didn't have time to get up. He
felt the cold prick of the needle somewhere in his side, then
the leaden sensation of an alien liquid flooding his blood
stream. Soon, he felt hot and shivery; his skin prickled all
over. He began to shake, his jaw chattering uncontrollably.

Now, for a moment, he thought he heard the ticking
over of the van's engine. He looked around but couldn't see
anything. Was it because it was too dark? Or were his eyes
closed? He could feel the drug distorting his senses.

The sound of the van appeared to get closer. He thought
he got a whiff of diesel; then it started to feel like he was in
the back of the van again, and they were moving. Bumping
along an uneven track… slowing down… pulling away.

He remembered thinking on the drive over here how
they must have arrived at their destination when the van
stopped. But now he wondered whether they hadn't in fact
arrived after all; that maybe they'd just stopped somewhere
temporarily and were now setting off again. Maybe he'd
been in the back of the van all along.

But what about the injection? Why were they giving

him drugs? he wondered. Was he sick? Had there been an accident? Maybe he was on his way to hospital. Maybe the van was in fact an ambulance, he thought.

For a moment, the sound of his heart pumping was all he could hear and he wondered if this was because he was hooked up to a mechanical ventilator. Maybe he was in hospital already, he thought.

He tried moving parts of his body, but couldn't feel anything – not even his fingers. As if he didn't have a body anymore, just thoughts.

He experienced memory flashes. The sun shining through pine trees; shadows across a lawn. He heard his daughter saying to him, 'Daddy, when are you coming home?' For a moment, he imagined he was back at home, looking from his bedroom window. Had the hospital released him? Then he saw himself walking across the golf club car park, the man standing behind him, his spread hands seeming to cut out the sun as he reached out and grabbed him. Then he saw himself back in the boarded-up room again, clutching his legs, his shoulders shaking, looking up at the boarded window, the bed, the table and chair; then feeling like this was where he now lived, a rented room somewhere, and the memories he had of his daughter were from one of her recent visits. Was he separated from Amanda now? Did he live here alone? Lawrence started to wonder if he'd lost his mind without knowing it (because you wouldn't know, would you?). Or whether he'd been in an accident and suffered amnesia.

Several hours seemed to have passed before Lawrence sat up and wondered where he was again.

Looking round, he recognised the table legs and chair and realised he was still in the boarded-up room. He was lying on the floor, and he wondered how he came to be there. He couldn't remember lying down. He felt different from earlier, though, when he thought he'd heard the van. Was it the injection wearing off?

He wondered where the two men were.

He got up off the floor, steadying himself against the wall, hands still tied, and walked across to the door and listened for any sounds of life downstairs.

He couldn't hear anything. He felt a rush of blood and started sucking in the tape on his mouth.

Where were they?

He told himself not to panic. He took in deep breaths through his nose and exhaled slowly. He was used to the tape on his mouth; he knew how to breathe with it there. It was okay.

He looked round the room, trying to think logically about this. Maybe the men were outside. He remembered the crack in the window board and dragged the chair across to climb up and look outside. But it was too dark to see much other than the shadowy slope of the field.

He got off the chair and tried to think what to do next.

Surely they wouldn't have just left me here? he thought.

But he couldn't hear anything.

He faced the door, breathing deeply. Maybe they'd popped out for something to eat, and wouldn't be back for an hour or so – in which case, was this his chance to escape? There was only one way to find out.

He tapped the door with his foot, gently at first, and listened to see if anyone responded. He was half-hoping it was just the young guy down there, in which case he could try talking him round, like he had with the phone number.

There was no response; no sound at all. Maybe they really had gone out.

He kicked the door again, a little harder this time, growing in confidence. Then listened out for a response. But none came.

Stepping back now, Lawrence lifted his leg and brought his foot down on the door as hard as he could.

His heart was beating hard as he listened for a response. But still nothing. They really had gone out, he thought.

He backed away from the door, then ran at it, shoulder first. The padlock and clasp rattled on the outside. But the door didn't open.

He went to the window next, turned his back to it and gripped the edge of the board and tried to move it, but it was screwed down solidly. He stood for a moment, thinking about the guy on the quad bike, how if he came back he could try getting his attention by banging against the window. Only the quad bike guy wasn't likely to be coming back until it was light, whereas the two men would probably be back any minute.

Concluding he'd no time to waste, Lawrence started kicking against the window board. He kept this up for several minutes, then tried with his shoulder, taking several steps back and throwing himself against it. But the board was as solid as the door.

He sat on the edge of the bed, breathing heavily. He was sweating and wiped his face on his shoulders. Sharp stabbing sensations ran down his side; his shoulder throbbed.

He wondered where the two men had gone and when the person who wanted to speak to him was coming. Was there really someone coming? Maybe this was it. They'd just left him here. What then?

19

Sean waited at a set of traffic lights on the edge of a small town. Roadwork barriers closed off one side of the road. Sean tapped the steering wheel. The lights changed, and Sean continued along the road for another hundred metres, then pulled into a pub car park, as planned. He parked the van against a low brick wall, pulled up the handbrake and turned off the engine. It was just beginning to drizzle.

'Okay,' Terry said, checking his watch, 'we've got an hour. Then we pick up the car.'

'What about the van?'

'We leave it here. Someone will pick it up later.' Terry held his rucksack on his lap and checked his wing mirror.

Sean watched the drizzle spot the windscreen.

Terry said, 'Right. Don't forget your things,' and, opening his door, got out.

Sean grabbed his backpack and jumped out after him. They went into the pub together.

Inside, at the bar, Terry said to the barman, 'a pint of Best, please,' then asked Sean, 'What do you want?'

Sean looked along the bar and everything looked a little blurry and unreal. He felt out of it for a moment. Someone hit the jackpot on a nearby fruit machine and coins chugged into the tray.

'Sean,' Terry said, nudging him. 'What do you want?'

Sean blinked and saw the barman was waiting for him. He said, 'San Miguel.'

'Right. And a San Miguel, please,' Terry said to the barman. Then to Sean, 'Go and find us a table, will you?'

Sean walked off and found a table in the corner. Sitting down, he took out his phone. Terry had said he could use it now. He stared at the screen for a moment before turning it on. He remembered the telephone number the cargo had given him. He pictured the guy back at the cottage, stuck in the room, all alone, his missus and kids out there somewhere. Was he the cargo's only hope of getting out of there? he wondered. He looked up and saw Terry waiting for his change and felt in his pocket for the number. It was still there.

Terry approached with the drinks and Sean removed his hand from his pocket and swiped the screen of his phone.

Setting down the drinks, Terry said, 'Thought it wouldn't take you long before you were on your phone.'

Sean ignored him and looked at his messages. But the smell of beer made him feel sick. He looked up and saw Terry sip the froth off his pint of bitter. He couldn't understand how Terry could drink that stuff – it looked like rusty piss. But then he couldn't understand why Terry smoked rollies and wore wax-proofed jackets.

He watched Terry draw the back of his hand across his mouth, then set down his pint. His eyes were puffy and bloodshot from lack of sleep; his greying stubble was thicker. He looked a year or two older than when they'd left.

'Aren't you going to drink that?' Terry said, gesturing towards Sean's untouched bottle.

'Yeah. In a minute.' He now regretted not ordering a Coke.

Terry shook his head and took another sip of his pint.

Sean picked up his bottle but couldn't bring himself to take a drink yet.

'What's the matter?'

'Nothing.' Sean looked round the room.

Terry said, 'I thought you'd be all excited about getting home.'

Sean shrugged, putting the bottle up to his mouth now, and letting the beer touch his lips.

Terry added, 'You can see your bird again. Tell her you love her. And all that.'

Sean lowered the bottle, swallowed, and thought what a prick Terry could be at times. 'Leave it out.'

'Oh dear, is someone in a strop?'

Sean ignored him and looked at his phone again.

Terry said, 'She not texted you? Is that it?'

Sean wasn't in the mood. 'Yeah, right,' he said.

'Cheer up. I'm sure she still loves you.'

Sean ignored him and looked at his phone.

Terry took another drink. Putting down his glass, he swallowed a belch, and said, 'Just remember what I told you. All right?'

'Which bit was that?' Sean muttered sarcastically.

'The chat we had. About keeping things to yourself… remember?'

'Oh, that… Yeah, I remember.'

Terry kept staring at him.

Sean said, 'What? I said I remember.'

'Sean, are you keeping something from me?'

'No!' Sean put the bottle to his lips again; Terry's eyes on him all the time.

Terry leant towards him, and said in a low voice, 'Sean, just forget about what happened, all right?'

'Yeah. I know.'

'What's happened is done with now. You move on.'

Sean swilled his beer and looked down the neck of the bottle. He sensed Terry knew what he was thinking – about the cargo, his wife and kids. Maybe Terry even felt the same way himself, just wasn't saying. Who knew? Because you didn't say anything, that was the rule. You forgot it and moved on.

Terry said, 'We drink this. Then get going. Just like we planned. Right?'

Sean took another swig of beer, jiggling his leg nervously under the table.

Terry said, 'Right?'

Sean said, 'Yeah, right.'

'You remember the plan, don't you?'

'We leave the pub and split up.'

'Then what?'

'I walk across town via the station. Then we meet up by the Shell garage.' Sean knew this was Terry's way of trying to find out if they were being followed, which Sean thought was a waste of time. But you didn't argue.

'And what about when you get home?' Terry said. 'What have you got to do then?'

Sean wondered how much longer he could put up with this shit. He said tiredly, 'We keep our heads down.'

'That's it,' Terry said. 'We keep our heads down. You order pizzas. Watch DVDs. Anything you like. Just keep out of trouble. You understand?'

'Yeah,' Sean said.

Terry lifted his pint, and said, 'Drink up.'

They finished their drinks and left through a side door by the Gents toilet. Outside, Sean pulled up his hoodie and Terry took out a half-smoke rollie from his pocket, put it in his mouth and lit it.

Sean crossed the road, holding down the flaps of his hood, while Terry, puffing on his rollie, kept walking straight ahead. A car zipped past in the wet. Sean turned down a side street without any lights. The air was cold and damp. He hunched up his shoulders and thrust his hands in his pockets. He crossed over the railway bridge. His breath smoked in the cold night air. He passed a line of shops with metal shutters pulled down. A fish and chip shop was open on the corner. Teenagers were hanging around outside, sharing a spliff. He walked past with his head down. He came to a mechanics yard, surrounded by a chain link fence and stopped outside, as rehearsed. The Shell garage was opposite. He saw a taxi filling up at one of the pumps. The taxi driver then went over and paid at the till window. Sean shivered with cold and folded his arms. The taxi driver bought a packet of crisps and a drink as well, then got into his cab and left the garage. A moment later, Sean saw Terry approach in a silver Vauxhall and pull into a lay-by.

Sean checked in both directions, then jogged across the road and got in. Terry accelerated up through the gears, beating a set of traffic lights. 'All right?' he said.

'Yeah. Fine.' The car smelt of cheap air freshener, like

it'd had a recent valet.

Terry said, 'No one follow you?'

'Nope.'

'Sure?' Terry checked his mirrors and re-gripped the steering wheel.

Sean noticed he was wearing his leather driving gloves with cut-out backs. 'Yeah. What about you?'

Terry said, 'I'm here, aren't I?'

They didn't speak for a while after that.

Sean looked out of the window at the passing roadside, where hedgeless fields sloped off into the darkness, his mind filling with images of the cottage and the cargo as he imagined different scenarios playing out: the guy on the quad bike breaking into the cottage, finding the cargo and calling the police, then the hazmat-suited forensic guys collecting DNA swabs and fingerprints. Maybe they'd trace the van. Link a CCTV image of them at the golf club. Or none of these things. Perhaps the guy on the bike would never go back. Or anyone else for that matter. The cottage would remain untouched for years to come, just be left to grow damper and more derelict, until someone came to knock it down and when they did – and this was what Sean feared most of all, above and beyond the police and forensics – they'd finally discover the cargo, just a decayed corpse by then.

The thought of the cargo just rotting away in that damp, abandoned house filled Sean with horror. This wasn't what he'd imagined when he agreed to do this job. He wanted money to open a restaurant. Now he had this guy and his wife and kids on his conscience. How was he going to live out his dream now? What had Terry said? 'What's happened is done with now. You just move on.' But Sean couldn't. He wasn't like Terry. How could he move on knowing the cargo was still in the cottage?

The car headlights lit up cat's eyes through a tunnel of trees. Finally, Sean began to feel sleepy and he nodded off. The car swayed hypnotically through corners. For a while, he fell in and out of consciousness, waking up to glimpse a different roadside or Terry re-lighting a rollie. The events of the last few days began to seem part of a different reality, more like a dream. Perhaps that was how he should think of it: like a dream. Maybe in years to come he could forget about it that way.

Sean was fast asleep when Terry shook his arm, saying, 'Sean! Wake up.'

He sat up and looked round. 'What?' he said, as if he'd just been dozing for a second.

Terry said, 'We're here.'

They were stationary. Sean looked out of the window, seeing streetlights, a bus stop, a main road, and recognised the outskirts of the town where he lived.

He said, 'Right,' but was still half-asleep and couldn't recall what he was meant to do next.

Terry said, 'Time to go home. Remember?'

Sean opened the door and got out. He was about to shut it when Terry said, 'Your bag.'

'Oh, yeah.' Sean reached in, picked his bag out of the footwell and shut the door. He held up his hand to wave.

Terry nodded at him through the glass, then pulled a U-turn in the road, and drove off.

Sean stood there for a second. He felt the cold night air and shuddered through his shoulders. He took out his phone and checked the time. It was just after midnight. He slipped his arms through the drawstrings of his backpack, pulled down his hood and started walking.

Entering the town, he could smell the sea. The odd car passed along the road. A homeless guy lay asleep under sheets of cardboard in a shop entrance. He headed uphill, getting a glimpse of the sea through a gap between buildings. A couple in fur-hooded parkas walked past him holding hands. The wind gusted.

Eventually, he came to a shabby four-storey terrace, with flaking woodwork, where he lived on the top floor. Stopping outside, he looked in both directions. A police siren sounded in the distance and receded.

He gazed up at the building, checking the windows for any signs of movement. He didn't want anyone seeing him coming home tonight. Pulling on the cords of his hoodie, he walked up the steps to his front door.

20

Even before Lawrence opened his eyes, he sensed there was someone in the house with him. Whether he felt a change in temperature or heard a noise, he wasn't sure.

He sat up on the bed, his eyes straining in the darkness, and recognised the room's peeling walls. For a second, he thought he noticed the light flex judder from the ceiling, and wondered if it was vibrations downstairs.

Had the two men come back?

He felt a cool draught, as if there was a window open somewhere.

He got off the bed, trying to make as little noise as possible. If someone was downstairs he didn't want them to know he was awake. His shoulder still ached from ramming against the door and window board earlier. He imagined it was bruised.

Lawrence went to the door but couldn't hear anything, then got up on the chair, and looked through the crack in the board. All he could see was the shadowy slope of the field, the dark line of the hedgerow. For a second, he thought he saw something move, maybe an animal, a rabbit or fox. He wondered where the nearest house was, thinking about the guy on the quad bike, who must live locally. He imagined a nearby village, with a pub, a church...

Either way, he had to do something.

He knew from his previous attempt that breaking down the door was impossible. But maybe if he got his hands free, he'd stand a better chance. At the very least, he could then remove the tape from his mouth and try shouting.

He got down on the floor, backed up against the bed and started rubbing the cable tie against the bed frame. He wondered why he hadn't tried this before now. He imagined getting his hands free, breaking out of here and walking across fields towards the lights of a village, where he'd phone Amanda and tell her everything was fine, that he was coming home.

More determined than ever, he started rubbing harder and harder against the bed frame. He wasn't bothered about not making any noise now. He was certain no one was coming to speak to him and the two men had done a runner. All he could think about was getting out of there as quickly as possible.

Sweat prickled on his forehead. Breathing was difficult with the tape on his mouth. For a moment, he stopped to catch his breath and wipe his head on his shoulders. Then he tried pulling his arms apart to break the ties. But it didn't work. The cable ties pinched into his skin and left his wrists feeling sore.

He wondered whether the guy on the quad bike would come again in the morning, and how he could try to attract his attention if he did. Maybe he should just wait until then. He turned to the door, again thinking he heard something.

Had they come back? Was there someone there after all?

Out the corner of his eye, he thought he saw a red light flicker across the wall.

He walked over to the window to look out, trying to be quiet again. It was then he heard footsteps downstairs.

Someone was in the house. Maybe they'd been here all this time and were just waiting for the right moment. But for what?

The footsteps came up the stairs. For some reason, they sounded different from the two men. There was greater urgency; purpose to them.

Lawrence didn't move, but remained standing with his back to the wall, his hands tied behind his back, his mouth gagged.

Someone wanted to speak to him. Was this them?

Lawrence backed away from the door. He saw torch light flash round the edges. He listened for the sound of voices but couldn't hear anything. He wanted to say something. To let them know he was here. Alive. And not to hurt him. Maybe it was the police. They'd received a tip off and had come to get him out. He imagined Amanda waiting in a police car outside.

He heard the door being unlocked. They had a key. Whoever it was. Then torchlight flooded the room as the door swung open. Lawrence screwed up his eyes, half-blinded. A voice said, 'Get down on your knees.'

Lawrence dropped to his knees as two men in black military combats and tight-fitting balaclavas entered the room. They stood there holding guns with mounted LED lights. One man was slightly taller than the other, otherwise they looked identical.

Stepping forward, the shorter of the two men frisked

him, while the other man checked over the room, flashing his torch under the bed and across the window boards. Then the two men nodded at each other and the man who'd frisked him remained standing there, pointing his gun at him, while the other one removed the rucksack from his back and got out a power drill. Inserting a drill bit, he quickly surveyed the walls, selected a spot and started drilling. Masonry dust spilt onto the floor.

Lawrence looked at the man pointing the gun at him. The man's mask had a slit at the top and Lawrence could see his dark, unmoving eyes and the bridge of his nose. There was something so well-organised and rehearsed about both men, suggesting a high degree of training, not like the two who'd brought him here.

Lawrence glanced at the man drilling as he finished what he was doing and removed the drill from the wall. His hands were covered in masonry dust. He pushed an insulated flex through the hole, then left the room for a moment. Lawrence looked at the man pointing the gun at him; his expression hadn't changed. The other man came back. He changed his drill bit over to a screw head, then removed a wall bracket from the rucksack and began screwing it onto the wall. Next, he affixed a camera to the bracket and below that a large monitor screen about 15 inches across.

Lawrence's heart was pounding in his chest and it was making him feel sick.

The man packed away the drill, shouldered the rucksack, then nodded at his partner, who removed a pistol from a holster on his waistband. Lawrence couldn't stop himself from shaking as he heard the man's footsteps come up behind him and felt his gun push at the back of his head.

"No!" he moaned through the tape, fearing the worst. He heard a snip and felt the cable ties come loose around his wrists. A cramping sensation ran up his arms.

The man came and stood in front of him, pointing the gun at the top of his skull now, then reached down and ripped the tape off his mouth.

Lawrence sucked in a lungful of air and nearly gagged. He started coughing; his eyes watered.

The man said, 'Take it easy.' And standing back, he returned his pistol to its holster, then emptied a plastic bag onto the table. It contained bottles of water and unmarked foil containers.

Lawrence said, 'What's going on?' The words sounded croaky and strange, as if someone else had spoken; it'd been a while since he'd heard his own voice.

The man screwed up the empty bag and put it in his pocket, then stepped backwards until he was level with his partner. Both men stood side by side, guns pointed at him, just as they had when they'd come in. Then the taller man took out a remote control device, pressed a button, and there was a bleeping sound.

Lawrence turned his head and saw a red light glowing on the front of the camera. It brought a little illumination to the room. Looking round again, Lawrence saw the two men backing out of the room, then closing the door.

Lawrence went to the door and heard their footsteps as they headed downstairs. He heard a door close and waited, expecting to hear a car engine. But there was nothing. Then out of the corner of his eye, Lawrence noticed the red camera light flashing.

Were they recording him now?

The pulsing red light lit up the room. Lawrence noticed the water bottles and silver packets the men had left on the table. He went over and picked up one of them. Small printed lettering on the side read, 'Chocolate'. He looked at other packets: 'Biscuits'; 'Energy Bar'; 'Sandwich'. He wondered how long it was meant to last him. He looked at the camera again and wondered if someone was watching him at that moment.

He walked back to the door and listened out for the two men. But there wasn't a sound. He put his hand on the door handle and turned it; then gave the door a push. It was locked. 'Hello,' he called out. 'Is anyone there?'

There was silence.

'Hello?' Louder this time. But still no answer.

'Come on,' he said, rattling the door. He hadn't heard any vehicles, so maybe they were just ignoring him. 'What is it you want?' Looking over his shoulder, he noticed the camera again. Speaking directly to it now, he said, 'What's going on?' He took a step towards it and could just make out his reflection in its lens. 'Can you hear me?'

The red light flashed intermittently. He imagined the two men in black military combats trekking across the fields to a vehicle parked up in a lay-by somewhere, engine running, where someone else was, right at this minute, looking at him on a monitor screen.

He tried to think about what had just happened. What it meant. He remembered the two men who'd brought him here – were they not coming back now? It seemed like a long time ago that they were here, he thought, part of a different version of events – in another reality. Maybe in that version he ended up back with his wife or in a police station giving evidence. While in this version he remained here.

The camera light flashed a little quicker for a moment, as if it was recording his thoughts now as well.

Lawrence sat on the edge of the bed and, feeling cold, put his arms round himself and rubbed his hands up and down, as if was drying one of his children after a bath. He told himself to keep calm. That everything was going to be fine. He pictured his children at home; Amanda saying goodnight to them; Georgia holding her favourite toy – a horse with a long white mane – and Amanda kissing her forehead, then turning off the light. Georgia asking her again, *'Will Daddy be coming home tomorrow?'* and Amanda telling her to go to sleep and not to worry; then next door, William nearly asleep, eyes half-closed, Lego pieces on the floor, and Amanda pulling his door to and going downstairs.

Lawrence tried to imagine what she was thinking… how she was going to cope… what she was going to tell the children… her parents… work. But when he looked up and was reminded of where he was, the walls tinged slightly red by the camera light, he felt another reality take its place, like he wasn't the person in his memories anymore – that they were someone else's now. So when his daughter asked when Daddy was coming home, she wasn't referring to him, the person in this room, but someone else, and it was he they'd miss, not the person he'd become.

Tears came to his eyes and he wiped them away. He could feel himself wanting to give in, that he'd had enough, but told himself he must hold on.

He looked up, thinking he heard the camera move. Was it tracking his movements?

He gazed at its red light. He heard something flapping

in the wind outside. He felt so tired, his body ached. He lay back on the bed and covered himself with the blanket.

He imagined Amanda at home again, pacing the kitchen, checking her phone, the kids asleep upstairs. Maybe she'd poured herself a glass of wine from a leftover bottle in the fridge. Then he saw himself and the kids sitting in the garden, the tall pine trees splintering the late-afternoon sunshine. Then everyone started to get mixed up in his head. In a reversal of roles, he imagined his son was sitting in his place and he was William – identities suddenly interchangeable, like there was only one of them.

Whether he had fallen asleep or not, he wasn't sure, but he heard a bleeping sound and a light came on from somewhere. Had the two men come back?

He sat up and saw light coming from the monitor screen on the wall. Somehow, it had turned itself on.

Lawrence gazed at the screen, and as his eyes came into focus, he saw a man sitting on a chair in the middle of an empty room. For a second, Lawrence thought it was a recording of himself. The room was sparsely lit like his and he couldn't identify the man's face properly. But it wasn't him. Lawrence saw the man's mouth move.

'Hello Lawrence. Do you remember me?' The audio was surprisingly clear that it would have been easy to think the man was in the room with him.

Lawrence sat up on the bed and looked at the man on the monitor. Who was he?

The man on screen, sitting quite still on his chair, said, 'It is Lawrence, isn't it?'

Staring at the screen, Lawrence said, 'Who are you?'

'You don't remember me, then,' the man said. The way

the light fell in the room seemed to emphasise the movement of the man's mouth.

Lawrence said, 'No. What do you want?'

'I've come to speak to you, Lawrence.'

'What about?'

'About you.'

Lawrence looked at the man's dark outline on screen, and said, 'I think you've made a mistake.'

'And what mistake is that?' the man said.

'I think you've got me mixed up with someone else.'

The man appeared to smile. 'I don't think so.'

Lawrence glanced towards the door. He remembered trying to get it open but it had been locked. Where were the two men who'd brought him here?

The man said, 'Are you expecting someone?'

Lawrence said, 'Can I phone my wife, please?'

The man smiled again. 'And what would you say?'

'Pardon?'

'That you've disappeared? Reinvented yourself?'

'I'm sorry?'

'Your wife will understand in time, you know. Women are good with change. They have the edge on us there, don't you think?'

Lawrence said, 'Who the hell are you?'

The man leant forward in his chair, coming closer to the camera, and said, 'Who are *you*, Lawrence?'

'I'm sorry?'

'You see, it's an easier question to ask than to answer, isn't it?' He sat back again.

Lawrence said, 'What is it you want?'

'I've already told you.'

'What?'

'Haven't you been listening?'

Lawrence hesitated, doubting himself for a second and what he might and might not have heard. 'What is it you want to talk to me about exactly?'

'Your disappearance of course.'

'What disappearance?'

'I need you to remember, Lawrence.' The man's eyes glinted in the shadows of his room. 'Can you do that for me?'

Lawrence said, 'Remember what?'

'The reason you're here.'

'Who are you?'

'You need to let go, Lawrence.'

'Let go of what?'

'Of yourself, of course.'

'What?'

The man bowed his head.

Lawrence waited for him to look up and say something else, but the screen went blank and switched itself off.

21

Lying on his sofa in his cottage, Mark yawned into his fist and switched off the TV from the remote. He'd just watched *Independence Day* for about the fifth time. He got up off the sofa, stretched, and carried a glass and empty beer can into the kitchen. Clare was in bed.

It was a rare pleasure to sit up late, something he could never do when he had pheasants in the woods and had to get up early to feed and check on the pens. He rinsed the glass under the tap and chucked the can in the bin. His terrier, Scruff, was curled up asleep on its cushion. 'Scruff,' he said. 'Come on.'

The terrier opened his eyes. Mark always took him out before bed.

Mark stood at the door and put on a muddy pair of work boots. He didn't bother lacing them up. 'Scruff,' he said, putting on his jacket.

The terrier, eyes open, hadn't moved. Mark said, 'Out.'

The dog stood up, stretched and trotted after Mark. Outside, the terrier walked round the perimeter of the garden, lifted his leg against the washing line, as per normal, and sniffed under the bushes.

Mark stood and watched his dog, then looked up at the downs and trees silhouetted against the horizon. Mark couldn't see Hillards Farm from here – it was the other side of the hill – but he thought about it now, wondering whether any lights were on in the windows or any vans were parked up in the lane. Mark's recurring nightmare consisted of trespassers of one kind or another descending on his beat.

Mark regretted not going out there and having a look tonight. Instead, he'd watched *Independence Day*. He promised himself he would go and have a look again in the morning.

A light went on behind him and Mark turned round. It was the bathroom light. He saw his terrier looking up at the window as well. Perhaps Ollie had woken up or Clare needed the loo. Mark turned to go in.

Inside, he locked the doors and turned off the lights, then went upstairs. Ollie was fast asleep. He pulled his son's door to and went into the bathroom to start brushing his teeth. The wind whirred in the window frame. The wood was swollen and the window didn't shut properly, so there was always a draught. It got pretty cold in the winter and Clare was always complaining about it. She'd made him say something to the estate office about getting it fixed, but nothing had happened and Mark didn't like to rock the boat by complaining too much. They could decide it was easier to replace him than spend money on his cottage.

Standing there brushing his teeth, Mark could smell the chalky soil of the downs along with the whiff of cow manure. Two smells that, whenever he went away on holiday – especially abroad, which admittedly wasn't very often – always made him feel like he was home when he returned. He thought about Hillards Farm again. For a fleeting moment, he considered jumping on the quad and shooting over there now. But he couldn't be bothered.

Mark ran the tap, rinsed his mouth, and splashed water over his face. He dried his face and hands with the towel hanging behind the door and went into the bedroom. He would go and have a look tomorrow, he told himself.

Clare was turned towards the wall. Mark took off his top, removed his socks, and got into bed. He lay there for a second before moving behind Clare and putting his arms round her. He knew she was still awake. He put his hand over her breast and felt her nipple.

Clare said, 'Go away,' in a sleepy voice.

'What?' Mark said, smiling.

'I thought you were going out lamping.'

'So did I. I ended up watching *Independence Day* instead.'

Clare groaned as Mark touched her now. 'Oh, by the way,' she said. 'Sue said she'd seen someone at Hillards Farm.'

Mark stopped what he was doing. 'Really? You spoke to her?'

'Yeah.'

'When?'

'Earlier.'

'Why didn't you tell me?' Mark sat up.

'I forgot. Why's it so important?'

'Who was it?'

'She didn't know. She said a brand-new Range Rover was parked up there a few weeks ago.'

'Really?' Mark looked towards the window and thought again about going up there after all.

He felt Clare's hand on his, steering it back over her breast. On second thoughts, he decided, maybe not.

22

When Sean walked into his flat, he didn't get that feeling of home he usually did when seeing his things. He dropped his bag on the floor and stood for a moment staring at the items in the room: TV, X-box, an unmade bed, scattered clothes, shoes, a half-drunk bottle of Coke. Although everything looked familiar, there was something different about it as well, as if he was seeing things through another person's eyes. He had only been away a couple of nights, but it felt longer.

He went into the bathroom and took a piss, then rinsed his hands and looked at himself in the mirror. He looked tired; his hair was greasy. He came out of the bathroom, pulling his sweatshirt off over his head, then squatted down beside the fridge and took out a half-drunk carton of milk and sniffed it to see if it was still fresh. It smelt okay, so he took a sip. Then, taking the carton with him, he wandered across his flat and sat on the edge of his bed, checking the time on his mobile. It was 1:23 in the morning. He took another swig of milk and plugged his mobile into a charger, then pulled off his jeans.

He'd planned to have a shower but now he couldn't be arsed. He stood up and turned off the main light. The street lighting and the flimsy curtain in his rented studio meant the room was never that dark. He looked from the window for a moment, slipping a hand under his T-shirt and scratching his stomach. His chain necklace lay outside his T-shirt and he put it inside. He parted the curtains and looked along the street.

Opposite was a run-down four-storey terrace decorated with 'To Let' boards. Further along the road, a chain-link fence enclosed an industrial estate where a metal trailer was parked up in an empty forecourt alongside a stack of wooden pallets. Cars lined both sides of the road.

On the corner, Sean thought he saw someone sitting in one of the parked cars, a blue Ford. He narrowed the gap in the curtains so as not to be seen. Was someone there? Or was it just the headrest? It was difficult to tell. He wondered what someone would be doing sitting in their car at this time. There was a university on the other side of town, which meant there were plenty of students living nearby. Maybe it was a student out on a bender, unable to make it home.

Sean closed the curtains and got into bed. He lay there with his eyes open and wondered what Terry was doing. Had he got home yet? Was he asleep? He imagined Terry camped out on his sofa, maybe reading his book or having a rollie. Somehow he couldn't imagine him slipping into bed beside his wife.

Sean noticed his Wi-Fi router lights flicker in the corner of the room. He piggybacked off his neighbour's Wi-Fi and never paid a penny on connection charges. Something which didn't impress Terry when he'd told him. He watched the lights flickering for a moment, then picked up his phone and checked his messages from Tash and thought about sending her something but knew she was working tomorrow and would be asleep, and besides, he was going to see her in the morning.

He saw that it was 1:42.

He put his phone back on the floor, but felt too wired to sleep. Closing his eyes, he pictured the farmhouse. He saw himself standing at the bottom of the stairs. It was like part of him was still there. He remembered the picture of the geese on the wall. He could recall it clearly – the geese coming into land on a river at dusk. It felt familiar, like he'd seen it before somewhere – on TV maybe or in a magazine. Then he remembered the cargo upstairs, calling to him. He sat up in bed.

The cargo's phone number, he thought. Where was it?

He got out of bed. Where had he left it? He picked up his jeans and searched the pockets. He felt his pulse quicken. He checked front and back pockets, remembering having it in the pub. But it wasn't there now.

Maybe he'd dropped it in Terry's car. He turned on his bedside light and looked on the floor. He looked in the bathroom and under the fridge. His mind went into a spin. What if it wasn't in Terry's car? What if he'd dropped it on the street? Or in the pub? What if someone was to find it? Would they link it back to him?

He emptied his bag and sifted through his clothes.

Where the fuck was it?

He stood there for a moment and tried to think when he'd last looked at it. He remembered looking at it in the van when he was waiting for Terry to leave the cottage, then in the pub.

He picked up his jeans again and checked the pockets a

second time. But it wasn't there.

What if it had fallen out in the pub, he thought. The barman, clearing up, might have spotted it. Would he consider it important? Would he think of ringing it? Or just throw it away? What if he stuck it behind the bar in case someone came back for it? Should he go back? What if the police were already there? And already had the number? Fuck!

Sean turned and looked towards the window, thinking he'd heard something. Was it the police? He felt all sense of reason melting away, and couldn't contain his paranoia.

He parted the curtains, remembering the blue Ford. He now wondered if the car had something to do with the phone number. Surely it wasn't beyond the realms of possibility, what with today's technology, that the police, or someone else, could have got hold of the number, linked it to him and tracked him back to his flat?

Sean saw the blue Ford was still parked in the same place, only now it looked like there wasn't anyone sitting inside. He wondered where the person in the car had gone. He wondered if they had been waiting for him to get home. And now he was undressed and at his most vulnerable, were they paying him a visit?

He turned to his flat door. Should he ring Terry before it was too late?

There was a tightness in his throat. He imagined the guy from the blue Ford walking up the stairs, using the hand rail to soften his footsteps…

Sean couldn't take it anymore and had to know if someone was there. Taking care not to make any sound, he walked towards his flat's front door, his heart racing. He listened for a second, but couldn't hear anything, then opened the door and looked along the corridor. There was no one there. He closed it. Was he just being paranoid? Like a weed trip that had taken a nasty turn.

He walked back to the window and looked at the blue Ford again. There was no one inside. Perhaps there never had been. He exhaled a couple of deep breaths and ran his hands through his hair.

Crossing the room, he entered the kitchen and gripped the sides of the sink, his stomach pulsating. Like he was going to be sick. He ran the tap, picked up a glass, filled it and took a drink.

Then he noticed a packet of cigarettes on the floor. They were from the last time Tash had stayed over. He'd given up smoking about a year ago, though he occasionally shared one with her. He bent down and picked up the packet. There was one cigarette left. He put it in his mouth and looked for a lighter. He found one in the kitchen and sparked it up. It took four or five attempts to get it alight, then he sucked the flame into the end of the cigarette and inhaled deeply. The nicotine gave him an instant head-rush.

He sat on the bed and turned on the TV. He turned the volume right down until it was almost silent, just in case someone was outside and they made a noise. He lay back on the bed, some motorbike stunt show on TV, and studied the lit cigarette between his fingers; then took another drag. He blew smoke rings towards the ceiling. He used the milk carton as an ashtray.

After a couple more drags, he poked the butt through the lid of the milk carton, hearing it fizz, and lay there watching the TV for a bit. The cigarette had left him feeling dizzy. But it had helped take his mind off things. After a while, he got up and went for a piss and drank another glass of water at the sink. When he came back, he turned off the TV and checked the time on his mobile: 2:08.

He tried to sleep. But when he did, he remembered the cargo, the picture of the geese, the phone number and the fact he'd lost it. Though maybe it was best he had, he now thought. If he was worried about people sitting outside his flat now, imagine what it would be like if he'd actually phoned it – the authorities would soon be after him. And anyway, what would he say to the guy's wife? '*Oh, hello love. I'm the guy who helped lock away your husband. But I don't want you to worry because he's all right.*' Yeah, right! What the fuck was he thinking?

No, it was a good thing he'd lost it. No doubt about it. He shouldn't have written it down in the first place. All that stuff about the guy's wife and kids. What the fuck! Terry was right. It wasn't their problem. Forget it and move on.

Sean felt better having decided this. It was like he'd turned things around in his head. Tomorrow, he thought, he'd get up, shower, go into town, have a fry up at Billy's, a coffee at Starbucks – because their coffees were better than Billy's – then drop in on Tash at the salon and surprise her. Everything was going to be all right after all, he thought. The cargo. The phone number. It was someone else's problem now.

How much Sean slept he wasn't sure. When he looked at his phone, it was just after six. He was tempted to send a message to Tash but decided to leave it and surprise her later. He lay there listening to the sound of seagulls and watching it get light round the curtains.

Before long, he got undressed and stepped into the

shower. He stood under the water and shut his eyes. Wiping the hair out of his face, he squirted shampoo into the palm of his hand and washed his hair, rinsed it, and then did the same with conditioner.

When he got out, he stood in front of the mirror and dried his hair with a towel, then tied the towel around his waist, brushed his teeth and gelled his hair. He checked himself in the mirror, pulling a couple of strands of hair forward so they hung over his forehead, and walked back into his bedroom and got dressed.

It was 8:03. He unplugged his phone and put it in his pocket. He saw his wallet lying on the table with his keys from last night. He picked them up. He checked his wallet, opening its Velcro fasteners, to see what money he had. As he did so, he noticed the receipt with the phone number flutter to the floor. He'd looked everywhere, he thought, how had he missed it? He felt relieved to begin with, but it was short-lived.

Sean bent down and picked it up, staring at the paper for a moment. He felt like he was about to shudder but didn't. He looked at the row of numbers and almost didn't recognise his own writing. It gave him an uneasy feeling to think he had written it in the farmhouse and now here it was. He wished he hadn't found it. What was he going to do with it?

He saw the lighter on the table and thought about burning it there and then. But quickly decided he didn't want any trace of it in his flat, picturing overall-suited forensic dudes putting it together with tweezers.

He folded it up instead and stuffed it back into his wallet.

He would go down to the beach, he thought, and burn it there.

23

MARK LEANT ON his garden fence, clutching a thermos cup, and watched his spaniels chase each other round the field at the back of his house. He hadn't been up long. His hair was ruffled from sleep; he hadn't shaved. There was a toothpaste mark on his chin. His wife had left ten minutes ago to take Ollie to nursery before she went off to work. 'You won't forget to pick him up, will you?' she'd said on her way out.

It was nearly eight-thirty.

Mark called the dogs and returned them to their kennels, then went back into the house, topped up his thermos cup, and took his .22 out of the cabinet. He would have a drive around before he continued with the coppicing. He looked in his pockets for a lighter, just in case he couldn't get yesterday's fire going from the embers, and locked up the house.

He got on the quad, slotting the rifle into the case and chucking a chainsaw and combi can on the back, and set off up a rutted chalk track at the back of his house. As he climbed the slope on the quad, he started to think about Hillards Farm again. He'd asked Clare again this morning what else Sue had said, aside from spotting the Range Rover. 'That was it,' she said, adding, 'I shouldn't worry about it.'

He reached the top of the slope and accelerated alongside a conifer plantation to a clearing in the trees where he could see Hillards Farm in the distance.

A damp mist hung over the fields. Mark turned off the quad's engine and took out a pair of binoculars. A cock pheasant crowed in the wood. He zoomed in on the farmhouse, pausing on the boarded-up windows, the flaking door, and the moss-covered roof, then scanned the farmyard, noting the missing tin sheets in the barn's roof, the broken glass in the windows and the flapping polythene in the old silage press.

It looked quiet down there, he thought, no signs of life.

Through the binoculars, he followed the track out of the farmyard and back towards the road. It was difficult to discern any fresh tyre marks at this distance, but he did notice a plastic shopping bag that he couldn't remember seeing before. The bag was hooked to a strand of barbed wire and flapped in the breeze. It could have dropped out of the footwell of a car, he thought, as someone got out to open the gate.

Mark looked back at the farmyard again. A gust of wind swept across the valley. Dust blew off the concrete. He moved the binoculars up to the house. Brambles covered the lower windows. It wouldn't be long before they swallowed up the whole house. Then, lowering the binoculars, he looked with his naked eye and wondered if it was worth taking a closer look. The plastic bag could have come from anywhere. But in the back of his mind was the fact that in about four months from now a delivery of two thousand pheasant poults were going to put into a pen about a ten-minute walk away.

He saw a crow land on the barn roof and lifted the binoculars again, adjusting the zoom. The crow, scanning the area, let out several long caws. Mark wondered what it was trying to tell him. For a moment, he considered firing a shot down there. That might get someone's attention.

Mark decided to take a closer look, and putting away the binoculars, he started the quad and set off down the slope.

24

IT WAS DEFINITELY the morning again. The birds' singing confirmed that. After the screen had switched itself off, Lawrence lay on the bed, wrapped in the blanket, trying to make sense of what the man had said. 'I want you to remember…' But remember what?

He was sitting on the edge of the bed, drinking from one of the bottles the men had left, when he heard the sound of the quad bike.

Aware now someone could be watching his every move, he proceeded to screw the lid slowly back onto the bottle, making it look like he hadn't heard anything. He was going on the assumption the camera couldn't hear the bike outside.

The bike was still some way off but getting closer all the time and Lawrence realised this might be his chance to raise the alarm.

He stood up and put the bottle back on top of the table, taking care not to look towards the window and give anything away. He must wait until the bike got closer, he thought, before doing anything. He may only get one chance.

He tried to think how he was going to get the guy's attention. Should he bang on the door? Shout out? And what about the camera? Should he cover it up? Rip it down? Or just ignore it? Whatever he did, they were going to know something was going on.

He decided he would cover the camera up. That way, if his attempt failed, he could always pretend there'd been a technological fault with the camera, whereas if he ripped it down there was no hiding what he'd done and they may not leave him alone again.

He started to pull off his jumper. As he did so, he kept an eye on the camera. He could hear the quad bike getting closer all the time. His heart rate quickened; his hands shook. He was aware he didn't have long. With his jumper off, he walked back across the room towards the camera, trying to look as natural as possible; not easy. Once in range, he flattened himself against the wall the camera was on, out of shot, and reached up and slung his jumper over the bracket. There was no turning back now.

He felt himself growing in confidence. He went over to the window, stood on the chair, and looked through the crack in the board. There it was – the quad bike coming across the fields towards him. He wondered if he should start banging on the window now. Would the guy hear him? He looked round at the camera. Then noticed the monitor. He hadn't covered it. But did he need to? Either way, it was too late.

He looked back through the crack again. The quad bike had stopped by a water trough at the far end of the field opposite the farmhouse. The guy got out a pair of binoculars and looked towards the house. He was about four hundred metres away.

'Come on. Over here,' Lawrence said under his breath.

The guy appeared to scan the surrounding area, taking

his time, then put his binoculars away and set off again. Accelerating, he continued down the edge of the field in his direction. Lawrence thought that this was it. That he would come all the way up to the house. But as he got nearer, it was clear he was just heading for a gateway a little further down the fence line. Making a wide turn, he passed through the gateway into the next field.

'Jesus! Come on,' Lawrence called out. He pulled back from the crack and wiped his eye with his sleeve because it was watering. When he looked again, he saw the guy on the quad standing up on the peddles, riding through a dip in the field, heading in the opposite direction.

Lawrence banged on the window board. 'Over here!' he shouted. But the guy didn't hear him. And Lawrence watched him go, clearing the brow of the hill, sitting back on the quad's seat again.

Lawrence smacked his hands against the window board. 'Jesus!' He got off the chair, went to the door, grabbed the handle and began pulling on it in the hope it would suddenly open. Of course, it didn't.

He listened for voices, but couldn't hear anything.

He kicked at the door out of frustration.

He glanced round at the camera. At the monitor.

Were they really watching him?

Lawrence knew he had to get out of there. The guy on the quad bike must live nearby.

He went back to the window, stood on the chair and peered through the crack. There was no sign of the bike now. He'd assumed the guy riding it was just a regular person, but suddenly wondered now whether he had something to do with him being locked up here. Maybe he was employed to keep an eye on him. Perhaps the same person who'd locked him up owned all this land. Maybe there was a perimeter fence topped with barbed wire and CCTV cameras.

But then he remembered the guy on the bike coming to the house and knocking on the door and calling out, and his captors panicking. Why would he have done that if he was part of this?

Lawrence now wondered what had happened to the first two men. He felt like he had been better off with them. Had the younger one rung the phone number yet? Surely, it was only a matter of time before the police swarmed the house and got him out of here?

Then he remembered the man on the monitor talking about his 'disappearance', saying, 'your wife will understand in time.' What had they told her? That he'd run off, to start a new life? But why? What for? And had Amanda believed them? It'd been several days now and no one had come looking for him, as far as he could tell. Maybe there was no investigation. No search.

He looked round the room, at the now-familiar walls and peeling wallpaper, and couldn't believe he was having these thoughts. But suddenly everything seemed open to doubt. Could he really be sure about anything anymore?

Then he thought of his children and what they might have been told. Thinking of them brought tears to his eyes. Without really making a conscious decision, Lawrence stood up, walked over to the camera and pulled down his jumper.

For a moment, he just stood there looking up into the now unobstructed lens, imagining someone watching him on a monitor the other end. Then, speaking directly to the camera, tears running down his cheeks, he said, 'What is it you want?' He stood there, shaking with emotion and wiped his face with his hand.

There was silence for a second.

Then he heard banging downstairs and turned towards the door.

Footsteps were coming through the house. They were running.

They came up the stairs and stopped outside the room.

Then a man said, 'Turn round and face the wall. Do it now.'

Lawrence did as he was told, wondering who it was this time. He heard the door being unlocked, then as it swung open, he looked over his shoulder. The two men in combats, who'd installed the camera, entered the room.

One of them said, 'Face the wall,' pointing a pistol at his head, black gloves on. The other one, preparing a syringe, had taken his gloves off.

25

BILLY'S CAFÉ WAS on the seafront; its specials and meal deals were written on coloured cards and stuck to the inside of the window.

The café's owner, Billy, said to Sean, 'I haven't seen you for a while. Have you been on holiday?'

'No, mate. Just busy.' Sean wondered who else had noticed he'd been away.

Billy said, 'The usual – full English, extra toast?'

Sean hesitated. 'Yeah, cheers,' he replied, his lips sticking together as he spoke. Maybe he should have gone somewhere they didn't know him, he thought.

Billy smiled. 'I'll bring it over.'

Sean sat by the window and got out his phone. It was 8:28 a.m. He had no messages. He looked round the café. A couple of workmen in Hi-Vis jackets were eating fry-ups. An old man in an overcoat and flat cap sat in a corner, sipping tea. One of the workmen got out a copy of the *Sun* and Sean half-expected to see his picture on the front cover.

When his breakfast arrived, Sean ate without putting down his knife and fork. He mopped up the egg yolk with his extra slice of toast, then pushed his plate aside and took a paper napkin from the plastic holder on the table and wiped his mouth. Then, picking bacon from his teeth, he stood up and walked out of the café.

He went into the newsagents a couple of doors down and asked for a packet of ten Marlboro Gold. He had Tash in mind when he bought them. But leaving the shop, he tore off the cellophane wrapper and silver foil and put one in his mouth. He got out the lighter, which he'd brought with him to burn the telephone number on the beach, and shook it a couple of times, then cupped his hands and sparked up the fag.

Puffing on the cigarette, he stopped at the seafront and leant against the metal railings. To his right, some steps led down to the beach. He could get this over with now, he thought, go down to the beach and burn the phone number. He looked round. He saw a police car turn down a side street. Watching it, Sean puffed on the cigarette, seagulls squawking overhead. The police car stopped and two policemen got out and entered an adjacent building. He turned and looked the other way, hunching up his shoulders. He leant over the railings and spat, the wind blowing his phlegm against the seawall. Then he heard a couple behind him, debating whether to walk along the beach or keep going on the pavement. Sean glanced over his shoulder. The couple, arm in arm, couldn't decide; they had a dog on a lead. What with the police car and now the couple, Sean decided the number could wait, and chucking the cigarette on the ground, he set off again.

He went into a Starbucks and ordered a skinny latte, telling the girl his name was 'Justin' when she asked him what to write on his cup. He used to meet Tash here in the early days of their relationship, sitting on a sofa together and having a smooch, sometimes going a bit too far – getting his hand on one of Tash's breasts, and Tash saying, 'Not here.'

He picked up his latte and went upstairs to sit in an armchair. Swigging his drink, he took out the receipt with the phone number on. Maybe burning it wasn't the best option after all, he thought. He might need it. He looked at the number and noticed the last two digits were 48. It happened to be his house number. Then he thought: what if all the other digits were connected to him in some way, as well? What if it wasn't a phone number at all? What if the cargo had been trying to tell him something?

Sean looked at the number again for other combinations that might mean something to him. But nothing stood out. He looked at his contact list on his mobile to see if he had any similar numbers. Then he wondered why he didn't just ring the bloody number and get this over with, picturing himself using the pay phone at the train station. No one was going to know it was him that way.

Sean took another swig of his latte and looked across the room. Three uni students came up the stairs carrying Apple Macs. Two girls, a blonde and an Asian, and a guy wearing a baggy beanie. He watched as they sat down and plugged in their Mac books.

Sean checked his messages. Still nothing. He wondered what Terry was up to and started typing him a message, but quickly deleted it. He knew Terry didn't appreciate texts that weren't essential. Sean looked across at the students working on their laptops – the blonde one kept hitching up the sleeve of her baggy top to cover her bra strap; while the Asian one pouted thoughtfully as she typed. Sean wondered if the guy in the beanie was doing them both. Good luck to him if he was.

Looking at the phone number again, Sean wondered if the cargo was still at the farmhouse and if he was alone or not. And what about his wife and kids – what had they been told? Sean imagined seeing the cargo's wife in one of those TV interviews when they make a plea to the public to come forward if they know anything.

Would he ring the number if that happened?

Fuck. Why hadn't he thought about all this before? He didn't have to agree to do the job; Terry could have got someone else. But he'd said he was fine with it. They were delivery drivers after all. He never thought it was going to be like this, worrying about whether the police were after him, or if the cargo's blubbering wife was going to appear on the news, or if he was going to see his picture in the newspapers.

Sean could hear Terry's voice in his head – not for the first time – telling him it wasn't their problem. To forget it. But he wasn't like Terry. He couldn't just put shit aside, forget about it and go fishing. He kept getting these thoughts, going round and round his head. Always had since he was a kid. Sometimes, he couldn't sleep because of them. That's why he didn't smoke weed anymore. Made him too paranoid. Booze was all right. But weed put him on edge. A doctor put him on some head pills once. Fucking things made him so sick, he never finished them. Better off without them, he'd concluded. Of course, he struggled to keep himself together sometimes. Which was why he remembered weird stuff like the picture of the geese in the farmhouse near where he'd found those damp envelopes. The situation was fucking with his head. He wished he'd given the number to

Terry now. Just told him the truth. Come right out with it. Then it would be out of his hands by now.

Sean folded up the receipt and put it back in his wallet. He checked the time on his phone. 9:49. Tash's salon would already be open. He stood up, finishing his latte, carried the cup to the bin and dropped it through the hole. He looked at the three students on his way past and envied them for only having essays to think about.

Outside, the sun was shining. Maybe it was the coffee, or thinking about Tash, but Sean felt less on edge now. He glanced at himself in a shop window, putting his hand up to his hair, tweaking a strand here and there, and thought how much he was looking forward to seeing Tash again. But as he was about to set off, he noticed a guy staring at him from the other side of the street. Wearing a black baseball cap, he was just standing there, with his hands in his coat pockets, like he'd been waiting for him.

Trying to stay calm, Sean told himself the guy wasn't really looking at him, but just happened to be staring his way at that moment. He kept walking, thinking the guy would just disappear. But he kept pace with him, glancing at him from across the street.

When they reached the end of the road, Sean turned left towards the high street, while the guy continued up the slope to a line of parked cars. Sean saw him stop beside a car, stare at him over the roof, and then get in. Sean thought there was something familiar about it, when the penny dropped. It was the blue Ford he'd seen parked outside his flat last night. He felt sure of it.

Sean picked up his pace, and was nearly running by the time he reached the high street. He sheltered in a shop doorway to catch his breath, then looked round the corner in both directions to see if he'd been followed.

Should he still go and see Tash at work? What if the guy followed him there?

He got out his phone again and considered ringing Terry. But what would he say? That he saw a car parked outside his flat last night and then again this morning. *So fucking what?* Terry would say.

If he was honest he couldn't even be sure it was the same car now. And what if the guy wasn't really looking at him but something else? A shop behind him perhaps. Or maybe he just liked his clothes. What if he'd imagined the whole thing?

Sean remembered the phone number in his pocket and wondered if it had anything to do with that. For fuck's sake, he thought, it was just a phone number. Wasn't it?

He rang Terry.

26

LAWRENCE OPENED HIS eyes. The monitor was on again and the man on screen, sitting in the empty room, was looking at him. It felt like they were somehow in the middle of a conversation and the man had just spoken. Lawrence said, 'Did you say something?'

The man said, 'The reason you're here. Is it becoming clearer?'

'Who are you?' Lawrence sat up on the bed, shivering, and put his arms round himself. 'Where are the two men who were just here?' Lawrence remembered the men in black military combats and balaclavas coming into the room, the gun against his head and the injection in his arm, then nothing much after that.

The man said, 'My name is Dvorak. Do not interfere with the camera again. Do you understand?'

Lawrence stared at the man on screen, and remembered covering the camera with his jumper after seeing the guy coming on the quad bike. It was after that the two men had turned up.

Dvorak said, 'Do you understand?'

'Yeah. I understand.'

Dvorak turned to his side, as if to look out of a window, although there wasn't one there, just bare walls. His outline threw a shadow on the wall. 'Do you believe in God?' he asked.

Lawrence hesitated, wondering what God had to do with this.

'It would be nice, don't you think?' Dvorak said, and turned to the camera again, his mouth moving visibly in the half-light as he spoke. 'To believe. In something. Don't you think?'

Lawrence said, 'What's going on?'

Dvorak turned away from the camera again. 'It all seems a bit meaningless otherwise. The things we do down here, the efforts we go to, as if any of it really matters in the end.'

'What's this about?'

Dvorak looked into the camera. 'I need you to remember, Lawrence.'

'I told you, I don't know what you're talking about.'

'You received some information. I need you to remember.'

'I don't know what you mean. What information?'

Dvorak looked down at his hands and appeared to massage them on his lap; then, looking up, he said, 'What is the code, Lawrence?'

'What code?'

'They gave you a code. What is it?'

'What are you talking about?'

'I need you to remember. What is the code?'

'I don't know any code.'

'Try to remember.'

'What?'

'Tell me what the code is, Lawrence.'

'I don't know any code.'

'Start from the beginning.'

'What?'

'The beginning,' Dvorak said.

'The beginning of what?'

'Of what you remember. You remember something, don't you?'

27

As the phone rang, Sean backed into the shop front.

Terry answered with, 'Yeah? What is it, Sean?'

'Hi, Terry.' Already he felt better for hearing Terry's voice. 'How are you doing?'

'What do you want, Sean?'

'Nothing.' Sean stepped forward to check along the high street for the guy in the black baseball cap. 'Just wanted to check you got back all right,' he said.

'Now you know.'

'Don't be like that.' Sean scanned along the high street. 'How's everything at home, all okay?'

'Goodbye Sean.'

'Terry! Listen – please.'

'What is it?'

'You're off fishing, aren't you?'

'Yeah. What are you doing, Sean?'

'I'm in town. Just picking up some things.' Sean looked across the street and saw a couple with a push chair leaving a shop. A man in suit held the door open for them.

Terry said, 'Go home and get some rest.'

'Yeah, I'm going to. It's just…'

'Just what?'

'I keep thinking about… you know…' Sean knew he couldn't mention the cargo, or anything to do with the job, on the phone. And he couldn't bring himself just to come out and say he thought he was being followed. It didn't sound right now he had Terry on the phone.

Terry said, 'Go home, Sean.'

'Yeah. I will,' he said, stepping a little further out of the shop front, emboldened by the fact he had Terry on the line. 'Just checking on my old mate, you know.'

Terry said, 'Have you been smoking something?'

'No! I told you, I don't do that anymore.'

'Where's your girlfriend? Shouldn't you be with her?'

Sean often wondered why Terry never referred to Tash by her name. It was like he was embarrassed to be that personal. As a result, Sean found himself constantly using Tash's name in conversations by way of a reminder. 'No, Tash's at work,' he said.

'So you're all on your own, then – is that it?'

'No,' Sean said. 'That's not it.' He could see the road where the blue Ford had been parked. But the car was no longer there. Perhaps he'd got the cars mixed up, he thought. Perhaps he'd imagined the whole thing. Now he was speaking to Terry he felt a lot calmer. He let out a deep breath.

Terry said, 'Just go home, Sean. And I'll speak to you later.'

Sean said, 'Yeah,' but didn't hang up.

Terry said, 'Did you hear me, Sean?'

Sean knew he had to snap out of it. That Terry could only be pushed so far and then he'd flip. 'Yeah, okay – speak later then. Enjoy your fishing.' He hung up.

The salon was a five minute walk. Sean checked in both directions along the street before pushing the door open.

As he went in, he saw Tash at the far end of the salon talking to a customer in the mirror. The receptionist asked him if she could help. He said, 'I've come to see Natasha.'

'She's with a customer at the moment.'

'Yeah, I know.'

The girl said, 'Do you have an appointment?'

Sean tried to distract Tash but she was too busy chatting to her customer.

The receptionist saw him trying to get Tash's attention and, smiling, said, 'Are you a friend?'

Sean said, 'Yeah,' and smiled back. She was cute, short, dyed blonde hair, black bra showing under a crop top.

She said, 'Do you want me to give her a message?'

'Yeah, can you tell her—' Sean saw that Tash had seen him. She was now explaining something to an assistant behind her. The assistant led Tash's customer over to the basin area and Tash came over towards him. Sean watched her approach. She was wearing her hair loose today, large silver hoop earrings, skinny jeans and ankle boots, a sway to her movements as she crossed the salon. Sean grinned at her.

He said, 'Hello babe.'

Tash said, 'What are you doing here?'

'Come to see you.' He gave her a kiss.

'I'm with a customer.' Tash grinned.

'I know. You coming round later?'

'Yeah. I said, didn't I?'

'What time?'

'About six.'

'Cool.' He thought about telling her about the fags.

Tash's assistant mouthed something to her across the salon.

Tash said, 'Look. I've got to go.'

The sun was out again. Sean realised now he had all day to fill. He walked down the high street with no particular purpose in mind. He didn't want to go back to his flat. It was too soon for another Starbucks.

He came to the end of the high street and turned left onto Prince's Square, where there was a small park with benches and a children's play area.

He sat down on one of the benches with some dead guy's name on a plaque and took out his phone to check the time.

Leaning forward, he juddered his legs. He saw an old man walking his dog on one of those extendable leads. He'd read somewhere that twenty-five percent of the population along the South Coast was over sixty-five. That was a lot of old people. What would happen when they all died? he wondered. Would there suddenly be a lot of empty flats? Or would they just be replaced by more old people? Fuck knows. All Sean was sure about was that by the time he was that age, he wanted to be somewhere else. Maybe abroad. He'd have several restaurants by then, he imagined.

He put his phone away and left his hands in his pockets. Seagulls swooped low overhead, squawking. The wind gusted in off the beach. He saw the old man picking up his dog's shit in a bag. He thought about hanging around and having a cigarette, but then remembered the guy in the baseball cap and thought it best he got going.

He headed back to his flat, remembering what Terry had told him in the pub, about keeping his head down, watching DVDs and ordering pizza. On his way, he stopped at the chippy, so he didn't have to go out later, and bought some chips, a pasty and a can of Coke, dousing the chips in salt and vinegar, and eating a couple on his way out.

He turned down his road. A forklift was loading pallets of cardboard boxes onto the side of a lorry in the industrial estate. He looked for the blue Ford in the line of parked cars but couldn't see it.

He reached his house, stopped on the steps and took out his keys, balancing the can of Coke on top of his chips in one hand and unlocking the door. He went in, letting the door bang shut, and trotted up the stairs to his flat.

The first thing he noticed when he got his door open was how dark it was inside. Hadn't he opened the curtain before he left? For a split second, he wondered if he'd got the wrong flat, but realised he wouldn't have been able to get the door open if he had.

Then he started recognising his things spread about the floor – black Adidas T-shirt, sofa cushions, CD cases – like someone had turned the place over. *What the fuck?*

His brain couldn't compute the images quickly enough before a man appeared out of the darkness, as if coming out of the wall, ready to grab him.

28

You remember something, don't you?

Lawrence looked at the monitor and at Dvorak sitting on the chair in the empty room. He sat quite still, with hands folded on his lap, in the half-light.

Lawrence saw himself standing in the golf club car park, with a man behind him. The man was wearing a cap pulled down low to cover his eyes.

Dvorak said, 'What do you see Lawrence?'

'The man at the golf club, who forced me into the back of the van and brought me here.'

Dvorak said, 'Go further back.'

Lawrence looked at Dvorak's unmoving outline on screen. 'What do you want from me?' he said.

'I want you to remember,' Dvorak said. 'You do remember, don't you, Lawrence?'

'Remember what?'

'Why you are here.'

'I told you – I don't know why I'm here.'

'They gave you some information. A code. Try to remember.'

'I think you've made a mistake.'

'And what mistake is that?'

'I don't think I'm the person you think I am.'

'Start from the beginning, Lawrence.'

'What?'

'You were given some information. A code. You've kept it safe. Think back.'

Lawrence could feel his chest rising and falling with each breath. He looked down at his feet; his head swirled.

Dvorak said, 'Look at me, Lawrence. What did they tell you?'

Lawrence looked up at the monitor and for the first time could make out Dvorak's face in the gloom, as if a shadow had shifted. His eyes were pale green and he had short greying hair. Lawrence said, 'Who are you?'

'I'm here to help you. Remember. You remember something, don't you?'

'I remember meeting clients. Then being brought here. That's it.'

Dvorak said, 'It was your daughter's birthday, wasn't it?'

'How do you know about that?'

'Tell me what happened.'

'I was walking to my car when a man grabbed me.'

'Go back a bit. Why were you there?'

'I told you. I was meeting clients.'

'What about?'

'About a property in France.'

'That's right. You're a property developer, aren't you? But you studied law at university.'

Lawrence said, 'Who are you?'

'You met Amanda there.'

'What is this?'

'But you lost contact after university. Then, quite by chance, you met up again in London. You were living on neighbouring streets, weren't you?'

'How the hell do you know all this?' Lawrence thought that he'd told the story enough times, though, perhaps he shouldn't be surprised Dvorak knew about it. It made him wonder whether Dvorak might be someone he'd dealt with through work, a client or contractor, someone he'd let down perhaps, who now had a grudge against him.

Dvorak said, 'A lucky coincidence – neighbouring streets.'

'Yeah,' Lawrence said, though he was beginning to suspect luck had nothing to do with it. 'What's this about?'

'Tell me about your school life.'

'What for?'

'You went to boarding school, didn't you?'

'Yeah. So what?'

'You did well there, if I remember – academically, in sports ...'

'I did okay.'

'But you lost both parents when you were still young. That must have been hard.'

'Who are you?'

'But, as you said, you did okay. You went onto university, graduated, got a job. Maybe it even gave you an edge, set you apart from your peers, matured you beyond your years. Have you ever thought that?'

'I had good adoptive parents. Where's this going?'

'I don't know. That's why we're here, Lawrence.'

'Well, maybe I've forgotten.'

'Maybe.' Dvorak looked down at his hands again, then looked up. 'What do you think happens when you die?'

'What?'

'Do you think it's the end?' Then looking away from the

camera, Dvorak said in a change of tone, 'Why don't you describe the view from your window?'

'What view?'

'At your home. You remember the view, don't you?'

'Why? What for?'

'It'll help take your mind off things.'

'What things?'

'What it is you're trying to remember. I find it helps. Distract yourself and what it is you're trying to remember often comes to you.'

'What is it you want me to remember?'

'Try it. Describe the view to me.'

'Just let me out of here.' Lawrence stood up.

'Try it ... It'll pass the time.'

'I don't want to pass the time. Just let me out of this room.'

'What room? There is no room, don't you get it?' Dvorak tapped his head. 'This is your room. This is where you are.' He lay his hands on his lap again. 'Describe the view to me.'

'You're crazy.'

'Don't you want to escape from here?' Dvorak said, tapping his head again.

'Just let me out.'

'Close your eyes.'

'Is this some kind of game?'

'Try it,' Dvorak said, closing his own eyes.

Lawrence looked at Dvorak with his eyes closed and had the feeling they were somehow in the same room now – that their two rooms had merged into one.

Dvorak said, 'Is it coming clearer now?'

Lawrence said, 'What is this?'

'You were there, Lawrence. Picture it. What is it you

remember?'

Lawrence felt his heart rate quicken. He had to get out of here. He looked round the room. He felt sick.

Dvorak said, 'Let go. What did they tell you? What is the code?'

Lawrence covered his ears with his hands and tried to block him out, but somehow Dvorak's voice got through.

'Listen to me, Lawrence. What is the code?'

'There is no bloody code,' he shouted. He turned away from the monitor and pressed his hands over his ears as hard as he could. He held them there for about a minute until there was silence.

When he looked round again he saw the screen wasn't on anymore, and for a moment, he felt like the conversation with Dvorak was something he'd imagined.

He glanced round the room, at the ration packs, the boarded window, the chair and the bed, and everything looked as he remembered it.

He went over and tried the door, hoping someone had come and opened it for him. They hadn't. He stood there for a moment, wondering what to do next. He felt sweat run down the inside of his shirt and his heart beating hard. Then he glanced back at the monitor, thinking he heard something. But the screen was still off. He recalled Dvorak tapping his head, telling him, 'This is your room. This is where you are.'

He noticed how dry his mouth was, his lips sticking together, as he struggled to swallow. He started towards the table to get himself a drink. He guessed that was when he must have blacked out because he couldn't remember anything after that.

29

SEAN COULDN'T UNDERSTAND why he hadn't seen the guy in his flat sooner. He was standing right there. It was the guy in the black baseball cap who'd been following him.

Sean rocked backwards, throwing up the parcel of chips, as the guy reached out to grab him. Sean had been in his share of scraps over the years and knew where his strengths lay and they weren't in hanging round with guys bigger than him. Slipping out from under his reach, Sean flung himself down the stairs, opened the front door and burst out onto the pavement and ran. As he ran, he realised he had been right about seeing the car last night and again this morning; he wasn't just paranoid. He should have told Terry.

He ran for about five minutes, glancing back over his shoulder, making several turns down side streets, until he felt safe to slow down. Checking behind himself again, he couldn't see the guy in the baseball cap, so he stopped in a doorway to catch his breath.

He bent over, clutched his knees, and sucked in air. He spat out a globule of saliva and it hung from his lip until he wiped it away. His heart pounded.

He looked round the corner and listened out for the

sound of footsteps but couldn't hear any. He thought of Tash at the salon and wondered if this guy was going to go there next and whether he should ring and warn her. Then he thought of Terry fishing and wondered if he should call him as well. And what about the police? Should he call them and all? Or maybe this guy just wanted to talk to him. Maybe he was here to help. A private investigator, perhaps, that the wife had hired.

Sean remembered the phone number. Maybe now was the time to ring it. He didn't want to ring Terry. He was sure he'd blame him for this. Could hear his voice already: *What the fuck have you done, Sean? Didn't I tell you to stay at home?* Then Terry would feel duty-bound to ring Mr Hayes. And then he'd be in the shit. They wouldn't give him another job. He'd be back valeting cars, which meant he wouldn't get to open his restaurant any time soon, or marry Tash.

No, he had to sort this out himself, he thought. He'd text Tash and warn her. But keep Terry out of it. Thinking this, Sean started jogging again.

Before long, he came to the main road and waited for a break in the traffic to get across. Cars raced past. He held his hood down over his face, expecting to see the blue Ford any minute, and worried if there were other guys in baseball caps looking for him as well, stationed at different points around town.

He walked out into the road, crossing one lane at a time. A car sounded its horn at him. Once across, he disappeared down a side street and entered a small park, looking back over his shoulder, and sat down on a bench to catch his breath again. He hung his head between his legs and spat on the paving stones. Looking up, he saw a woman pushing a buggy along the path and two teenagers riding bikes.

Sean got out his phone and started texting Tash, telling her not to leave the salon on her break, that he'd pick her up later and explain then. Sean wondered if he should go back now and see what this guy wanted. He couldn't keep running. He was going to have to go and pick Tash up later anyway.

The woman pushed the buggy past his seat. Sean got out the packet of cigarettes, feeling the need to do something, and sparked one up. Exhaling smoke, Sean looked at his phone again and wondered if he should call Terry and tell him what had happened. He knew Tash wouldn't look at her phone until at least her break at twelve. Wouldn't someone be after Terry as well? Shouldn't he warn him? Maybe he could help.

Sean recalled Terry on the phone this morning telling him to go home. Sean remembered this was just before he'd found the guy in his room. Did Terry know something he didn't? Was something going on between Terry and Mr Hayes? Could he really trust Terry to tell him everything? He remembered the gun in Terry's rucksack. He'd never seen him with a gun before. And how Terry had asked him to go wait in the van while he locked up the farmhouse. He was gone several minutes. The cargo was already shut up in his room. He'd thought it odd at the time. Terry didn't go back in and shoot the guy, did he? The thing was, Sean reckoned Terry was perfectly capable of it. If Mr Hayes had asked him, then Terry would have done it – no question.

Sean took two quick successive drags on the cigarette, then dropped it on the tarmac and stood on it. Looking round, he saw the woman with the buggy leave the park. The two teenagers were sitting on a bench opposite him, gazing at their phones. Sean didn't feel he could trust anyone at that moment. He stood up and headed for the exit.

Leaving the park, he set off down the pavement. He wondered if he should find somewhere to hide for a while. A safe place, out of the way. He knew of a student halls of residence not far away. He could hang out there for a while. He knew a way in through the back. No one would bother him there. But then what? What about Tash?

The police were out of the question. Jesus! Maybe he shouldn't even go and pick up Tash. Now he thought about it, Tash had seemed a bit off with him this morning. Was this because she was just busy? Or was something else going on? Had she had a visit from this guy? Were they using her to get to him? Or was she just getting bored waiting for his plans to work out. Maybe Terry was right all along and she had him where she wanted him.

Sean felt alone. He thought about getting out of town, going up to London maybe; anywhere that wasn't here. He looked in his wallet and checked how much money he had – not enough to get him very far. Fuck!

He thought about Terry, who he'd always relied on in the past, picturing him fishing, the plop of the lead weight as he cast out his line, far away from all this. Or maybe he wasn't fishing at all. Perhaps he was in a van somewhere, parked up in a lay-by, or bombing down a motorway, or even back at the farmhouse for some reason. What was going on here?

Perhaps he should just hop in a taxi, Sean thought, and go to the lake and see if Terry was there. If he wasn't, then he would know. And if he was, he could pretend like he'd just come to see him (he had before) and, depending on Terry's mood, maybe tell him about the guy following him, see how he reacted. He could ask about the gun as well and find out what really happened at the farmhouse. Get it all out in the open.

Sean came to the end of the street and thought about where the nearest place was he could get a taxi. The station, probably, he thought. He stopped and looked round, trying to get his bearings. It was then he saw the blue Ford Focus parked along the street.

The guy in the baseball cap had the window down, with his arm resting on the ledge, and was speaking on his phone.

Sean saw him first and froze. A split second later, the guy clocked him as well. That was when Sean started running again.

As he ran, though, he could hear the car closing in on him. Then, glancing round, he saw it draw level and the guy looking across at him. The next thing he knew, the car accelerated past, banked the pavement and he was flying over the bonnet.

He tried getting up but the guy was on him in a flash, pinning him to the ground, and twisting his arm up behind his back.

'Fuck! That hurts!' he cried out, and saw the guy check along the street, his baseball cap pulled down low to his eyes, as he reached round and pulled a gun from his waistband.

'Jesus!' Sean said, as he felt the gun press against his head.

'Shut it,' the guy said. He frisked him and took his wallet, phone and keys. 'Stand up.'

Sean stood, raising his arms. 'Please, don't hurt me.'

The guy scanned the area, almost robotic in his movements. 'Get in the car.'

Sean, hypnotised by him, didn't move.

'Do it now,' he said, lifting the gun slightly. 'You're driving.'

Sean got in. The engine was still running.

The man got in beside him, checked over his shoulder, and said, 'Okay. Drive to the end of the road,' pointing his gun at him from his lap.

Checking his mirrors, Sean reversed off the pavement and set off along the road. He could feel his hands shaking as he changed gears. He approached the T-junction.

The man said, 'Turn left.'

Sean checked the oncoming traffic, the gunman doing the same, like he was a driving instructor, only he had a gun. When a gap appeared, Sean pulled out into the road. 'Where are we going?' he asked.

The gunman, taking out a phone, memory-dialled a number. 'Just keep driving.' He put the phone to his ear, giving a glance to his wing mirror.

Sean gripped the steering wheel; his arms shaking.

On the phone, the guy said, 'Yup. We're on our way,' and hung up.

They approached a set of traffic lights.

The gunman said, 'Get into the right-hand lane.'

Slowing down, Sean looked up at the signpost and saw it was the way to the recycling centre; a dead end. Stopping at the lights, Sean wiped his hands on his trousers then put them back on the steering wheel. He glanced at the man in the car next to him, suit jacket hanging up in the back, then looked up at his rear-view mirror where he saw a woman in a Mini checking her phone. Sean wondered how he could let her know he was in trouble when the guy motioned with his gun to show him he was watching him.

The lights changed and Sean pulled forward.

The gunman said, 'Take the next left.'

Sean turned left towards the recycling centre and noticed the woman in the Mini carry straight on. Now there was no one behind them.

Sean said, 'Can I ask what this is about?', his lips sticking together as he spoke. 'Because maybe I don't know anything.'

The gunman ignored him, looking straight ahead.

Sean said, 'Seriously. You saw my flat. There was nothing there, right?' Still he got no reply. 'I swear, I don't know what this is about—'

'Be quiet,' the gunman said, and he looked over his shoulder.

Sean glanced up at the rear-view to see what he was looking at but the road was clear. They were on the outskirts of town where the ring road cut across fields at varying stages of development into new housing and business parks.

The gunman then pointed ahead of them, and said, 'Pull in over by that gateway.'

Sean spotted the gateway, rubble piled in its entrance. 'What – there?' he asked.

'Yeah,' the gunman said, checking round again.

Sean ran his hand through his hair, his heart racing out of control. He pulled up in the gateway, almost hyperventilating.

The gunman said, 'Now turn off the ignition.'

Sean did as instructed and just sat there without taking his hands off the steering wheel. I'm going to get shot, he thought.

The gunman said, 'Put your hands on your head.'

'Why?'

He gestured with the gun.

Sean put his hands on his head, shaking.

'Now lean forward.'

Sean moved forward until his forehead touched the steering wheel, then felt the gun against the back of his head.

The gunman said, 'Now tell me where he is.'

Sean felt a wave of nausea rise up through his stomach. 'Seriously, I don't know what you mean.'

'I'll ask you one more time…'

Sean swallowed. 'I think I'm going to be sick.'

30

Lawrence opened his eyes, not realising they'd been closed. Had he been asleep?

He was sitting in the chair in front of the monitor again. He saw Dvorak on screen in the shadows. It felt like they were in the middle of a conversation again. Was it the same conversation as before?

Lawrence said, 'What happened? '

'You were trying to remember something.'

Lawrence tried standing up but couldn't move. He looked down and saw his hands were tied to the chair. He couldn't remember how he'd got here. 'What's going on?' he said.

Dvorak said, 'It's for your own safety.'

'How long have I been like this?'

'We came just in time.'

'What did you give me?'

Dvorak leant towards the camera, and said, 'What is the code, Lawrence?'

Lawrence gazed at Dvorak's face – the clean, symmetrical lines of his cheekbones, the pale green eyes, the recently trimmed greying hair. He appeared almost inhuman, synthetic. 'What code?' Lawrence said.

'The code,' Dvorak repeated. 'What is it?'

Lawrence felt his mental resistance giving way, like a wall of sand toppled by seawater, a melting sensation spreading through him. His eyes stung. 'Please,' he said, feeling the tears run down his face but being unable to wipe them away. 'I don't know what you want.'

'What is the code, Lawrence?'

Lawrence experienced memory flashes of the two men bursting into the room, dragging him onto the chair, tying his hands, then injecting him in the arm… whether this was a few minutes ago or several hours he had no idea. Time looped back on itself, dismantling any chronology.

Dvorak said, 'Try and remember.'

Lawrence wiped his chin on his chest. 'I don't know!'

Dvorak said, 'What is the code, Lawrence?'

'I don't know any codes. *Please!*' Lawrence flexed his arms, trying to break free from the ties that held him to the chair. 'What else can I say?'

Dvorak said, 'Say what's in your head. There's something in your head, isn't there?'

'I don't know what you mean.'

'Just say what you see.'

'I don't see anything.'

Dvorak said, 'Close your eyes.'

'What?'

'Close your eyes. Go on.'

'Why?'

'So you can see better. Do it.'

Lawrence closed his eyes, afraid the two armed men might return if he didn't.

Dvorak said, 'Now tell me what you see.'

Lawrence said, 'Nothing.'

'Try harder.'

With his eyes closed, Lawrence pictured the walls of the room he was in. He said, 'All I can see is this room.'

'What else?'

'Nothing.' Lawrence opened his eyes.

Dvorak leant forward on his chair, his face coming out of the shadows, so Lawrence could see his eyes. 'Have we met before?'

Lawrence said, 'No.'

'Are you sure?'

'Yeah.'

'Maybe you're forgotten. You don't remember everything, do you?'

'I think I would remember.'

'Really. Why is that?'

Lawrence didn't answer, starting to doubt himself.

Dvorak said, 'What *do* you remember?'

Lawrence said, 'I remember what's important.'

'What if you don't know if something is important or not?'

Lawrence shook his head. 'Am I supposed to know who you are?'

Dvorak said, 'How did you meet Amanda?'

'What's this got to do with her?'

'Just answer the question.'

'You already know – at university.'

'Do you trust her?'

Lawrence hesitated. 'Yeah.'

'Does she trust you?'

'Yeah. Why?'

'No indiscretions then?'

Lawrence hesitated, wondering where this was going. 'No,' he said.

Dvorak said, 'Never been tempted?'

'Not really.'

'What about before you were married?'

'What about it?'

'Did you have lots of women then?'

'Not particularly.'

'You went travelling for a bit. What about then?'

Lawrence stared at Dvorak for a moment, wondering how he could know so much about him.

'Was there anyone then?'

'Probably – I can't remember.'

'What about your time in France?'

Lawrence hesitated, shocked again by what Dvorak knew. After graduating from university, he'd spent time travelling around Europe before taking a job in France.

Dvorak said, 'Didn't you live there for a while?'

'How do you know all this?'

'What about at that time? Was there anyone important to you?'

'I don't remember.' He had been renovating an old shooting lodge in the Dordogne region for a wealthy client of his adoptive father. The work had taken him all summer. Working ten hour days, in baking sunshine, sleeping on a mattress on the floor. The experience had inspired him to set up his own business in property development.

Dvorak said, 'You don't remember a girl called Suzanne, then?'

He looked up at the monitor. 'Who?'

'A girl called Suzanne.'

'No.' Lawrence recalled the lodge was set in the grounds of a large country estate and was a mile from the nearest village. Apart from the family living in the big house, he'd hardly seen anyone that summer.

Dvorak said, 'Or was she "Anne"?'

'Who?'

'Or perhaps Lucy?'

'What are you talking about?'

Dvorak said, 'It was Lucy, wasn't it?'

'What?' Lawrence remembered there was someone – a girl who rode a horse. She knew the family up at the house. He met her there after a swim one evening and they got drunk and walked home together. But was her name Lucy? He said, 'Is this what this is about? Me living in France?'

'So you remember now?'

'Remember what?'

'Does Amanda know about Lucy?'

'Why should she?'

'You didn't tell her?'

'We weren't together then.'

Dvorak turned his head, as if he was checking to see what the weather was like outside. 'You see,' he said, 'you don't remember everything you think you do.'

'There's nothing to remember.'

Dvorak turned and looked at him again. 'That's not very kind to Lucy.' He smiled.

Lawrence said, 'I expect she doesn't remember me either.'

'But what if she did? What if you were the most important part of her life, a part she couldn't forget?'

'Is this what this is about?'

Dvorak lowered his gaze for a second then looked up at the camera again. 'Tell me about Lucy,' he said.

'There's nothing to tell.'

'Are you sure?'

'Yeah. I hardly knew her.'

'Really? Before I jogged your memory just now, you'd forgotten she ever existed. Why should I believe you now you say you hardly knew her?'

'I remember her now. She just wasn't at the forefront of my mind before, that's all.'

'*The forefront of your mind*. That's nice. What about the forefront of other people's minds? Like Lucy's or Amanda's?'

Lawrence said nothing.

Dvorak went on, 'Something deemed unimportant to you, and therefore *not* at the forefront of your mind, could be important to them, and on their minds all the time. Don't you think?'

Lawrence stared back at Dvorak, unable to think anything at that moment.

Dvorak added, 'Simply put, an event deemed unimportant to you is not necessarily an unimportant event to others.'

Lawrence said, 'What's this got to do with me?'

Dvorak came back at him quickly, like he had his answer memorised. 'We are who we are because of the version of events we choose to remember,' he said. 'But buried deep inside us is another story that, for one reason or another, we choose not to tell.'

'I'm not telling you a story,' Lawrence said. 'I knew Lucy, very briefly, ten-to-fifteen years ago. That's it.'

'Which is *your* story.'

'No. It's what happened.'

'To you maybe.'

'Well, I can't speak for anyone else.'

'No, you can't – that's right. You have *your* story and others have theirs. But how many different stories could we tell ourselves? And indeed, how many different stories could others tell about us?'

'Like Lucy, you mean?'

'Yes, like Lucy. Isn't she one of the stories you didn't tell?'

'Well, now I have. Can I go now?'

Dvorak looked down at his hands for a moment, massaging the palms. Then, looking up, he said, 'I want you to close your eyes again.'

Lawrence tried moving his arms. 'Just let me go. I can't help you—' He tried standing up, forgetting he was tied to the chair.

Dvorak said, 'Close your eyes, Lawrence.'

Lawrence looked towards the door, thinking he heard footsteps outside. Were they going to inject him again? Was he about to pass out and not remember this? He looked back at Dvorak on screen, and said, 'Please,' he said. 'Just let me go.' He felt exhausted; tears ran down his face once more.

Dvorak said, 'You need to listen to me, Lawrence. Close your eyes.'

Breathing heavily, Lawrence said, 'Why?'

Dvorak said, 'I'm here to help you.'

'Then let me go.'

'In good time. Close your eyes.'

Again, Lawrence thought he heard the sound of footsteps outside the door and pictured the balaclava-clad men and their needles. 'Please,' he said.

'Close your eyes.'

He did so, feeling tears running down his cheeks.

'That's it. Relax. Breathe in.'

Lawrence took a deep breath.

Dvorak said, 'Now let it go.'

Lawrence let it out.

'Now keep breathing.'

Lawrence took in several more deep breaths, exhaling slowly, and felt his heart rate slow down. Dvorak said, 'Now tell me what you remember.'

'What – about Lucy?'

'If that's where you want to start.'

'There's nothing to remember.'

Dvorak said, 'Just try.'

With his eyes closed, Lawrence tried to think of something. But his mind was blank.

Dvorak said, 'Concentrate. You need to listen to me, Lawrence. Go back.'

In his head, Lawrence experienced a sudden flash of light and felt himself sway backwards. He opened his eyes in alarm. 'What's going on?' he said. He glanced round the room. Was someone there?

'Close your eyes again,' Dvorak said. 'Stay with it.'

Lawrence looked back at Dvorak and felt his eyes close of their own accord. Was he being hypnotised?

Dvorak said, 'That's it. Now tell me what you see.'

Things slowly came into focus and Lawrence realised he was looking at the night sky. He could see the stars and moon, a church tower and the shadows of trees. And Lucy was there with him.

Dvorak said, 'Tell me, Lawrence. What do you see?'

Lawrence said, 'That night.' He saw them sitting on the

grass together, Lucy and him. She was smiling, resting her head on his shoulder, her bare shoulder poking through her loose-fitting top. They were passing a bottle of wine between them. 'We're sitting in the churchyard,' he said.

'Go on.'

He saw Lucy running her hand through her fringe of hair, the sparkle of her brown eyes in the moonlight. She swigged from the bottle again; then about to laugh, put her hand over her mouth to stop herself spitting out the wine. Once again, there was a flash of light in Lawrence's head and the picture went blank.

Lawrence opened his eyes.

Dvorak was looking at him from the monitor.

'What happened?' Lawrence said.

Dvorak said, 'I'm here to help.'

'Who are you?'

'I'm just like you – another untold story.'

'Are you a friend of Lucy's or something?'

Dvorak said, 'Lucy disappeared a long time ago.'

'So you're looking for her?'

'In a way. Do you remember this?' Dvorak held up a photo to the camera.

Lawrence saw the photo was of him and Lucy. They were sitting outside the big house on the veranda wall, Lucy perched on his lap, looking suntanned and a little drunk, while others were dancing in the background. He said, 'Is this what this is all about? You think I know where she is?'

Dvorak returned the photo to his pocket. 'No. I'm just telling you a story – the story about Lucy… It's got a ring to it, don't you think? "The story about Lucy".'

Lawrence tried moving his arms, but felt the resistance

of the cable ties again.

'You're tired,' Dvorak said. 'You need to rest.'

Lawrence heard footsteps outside and imagined the two men in military combats were back to give him another injection. 'No – please,' he pleaded.

31

SEAN LEANT ON a gate post as he spat on the ground. He wiped his mouth. Saliva hung in the blades of grass at his feet. There were some red and yellow globules mixed up in it. Probably what was left of his fry-up from this morning, he thought. His throat felt sore. He needed a drink of water.

The gunman was sitting in the car with the window down. Traffic passed along the dual carriageway in the distance. Sean stood up, clutching his sides, and looked across the field in front of him. The breeze blew into his face. He tasted car fumes and felt sick again.

The gunman said, 'Are you finished?'

Sean spat on the ground again. 'Yeah.'

'Get it the car then.'

Sean wiped his mouth with his sleeve and, looking across the field, considered making a run for it. 'Okay,' he said.

The gunman said, 'Hurry up,' and pointed the gun in his direction.

Sean could just make out the man's eyes under his cap; he didn't blink. Sean started back towards the car. The man didn't take his eyes off him and Sean had no doubt he would shoot him if he had to. He got in the car and closed the door.

The gunman said, 'Let's start again. Where did you take him?' He lifted his gun slightly, pointing it towards his chest.

Sean could just make out the black hole of its muzzle from where he imagined a bullet appearing before rupturing through his body. 'Who?' he said, but not very innocently.

'Come on. You can do better than that.'

There was the sound of an approaching car. The man looked at his wing mirror, then said, 'I want you to drive me to him.'

Sean saw the car in the rear-view mirror.

The gunman said, 'Do you think you can do that?'

Sean thought about jumping out in front of the car and waving it down. 'I don't know what you're talking about,' he said, waiting for the car to get closer.

The gunman said, 'Yes you do.'

The car was approaching. Sean could feel sweat running down his back. He moved one hand across his lap and up to the door handle.

The gunman saw what he was doing and jabbed the gun into his side. 'Not a good idea,' he said. He kept the gun there until the car went past, then he grabbed Sean by the back of his head, tugged him towards the middle of the car and rammed his face against the dashboard.

'Fuck!' Sean cried out, as pain flooded his system.

The gunman pulled his head back.

Sean said, 'Jesus! There was no need for that.'

The gunman drove his head into the dashboard again, pushing harder this time on the back of his skull. Sean tried to reach round and grab the man's arm to try to restrain him but he was too strong. 'All right,' he groaned, his nose bent up against the air vents. 'I'll take you there.'

The gunman pulled Sean's head back again. 'You try anything stupid again, and I will kill you. You understand?'

Sean felt blood running from his nose. 'Yeah. I understand,' he said, wiping his hand across his face and wondering if his nose was broken.

The gunman said, 'How far is it?'

'About three hours.'

'You remember the way?'

'I think so.' Sean wondered what he wanted with the cargo. Was he the guy who was supposed to be coming to talk to him? He was a bit late, if he was.

'You're going to drive me there. Okay?'

Sean said, 'Yeah. You want to talk to him, right?'

'Yeah. That's right. I want to talk to him. Now drive.'

32

LAWRENCE THOUGHT HE was standing by the door. *Were his arms no longer tied to the chair?*

He wondered if he was dreaming this or just imagining it, and how he might know the difference. He decided to check to see if his eyes were open or not, and told himself to open them. But nothing seemed to change. Maybe they were still closed and he was seeing all this inside his head. How would he know?

He saw himself sitting in the chair in front of the monitor talking to Dvorak, as if he was looking down on himself from outside his body. How was this possible? If that was him down there – who was it having these thoughts? Were there two of him now?

Lawrence wondered whether they had planted some kind of device in his head, to access his thoughts. If this was true, how long had it'd been there? He hadn't been aware of any operation taking place. Surely it would require some kind of procedure.

He tried to remember when it might have taken place. He recalled arriving here in the van, the quad bike, the first two men. But couldn't be sure if he'd experienced these things with his eyes open or closed. Maybe his eyes had always been closed, and everything that had happened to him had just been going on inside his head. Like he'd been watching his life on a screen without actually taking part. Maybe that's all life was, he thought: just imaginings in our head.

Maybe he existed just as thoughts now. He no longer occupied any physical space.

In this 'blind seeing', Lawrence saw Dvorak on the screen again, sitting in the chair in his dark room. He looked at him for a while. Dvorak didn't move. Was he asleep?

Lawrence felt a reality beyond his thoughts, like a sound first heard in a dream that turns out to be coming from your room. Eventually he said, 'Is that you?'

Dvorak lifted his head. 'Hello, Lawrence.'

'How long have you been there?'

'I've been here all along,' he said.

Lawrence glanced round and saw he was sitting on the chair in the room, back in his body again, his hands tied behind his back, like before. He said, 'What happened?'

'You drifted off.'

Lawrence looked at Dvorak on screen again. 'Was anyone here?' he asked.

'No, just us.'

Lawrence noticed Dvorak looking back at him like he knew everything he was thinking – that it was almost as if Dvorak was inside his head. 'You know everything, don't you?' he said, and had the feeling he was back in his thoughts again and was imagining this conversation.

Dvorak said, 'Yes.'

Lawrence gazed at Dvorak, wondering if he was real, or if he was imagining him. Or if he would know the difference anymore.

Then Dvorak said, 'You remember Lucy, don't you?'

Lawrence hesitated. 'Yes,' he said.

'Tell me about her.'

33

Sean had been driving for about ten minutes when he heard his phone buzz. He did his best to ignore it and, with sweaty hands, gripped the steering wheel and looked at the road ahead.

The gunman said, 'Are you expecting to hear from anyone?'

'No,' Sean said, and he watched as the gunman reached for his phone and looked at the screen – a photo of him and Tash set as background.

'What time are you meeting her?' he said.

Sean asked, 'Who?', trying to play the innocent.

The man flashed the screen in his direction, which showed a message from Tash.

'Tonight,' Sean said.

'Anyone else?'

'What do you mean?'

'Are you meeting anyone else?'

Sean immediately thought of Terry. 'No,' he said.

The man looked at him. 'You've made no other plans?'

'No.'

'No one is expecting you some place?'

'No,' Sean said.

The man looked at the photo of Tash on his phone again. 'What time tonight?' he said.

'After work.'

'What time?' He gave him a glance.

'Six. It depends… About six.' Sean glanced at the man, whose face was part-hidden under the baseball cap, and wondered what he was thinking. 'Can't I just drop you off and go?' Sean said. He could still taste vomit in his mouth as he swallowed. 'Seriously, I'm not going to say anything.' He glanced at him again, trying to gauge his reaction, but the man just pocketed his phone and ignored him.

Sean looked back at the road and, removing a hand from the steering wheel, ran it through his hair. He felt light-headed, shaky. He let out a deep breath. He said, 'I knew I shouldn't have taken this job.' He glanced at the man again. 'It was the money, you know? It got me. All I want to do is open my own restaurant, you see. That's all.'

The gunman looked at the road ahead, blanking him out.

Sean said, 'You have anything like that? Something you want to do. A dream. Some people think its bullshit. "*You can't do this, you can't do that.*" I don't.' Sean straightened his arms on the steering wheel, then said, 'Maybe you don't. Which is fine. Maybe your job gives you satisfaction. Which is great. I respect that. I wish I was more like that sometimes, you know …' Sean felt himself burning up; he stroked back his hair again. 'Fuck,' he said, breathing out heavily. 'Do you mind if I open the window?'

The gunman said, 'Go ahead.'

Sean opened the window, felt the breeze on his face, and let out several deep breaths.

'Better?'

'Yeah, I'm sorry.' Sean closed the window. 'I tend to talk a lot when I get nervous. I'm not trying to piss you off or anything.'

'Glad to hear it.'

'I want to help you, you know. Just don't want any trouble.' Sean checked to see if the man was reacting. But taking his eyes off the road, he veered off course slightly and clipped the middle line.

The man said, 'Careful.'

Sean straightened up the car again and checked his mirrors. He saw a car close behind them and for a second thought it might be the police. He noticed the man check his wing mirror as well.

The gunman said, 'Just slow down a bit. And let him pass.'

Sean slowed down and the car zoomed past.

The gunman checked his watch and said nothing.

They sat in silence for a while and Sean wondered what Tash had said in her message. Did she know anything about this? He remembered thinking Terry might be involved in some way. Him and Mr Hayes. Maybe the guy next to him was, in fact, the only person he could trust now. Perhaps he should strike up a bond with him before it was too late. Thinking this, Sean remembered the cargo's wife's phone number and wondered whether he should tell him about that. Maybe if he did the guy would trust him, and then let him go.

Sean drove through a dip in the road, passed a field of sheep, a line of pylons running through a clearing in the trees in the distance, and remembered coming this way with Terry when the sun was setting and Terry was smoking his rollie.

The gunman said, 'What is it?'

'Nothing.'

'You recognise it?'

Sean said, 'Yeah.'

The gunman glanced out of the window.

Sean did too, wondering what would happen if he just drove the car off the road into the field and took his chances. Would the guy shoot him as he tried to run away?

Sean gripped the steering wheel a little harder, feeling his heart flutter nervously, as if he'd actually decided he was going to do it. For a second, Sean imagined what it would be like getting shot – the bullet entering his back, drilling through flesh, splintering bone, and then exiting the other side with a squirt of blood. Would it sting? Would the shock cancel out the pain? Sean felt his scalp tingle and he ran his hand through his hair again, trying to clear the image.

The gunman said, 'Are you all right?'

Sean replied, 'Yeah. I'm fine,' not wanting the guy to think he was shitting himself. It'd make him feel he couldn't trust him. He'd be a liability then. An inconvenience. He wanted to make him think he was cool and that he could count on him. 'I'm Sean, by the way,' he said, realising how stupid it sounded introducing himself like this but wanting to show he was ready to do what he was told and wasn't a threat. Then maybe he'd get out of this alive.

'Yes, you are,' the gunman said.

'What shall I call you?' Sean said, feeling his mouth drying up again. 'You know, if I have to get your attention or something.'

'I don't know,' the man said, playing along. 'What do you think?'

Sean said, 'I don't mind. Anything.'

The gunman shook his head, like he was finding it funny. 'You want to give me a name?' he said.

Sean tried to smile, wanting to be in on the joke, if there was one. 'Yeah,' he said. 'Why not?'

The gunman said, 'That's nice. Like my mother.'

'Yeah. Anything you like.' Thinking this was good, and that they were getting on now, Sean said, 'How about John?'

The gunman lifted the gun and pointed it at Sean's stomach. 'How about you just concentrate on the driving and shut the fuck up? How about that?'

Sean said, 'Yeah. Sure.'

34

TELL ME ABOUT her.

'What is it you remember?' Dvorak said, once again the movement of his mouth strangely emphasised in the light.

'I remember Lucy riding her horse along the lane,' Lawrence said. 'I was working on the barn roof.' In his mind's eye, Lawrence saw Lucy approach on her horse. She was wearing a black riding hat, jodhpurs, and a sleeveless T-shirt. She bobbed up and down in rhythm with the horse's movements; the sun shining through the trees; the sound of hooves on the stony ground. He could see the scene so clearly, like a film of it was playing in his head. He said, 'She didn't see me to begin with. There were trees along the lane.'

Dvorak said, 'What were you thinking?'

'That she looked good on a horse.'

'What else?'

'That I…' He hesitated. He saw Lucy lean forward to get out the way of an overhanging branch. She was wearing a necklace; it lifted off her chest.

'What else, Lawrence?'

'Nothing. I was just watching her.' He watched Lucy move in and out of the shade of the trees, her sleeveless

T-shirt showing off her suntanned arms, her coloured bra visible underneath. She held the reins lightly in both hands, occasionally giving them a flick when the horse turned its head.

Dvorak said, 'Keep going.'

'Then she saw me.'

'What did she do?'

'Nothing. Just smiled.'

'Did she stop?'

'No. She kept going.' He saw her enter a field up the road, leaning forward on her horse to open and shut a gate, then trotting off into the distance.

Dvorak said, 'You wanted to see her again?'

'I don't know – maybe.'

'What happened then?'

Lawrence saw himself standing outside the barn, drinking from a bottle of water and looking across the vineyard at the back. He was covered in dust and sweat. He'd just finished work. A buzzard turned in the sky above a block of conifers in the distance. 'I got a call a few days later,' he said. 'Would I like to come for a swim up at the house?'

'And did you?'

'Yeah, I drove up after work.'

'Was she there?'

'No. No one was there when I arrived.' He saw himself driving up the track to the manor house, getting out of the car, and knocking on the front door and getting no answer, then walking round the back, the rusty sun beds and ashtray on the patio, and calling out to see if anyone was there. But there wasn't.

'What did you do?'

'I went for a swim.' Lawrence remembered how beautiful the water was, floating on his back and looking up at the sky, so blue, not a cloud in sight, swallows flying to and fro.

'Where was everyone?'

'They'd gone into town, to pick someone up from the station. I was just getting out from the pool when they came up the drive.' Lawrence paused, seeing the trail of dust rise above the rows of vines as the car approached; then as the car got closer, hearing voices, music, and laughter.

Dvorak said, 'What did you do?'

'Nothing. I got changed and ready to go.'

'And Lucy? Was she there?'

'Yeah.' He saw the car pull up in front of the house, music going off with the engine, doors opening, and people clambering out. Lucy was last out the back, holding her shoes.

'What did you think?'

'Nothing.'

'Did she recognise you?'

'I think so.'

'Then what?'

'I said I'd better get back – I had work tomorrow. But the others said I must stay. They were having a barbecue.' Lawrence saw them holding up cans of beer and bags of food with baguettes sticking out. He glanced at Lucy, quieter than the others, and saw her looking at him. What were her eyes saying?

Dvorak said, 'You said yes.'

'Yeah. Why not?'

'You wanted to get to know Lucy?'

Lawrence hesitated, remembering Lucy bending down to stroke a cat that had just appeared from out of the bushes.

'Yeah, I suppose,' he said.

'And did you?'

'Yeah.' Lawrence saw the others standing round the pool. Someone was lighting two cigarettes at once. Music was playing. The smell of meat frying on the barbecue. Lawrence saw Lucy sitting on a wall, helping cook the food. He approached her and they started speaking. She was wearing cut-off jeans, T-shirt, and a bikini top with a necktie. It was still light, though the sun was going down.

Dvorak said, 'What did you speak about?'

'You know… what we were doing… the holidays…' Lawrence watched Lucy open a bottle of beer on the side of the wall, then serve food for others, laughing as she dropped meat between the grill.

'Keep going.'

Lawrence remembered chucking a frisbee with two of the guys, then sitting on the lawn with them and drinking shots. After a while, Lucy and another girl joined them. They lined up more shots. Downing her shot, Lucy smiled at Lawrence and they got chatting again. It was getting dark. The others got up to dance. 'We were having fun. You know, it was a good party.'

'Who were you with?'

'Just Lucy.'

'Where were the others?'

'Around. Swimming. Dancing. Playing table tennis.'

'You didn't want to join them?'

'We were enjoying ourselves. Just talking.'

'And later?'

Lawrence saw Lucy sitting on his lap. Together they were sharing a joint with some of the others. A couple were kissing on the steps of the house. A guy had taken his shirt off and was lying on his back on the lawn under the stars. Lawrence said, 'It was getting late. I was pretty out of it. We decided to leave.'

'You left with Lucy?'

'Yeah.'

'What happened?'

'I don't remember exactly. We were both pretty drunk.' Lawrence saw them leaving the house, stumbling over people crashed out on the floor, empty bottles on the tables, guttering candles.

Dvorak said, 'Where did you go?'

Lawrence saw the moon above the church spire. He was holding hands with Lucy. They passed through a broken wooden gate, Lucy leading the way. 'The churchyard,' he said. He felt the dry grass against his arms, noticed Lucy's necklace catching the moonlight, the gleam of her tanned face, her eyes.

'What did she say to you?'

Lawrence was looking inside himself but couldn't see anything; the film had stopped. Everything had gone dark. For a moment, he felt like he was still there, with Lucy, in the churchyard, but just couldn't see. He wanted to call out her name to see if she was there.

'Stay with it. What do you see?'

He looked again. But it was pitch black. He couldn't even see his hands; and the air felt cooler now, like he was somewhere else.

With his eyes closed, he gazed into the darkness inside himself, trying to see where he was now. Then slowly, his eyes began to adjust to the dark. He started seeing shadows ripple at the edges. He wondered what he was looking at.

He got the feeling he was lying down and tried to think where he could be. Then he saw himself turn on his side, looking about, and realised he was still in the boarded-up room. He was lying on the bed, his eyes open. The monitor was off, and the chair was in the middle of the room, facing it.

He lay there for a moment, conscious of his heart rate and his breathing. There was no other sound. He wondered what had happened to Dvorak, and how he came to be on the bed.

Lawrence got up, walked across the room and took a bottle of water from the table. Breaking the seal, he stood there and drank. The water tasted cold and he wondered if they'd delivered it recently.

Screwing the lid back on the bottle, he noticed his hands were shaking. He held them together for a moment. He remembered them being tied to the chair. But when was that? He looked across at the monitor and tried to think what could have happened.

Then he heard a noise downstairs and looked towards the door. It sounded like a window had worked itself loose and was banging in the breeze.

35

SEAN WAS TOLD to pull into a field gateway, ten minutes away from the farmhouse. He did so and, turning off the ignition, held onto the steering wheel.

The gunman said, 'Describe the place.' He had one hand on his gun.

Sean said, 'How do you mean?', nervous as fuck at having been asked to pull over again. He could feel his hands shaking.

'The place – what's it like?'

'It's just a small farmhouse.'

'Any other houses about?'

'No, just fields. It's a farm.'

'How close is it to the road?'

'Not that close. It's up a track. About half a mile maybe.'

'What about this farmhouse?'

'What do you mean?'

'What's the layout inside?'

'There's a kitchen as you go in. A sitting room. A downstairs toilet. Then the stairs...' Sean hesitated, remembering the picture of the geese on the wall and the damp envelopes, then writing the phone number on the back of the receipt.

The gunman asked, 'Where is he?'

'Upstairs. In the first bedroom.'

'At the back or front?'

'At the back.'

'Is he restrained in anyway?'

'What do you mean?'

'Is he tied up?'

'No. I don't think so.'

'What do you see from his window?'

'Nothing. The windows are boarded up.'

The man nodded.

Sean added, 'It's quiet,' as if he was recommending it as a holiday let.

The gunman said, 'What else do you remember?'

Sean thought about the picture and the damp envelopes again. 'Nothing,' he said.

'Did you see anyone else while you were there?'

Sean tried to think. Had they? 'No,' he said.

'Are you sure about that?'

Sean then remembered the man on the quad bike and realised he should mention him if he wanted this guy to trust him. He said, 'Actually, there was someone driving around on a quad bike, now I think about it. I forgot. Maybe a farmer or something.' He couldn't remember what Terry had said he was.

The gunman said, 'Did he come to the house?'

'Yeah, but we ignored him and he went away.'

'This was you and your mate, yeah?'

Sean realised he'd said 'we'. 'Yeah,' he replied, realising it was too late to take it back.

'Where's your mate now?'

'He's at home.' Sean knew there was no point lying to him about Terry. He probably already knew about him anyway.

The gunman sniffed and said, 'He's not going to be a problem, is he?'

Sean thought about this for a second. If there was anyone who could be a problem it was Terry. 'No,' he said.

The gunman nodded. 'Right. I'm going to make a call. Give me the car keys.'

Sean handed him the keys, and the gunman got out of the car and walked over to the fence.

Sean watched him take out his phone, tap the screen a couple of times, then put the phone to his ear. He guessed the call was about the farmhouse. It lasted no more than a minute. When he got back in the car, Sean asked him, 'Is everything all right?

The gunman checked his watch, saying nothing.

Sean said, 'Do you want me to drive you there now?'

'Not yet.'

Sean looked across the ploughed field in front of them, wanting to keep the conversation going, but not knowing what to say. He didn't like silence. Too many thoughts occurred to him when it was quiet. That was why he was always talking. Sean knew it got on people's nerves. Terry had once said to him, 'Didn't your mum listen to you or something?' That's how it had come up that he was an orphan. Sean even talked to himself sometimes.

Sean started to jiggle his leg in the footwell. He watched a flock of rooks take off from the ploughed field and then land again. Terry had taught him the difference between rooks and crows. He wished Terry was here now.

The gunman said, 'Keep still.'

'Sorry.' He knew he couldn't push this guy with his no-nonsense attitude. He reminded him a bit of Terry in that way, though Sean would have preferred Terry to him any day of the week. Although Terry was a royal pain in the arse a lot of the time, he was about the only person who'd stuck by him over the years. Even if Terry had something to do with this, Sean thought, it probably wasn't his fault; he was just doing what Mr Hayes told him to do. And Sean could forgive him for that. Anyway, Sean thought, it was about time he stood on his own two feet for a change and not rely on Terry.

Looking about, Sean caught his reflection in the rear-view mirror and for a second found it hard to recognise himself. He looked again, to double check.

The gunman said, 'What is it?'

'Nothing.'

The gunman checked his watch again; then his phone rang and he answered it with, 'Yup?'

There was a long pause; then he said, 'Understood.' He put his phone away again, and turned to Sean. 'Okay. Let's go.'

36

'WILL YOU WANT something when you get back?' Pam asked Hayes on his way out. She was holding Adam in her arms, having just finished feeding him. There were damp patches round her nipples.

'Probably not,' Hayes said. 'I'll have eaten with Jamie.' He glanced at Pam's breasts, her nipples studding her top – like spark plugs, he'd joked to her once, but Pam hadn't known what spark plugs were and by the time he'd explained, it didn't seem so funny. If something happened to him, like it did his father, he wondered how Pam would manage. Despite not speaking English very well and being away from her culture, he suspected she'd manage just fine. She was far more resilient that he was.

'Okay,' Pam said, smiling. 'Well, have a nice time.'

'Thanks.' For a moment, Hayes felt unable to move, as if his departure represented something more final. He was only off to see his son. What was wrong with him?

'Say hello to Jamie for me,' Pam said.

'I will.' Hayes was often struck by how Pam always thought of others above herself. Jamie had never really accepted her but still she treated him in the same good-natured way. As

Hayes started towards the car, Pam called out, 'And don't forget to tell him about your birthday!'

Hayes stopped. 'What about it?'

'You were going to invite Jamie and Chloe down, weren't you?'

'Oh, yeah.' He'd forgotten. He'd been so distracted thinking about his father's death. 'What do you think?' he said. 'Shall I still ask them both?' Never in his life could he remember being so indecisive about the smallest of things. He hated it. Asking Pam didn't usually help in these situations either, as she wasn't inclined to give direct answers if pressed on something, except on matters of food. Sometimes he wondered what would happen if he lost the ability to make decisions altogether. He reckoned they just wouldn't do very much. Except eat of course. She'd keep feeding him.

Pam said, 'I don't mind,' and smiled.

Even her smile gave nothing away. Hayes said, 'I'll see. They're probably both busy.'

'Why don't you ask anyway?'

'Yeah, maybe.' He climbed into the VW Golf, belted up and turned the ignition. The radio came on and he turned it straight off again, then backed up the car in the driveway and waved to Pam, who was standing in the doorway, waving back to him. Seeing her in his rear-view, still waving, he pulled out onto the road.

Hayes didn't know what Pam thought about dying, as he hadn't asked her. But he suspected she would treat it with the same good humour and acceptance as she did everything else in life. He wondered what her secret was and why he couldn't be more like her. Why did he have to keep thinking about dying? He didn't want to. The thoughts just kept coming. As if someone else was doing the thinking for him.

Hayes popped a piece of gum in his mouth and changed gear. He couldn't remember feeling so crap when he had cigarettes to smoke. Or whisky to drink for that matter. That was doctors for you, always advising you to cut back. He had been doing fine up until then …

Hayes accelerated on a straight section of road. In the field next to him, he saw a tractor towing a muck spreader, the outside of which was so caked in crap you couldn't see what colour the paint was underneath. As he went past, he looked at the field. The sun was shining. Rooks swooped behind the muck spreader. Accelerating, he cut through the middle of an S-bend, the speedometer tipping fifty mph. As he came round the next corner, he saw a red car stopped in the middle of the road ahead of him.

What the…? He started to brake, as he couldn't get past otherwise. Slowing right down, he noticed the car was missing a wheel cap and the sides were splattered with mud. There were two men sitting upfront.

Something wasn't right, Hayes thought. At that moment both men got out of the car and came towards him. They were wearing jeans, quilted jackets and trainers. As they walked towards him, they reached inside their jackets.

Hayes slipped the car into reverse and was about to back up, when glancing up to his rear-view, he saw a black Range Rover come to a stop in the road behind him. He knew it was no coincidence. Hayes looked ahead again. The two men pulled out Glock 17s and pointed them in his direction. They struck him as highly-trained individuals – perhaps Special Branch officers.

Hayes lifted his hands off the steering wheel. Looking

up at the rear-view, he saw the Range Rover hadn't moved. It had tinted windows, so he couldn't see who was inside.

Hayes heard one of the men say, 'Keep your hands up and get out of the car.'

Hayes opened the car door and got out, keeping his hands above his head. He had his cap in his coat pocket and would have normally put it on when getting out of the car, but resisted the urge on this occasion.

The approaching man said, 'Turn around. Put your hands on the roof.'

Hayes did so, and felt the man frisk him.

The guy then said, 'Okay. Turn around.'

Hayes turned round and saw the man behind him nod in the direction of the Range Rover, which then accelerated towards them.

The man said, 'Okay. You can put your hands down now.'

The Range Rover stopped alongside them.

The man said, 'Get in the back,' motioning with his gun.

Hayes hesitated, hearing the sound of an approaching car in the distance. For a second, he thought it might be Pam on her way to the shops. But the sound of the car soon faded into the distance.

The man shoved Hayes in the back, and said, 'Get in.'

Hayes climbed into the back of the Range Rover. Inside, there was a middle-aged man, smartly-dressed in Chinos and V-neck pullover, sitting on the seat beside him. The man didn't look round when he got in. Hayes could only think he was some kind of government intelligence officer. Upfront there was a driver wearing sunglasses and a gunman finishing a call through an earpiece. The driver then pressed a screen-tile on the Sat-Nav, glanced at his mirrors and accelerated off.

Still without looking round, the smartly-dressed man next to Hayes said, 'We need you to cooperate. Do you understand?'

37

CLICKING BACK THE bail arm of his Shimano reel and holding the line under his finger, Terry tipped his rod over his head and, picking a spot by the edge of the lilies, cast it out. The line fizzed across the lake in a looping arc. Terry pointed the rod tip after it. The 2oz ledger weight plopped into the water beside the lily pads and a small bubble of water broke at the surface.

Terry dipped his rod tip in the water and sunk his line, then set the rod in its rest and tested the bite alarm. All set. He picked up the landing net and lay it on some rushes to overhang the water. The net glistened with fish slime. He'd just had a small one out, a mirror carp of seven pounds. He then loaded his catapult with bait – 20mm boilies – and fired them towards the spot where he'd just cast. They showered the water. He stood there for a moment surveying the lake. Hazy sunshine splintered through trees as mist rose off the water. Perfect conditions, he thought.

Walking back up the bank, Terry sat down on his chair in the entrance to his bivvy, picked up the rollie he'd been making before the bite alarm had interrupted him, and finished rolling it. He took his time, tapping the rollie on top of his tackle box and removing loose strands of tobacco, before putting it in his mouth and lighting it. He looked out across the lake, smoked, and sipped tea from his thermos cup. Ducks skidded into land on the water. Only one other guy was fishing and he was down the other end. Just how Terry liked it. He avoided the busy times – weekends, bank holidays, half-terms – to experience this. Part of the pleasure of fishing, in Terry's opinion, was not to see another human being. He sat back in his chair, crossed his legs and rested his thermos cup on his lap, watching the ducks swim across the water, leaving bow waves in their wake.

A minute or two passed like this before Terry glanced at his rods, thinking he saw the line twitch where it entered the water. But the bite alarms were silent. Maybe he was mistaken. Just then, several pigeons flew out from the trees across the other side of the lake and Terry looked up, wondering what had disturbed them. He saw a man wearing a beanie and hoodie pass between the trees. Terry didn't recognise him as one of the bailiffs and wondered if he was a fisherman come to check out the lake, but somehow he didn't look the type. He then heard footsteps coming along the track, with an urgency about them, that didn't fit the surroundings. Something wasn't right.

Putting down his thermos cup, Terry reached down and picked up a Bowie knife from the side of his tackle box. Seconds later, two men came round the corner and, seeing him, stopped in their tracks. One of the men, wearing a black windbreaker, said into an earpiece, 'He's here.' The guy behind him, wearing a grey hoodie with the hood up, checked along the track. The man in the windbreaker, then said to Terry, 'Get up. We need you to come with us.'

Terry said, 'You *what?*'

'I'm not going to ask again. Get up. Now.'

Terry, rollie in his mouth, replied, 'No – I'm fishing.'

The guy stepped forward and kicked over Terry's rods.

'What the fuck?' Terry said.

The windbreaker guy reached inside his jacket and drew out a gun. But Terry was on him before he had a chance to rack the slide. Knocking his gun out of his hand, he got him round the neck, and pressed his Bowie knife against his stomach.

The hoodie guy span round and, seeing what was going on, went for his gun.

Terry said, 'I wouldn't if I was you.' He ratcheted up his hold round the other man's neck, and the man started spluttering.

The guy in the hoodie showed him his hands. 'Put the knife down,' he said. 'We just want to talk.'

Then Terry heard a rustle in the undergrowth and looked round to see the man in the beanie from the other side of the lake step into the clearing, pointing a gun at him.

The beanie guy said, 'Do as he says.'

Looking round, Terry noticed the guy in the hoodie side-stepping round him, putting distance between him and the other gunman, making it harder for him to cover them both.

Terry tried backing off to keep them both in his eye-line, dragging his hostage by his neck.

The guy in the beanie said, 'Let him go.' His finger curled round the trigger of his gun, a Glock 17.

The look in the guy's eye told Terry he wasn't messing around and he shoved the windbreaker guy away from him. The guy rolled down the bank and splashed into the water.

Terry stood there holding his knife at his side, the two other guys either side of him.

The guy in the beanie motioned with his gun, and said, 'Put the knife down now.'

Terry started to bend down, taking his time. He could see the windbreaker guy's gun lying on the dirt not far away. Terry thought he could make a dive for it.

The guy in the beanie, clearly seeing what he was thinking, said, 'Just drop it.'

Terry hesitated, then placed the knife on the ground.

'Now kick it away from you.'

Terry prodded it gently with his foot.

The beanie guy said, 'Stop fucking around.'

Terry kicked the knife away.

The guy in the windbreaker now came up the bank, dripping wet, and picked up the knife and his gun. Pointing the gun at Terry, he grinned, as if to let Terry know who had come out on top here.

The guy in the beanie said, 'Now get on your knees.'

Terry remained standing.

Windbreaker guy gave him a shove from behind.

Terry fought the urge to turn round and slug him.

'Come on, Terry,' the guy in the beanie said, 'we need you to hurry up.'

They knew his name, Terry noted, which was never a good sign.

The guy in the beanie motioned with his gun for him to move.

Terry lowered himself to his knees. Behind him, the guy in the hoodie said, 'Hands behind your back.'

Terry did as he instructed and felt a cable tie drawn tight

round his wrists.

The guy in the beanie, who was obviously the one in charge, said, 'Now up.'

Terry hesitated. 'What about my fishing tackle?'

'We'll take care of it.' The guy in the beanie nodded at the windbreaker guy, who grinned at Terry before tucking his gun into his waistband and walking back down the bank to where Terry's things were.

The hoodie guy then grabbed Terry by the crook of his arm and yanked him up. Terry, glancing back over his shoulder, said, 'If he breaks anything, I'll kill him.'

The guy in the beanie said, 'Just move.'

Terry moved on reluctantly. The thought of someone handling his fishing equipment upset him greatly. The rest – the tied hands, the guns, the arrest – he could deal with.

They led him along the dirt track through the rhododendrons and conifers back to the car park where there was a van ready, its engine running, and someone standing there holding the side door open.

Terry had lived with the thought of his past catching up with him for more years than he cared to remember. He guessed that time had come.

38

LAWRENCE OPENED HIS eyes. Or at least thought he did. Maybe he was seeing this inside his head again. The banging sound downstairs had stopped.

He saw himself sitting in the chair and Dvorak on screen. 'What happened?' he said.

Dvorak said, 'You were telling me about Lucy.'

'Was I?'

'Yes.' Dvorak looked at him and smiled. 'Is she still there?'

Lawrence saw himself sitting in the chair looking at the image of Dvorak on screen, as if he was having an out-of-body experience, but then became aware he was closing his eyes and seeing all this internally.

It was dark to begin with, but then his eyes – or rather, his mind's eye – grew accustomed to the light and he started to discern shadows and shapes in the dark.

He heard Dvorak say, 'Tell me what you see.'

Lawrence looked around, saw the stars, moon, and church spire and realised he was back. 'We're sitting on the grass,' he said. He saw Lucy sitting beside him, legs crossed, a wine bottle resting between them, her necklace catching the moonlight.

Dvorak said, 'Who's there?'

'Lucy. Me and Lucy.' He saw her tip up the bottle, her full lips pressed to the end, the wine running down the stem. She wiped her hand across her mouth, smiled and passed the bottle to him. He took a swig; it had the consistency of blood.

Dvorak said, 'What can you see?'

Lawrence hesitated. 'Everything… the moon, the stars. It's beautiful.'

'What's happening?'

He saw Lucy relighting a spliff, her hair falling forward as she sparked the lighter, then stroking it back, exhaling, before looking at him and laughing. 'We're smoking a joint,' he said. 'Laughing about something.'

Dvorak said, 'Go on.'

Lawrence saw Lucy resting her head on his shoulder; then she turned and looked at him. 'She's looking at me,' he said. He noticed Lucy's eyes and how they glistened in the moonlight, then her lips, coloured with wine, moving as she spoke. 'She's saying something.'

'What's she saying?'

'I can't hear.' Lawrence saw Lucy's lips moving but couldn't hear anything; like the sound was turned off.

Then everything went dark. Lawrence wondered where he was, what was happening, when he heard Dvorak's voice say, 'Stay with it. What do you see?'

Lawrence blinked, and slowly the image returned. Lucy was passing him the spliff. She smiled, pursing her lips, as he took it. He was back again. 'We're getting high,' he said.

'Go on,' Dvorak said.

Lawrence saw them lying on their backs now, counting

the stars. 'We're looking at the sky,' he said to Dvorak. 'I can see stars all around us… millions and millions of them… like dust. It feels like we're up there with them… in the stars… floating.' He hesitated. He saw himself roll over and look at Lucy, close-up. He could see the stars reflected in her eyes, and for a moment it was like he was looking into space; then he saw Lucy's lips part, the moist undersides, and they started kissing, gently at first, Lucy's tongue curling round his, then stronger, deeper… until he could no longer tell whose tongue was whose… like they had become one person.

For a moment, Lawrence's vision flickered and blurred.

Dvorak said, 'Stay with it, Lawrence. Tell me what you see.'

Lawrence blinked, trying to get the image back, but seeing nothing but a blank screen now, and wondering whether this was the monitor on the wall or the image inside his head. Then all of a sudden, bursts of light streamed into the darkness and he was back. But somewhere else now. Bright sunshine was shining through slated blinds. He was lying on a mattress on the floor. He realised he was in the converted barn where he had been staying in France… dust sheets, piles of cut timber everywhere.

Dvorak said, 'Where are you now?'

'I'm at the barn. It's the morning.' He saw himself wander outside and stand on the patio, the sun in his eyes making him squint.

Dvorak said, 'Are you alone?'

'I think so.' He was walking back inside the barn now. In the kitchen, he took a drink from the tap, then splashed water on his face.

'What are you doing?'

He was checking in the fridge for food. 'I'm feeling hungry. I'm looking for food.' But the fridge was empty. Then he saw himself walking down the road, in the shade of the trees. Birdsong; the smell of pine needles. 'I've left the barn.' He passed the churchyard.

'Where are you heading?'

'I'm on my way to the shop. I want to buy some bread.'

He saw a police car parked outside the village shop, its windows left open. Walking past it, he heard the crackle of broken French over its radio.

Dvorak said, 'What is it?'

'There's a police car.' Lawrence saw himself go into the shop. He saw the policeman standing by the till, talking to the owner, and then looking up at the TV in the corner of the shop as the news came back on after an ad break.

'I'm picking up some bread.' He noticed the policeman and the shop owner turn and look at him as he came in.

Dvorak said, 'Has there been some trouble?'

'I'm not sure.' He saw the TV showing images of a crashed car, police tape tied round trees, a buckled crash barrier in the mountains somewhere.

'What can you see?'

'There's been an accident. They're showing it on TV.'

'What happened?'

'People have died. There's been a shooting.'

'Where are you now?'

'I've just paid for the bread. I'm leaving the shop.' Lawrence saw himself under the trees again, walking along the roadside. He heard a car approaching and turned round. 'There's a car coming,' he said.

'The police?'

'No. It's one of the girls from the house. She's stopping.'

'What does she want?'

'It's about Lucy.' He saw the girl speaking to him. She was wearing sunglasses and an off-shoulder top. He could see white strap marks where she'd tanned in her bikini. She was telling him about Lucy going back to the UK and how she was sorry she couldn't get to say goodbye properly. Then the girl leant out of the window and kissed him on both cheeks and drove on.

Dvorak said, 'What did she say?'

'That Lucy had gone back to the UK and was sorry she couldn't say goodbye.'

'How did you feel?'

'Sorry, I suppose.'

'What do you think happened between you?'

For a second, Lawrence saw himself looking down the road as the girl drove off; then the image flickered and several competing images intruded. He saw Lucy sitting in the churchyard, tipping up the wine bottle, then Lucy and him kissing. Then he was back at the roadside again. The sun was shining through the trees. 'I don't know what happened,' he said. 'We must have passed out.'

'You don't remember what happened?'

The roadside image vanished. There was just darkness. Lawrence strained to see something. But there was nothing there. Then opening his eyes, he saw Dvorak on screen looking at him, hands on his lap, exactly as before. Lawrence said, 'What happened?'

Dvorak said, 'Close your eyes again.'

And before he knew it, Lawrence did so.

'Try to remember. You're walking back from the shop.

What did you see?'

Images flickered inside Lawrence's head, then he saw the police car going past. 'I can see the police car,' he said. 'Its lights are flashing. But there's no sound.'

'That's right. There's been an accident. Remember?'

Lawrence said, 'Where's Lucy?'

'Lucy has been staying with you these last few days.'

Lawrence saw a flickering image of Lucy walking through the barn in a loose-fitting T-shirt and black knickers.

Dvorak said, 'It's been two days since the party. Can you see now?'

Lawrence saw Lucy bending down to look in his fridge. He was looking at her from the mattress on the floor where he slept. He was lying propped up on his elbow, covered with a sheet from the waist down. He was admiring Lucy's arse as she bent over.

Dvorak said, 'You let her stay on. You've told no one. It feels like a secret.'

The image disappeared suddenly and Lawrence saw himself back in the room with Dvorak again. 'Who are you?' he said.

'Close your eyes, Lawrence. Concentrate.'

Lawrence closed his eyes again, without thinking about it. Once more, images of Lucy flashed up in his head, with Dvorak speaking over the top of them, like a narrator in a film, telling him, 'I'm just like you, Lawrence – another untold story. Let go, now. Remember.'

In the next moment, Lawrence was back in the room, sitting in the chair, with Dvorak looking at him from the monitor. Then, a second later, he saw himself huddled in a corner of the room, covering his face with his hands, crying.

He then removed his hands, looked up, and there was Dvorak standing in the room with him. This time, Lawrence felt sure what he was seeing was real and not a hallucination, the reality just seemed different, more focused, clearer, the accompanying sound, too, was sharper.

'I am you, Lawrence,' Dvorak said, walking across the room towards him. 'Just as I was Lucy. And will be you again.'

Lawrence said, 'No. I don't know you.'

'Yes, you do. I look after you both.'

Lawrence pleaded. 'Let me go.'

'Close your eyes,' Dvorak said. 'Concentrate.'

Lawrence wasn't sure whether his eyes were open or closed now, or if there was even a difference anymore. He was back in the barn again in France. He saw Lucy in her T-shirt and knickers walk across the room holding a gun. She held the gun loosely, casually, like it was a mobile or TV remote. She sat down on the mattress next to him and held the gun on her lap. Her silver necklace hung outside her T-shirt – her breasts, with that upward tilt, holding up the fabric. She passed him the gun and showed him how to hold it, folding her hands around his, and awakening feelings in him that he'd kept hidden for so long. He knew, then, this was his initiation into a world he somehow already belonged.

Dvorak said, 'You're my lovely little greylags. My sleeper agents. Can you see now, Lawrence?'

Lawrence said, 'No. I can't see.'

'Yes you can. Let go, Lawrence.'

He saw Lucy standing next to a crashed car on a hairpin in the mountains, wearing her riding boots and jodhpurs, with blood smeared down one side of her face.

Dvorak said, 'I am your moments of solitude… your

moments of joy…'

Lawrence saw himself holding his hands over his ears, trying to block out Dvorak's voice.

Dvorak saying, 'It's time for you, my little greylags, to come home.'

Lawrence saw Lucy shooting at the car. Saw the twisted faces inside, the mouths crying out in pain, their blood splashing the inside of the glass, bullets tearing up flecks of seat foam and plastic. Then saw himself back in the room, huddled in a corner, head buried in his hands, muttering to himself, 'I know who I am… I know who I am,' thinking that these weren't his memories… it wasn't him.

Dvorak saying, 'We are what we remember.'

Then Lawrence saw a moped cutting through the corners of the S-bends and Lucy, seeing it too, lift her gun and take aim. He remembered thinking the boy on the bike was just a teenager, wearing shorts and flip-flops, with his dark curly hair and dark skin. Lucy firing, once, twice, the boy slumping forward, like he'd had the air sucked out of him, then the bike skidding off at an angle, the red light casing shattering on impact, the bike bouncing off the crash barrier, blood pooling round his limp body on the tarmac.

'*No!*' said Lawrence, holding his head in his hands and shaking his head as if trying to free himself of the images.

Dvorak said, 'You are my lovely little greylags. You and Lucy. But it's time you came home.'

'No,' he said. 'I know who I am.'

'Do you?'

Now Lawrence saw himself years later sitting in a hotel bar, a business trip somewhere, when a girl sat down next to him. Her hair was cut short and dyed blonde. He smiled at her and said, 'You remind me of someone.' It was Lucy.

'No,' Lawrence said. 'No!'

Dvorak said, 'Yes, Lawrence. In the end, we remember everything.'

A series of images flashed before him, whether on screen or in his head, he wasn't sure now. He saw a body lying on a muddy track in a wood, sunshine shining through trees; saw himself fucking Lucy on a bed somewhere, her hair dyed black now; then attaching a silencer to a gun and driving a car at night; he saw conifer-clad mountains, ski lifts, falling snow… then he saw himself sitting on the floor back in the room where he was now clutching his stomach, with blood filling his hands.

Lawrence looked down. It looked like he'd been shot.

A second later, he saw himself standing at the window looking through the hole in the board; the sound of the quad bike in the distance.

Then he heard the door opening behind him, like it'd been unlocked all this time, and saw Lucy come into the room. She had a towel tied round her middle; it only just covered her breasts. Her necklace stuck to her cleavage, her hair wet, soap bubbles clinging to her skin. She walked towards him. Lawrence noticed there was a rug and mattress on the floor now.

He saw himself go over and kiss her. Then the picture changed and he saw himself slumped against the wall again, with blood filling his hands. He heard Dvorak's voice. 'It's time to come home, my little greylags.'

Lawrence span round. He saw Dvorak on screen, sitting on the chair in the empty room. 'You've been gone too long,' he said, smiling. 'I need you back.'

Lawrence watched Dvorak stand up now and walk across the room on screen. The camera followed him. There appeared to be light coming in from somewhere now. There was something familiar about the room that made Lawrence look again. It looked like his bedroom at home. He saw Dvorak standing at a window, venetian blinds filtering light into the room. He stood there and looked outside, the camera now swooped in over his shoulder to see what he was looking at.

Through the window where Dvorak was standing, Lawrence could see Amanda and their two kids in their garden at home. The kids were playing catch on the lawn and Amanda was talking to a man in a dark suit. He said to Dvorak, 'What's going on?'

The screen returned to Dvorak standing in the empty room. The camera panned round the room, with only the chair in it, but now it wasn't his bedroom at home, but the barn in France. What was happening? Lawrence felt tears run down his face.

Dvorak said, 'What you have to understand, Lawrence, was that I was there for you. I gave you something to believe in.'

'No,' Lawrence said. 'I don't believe in you.' Then on screen he saw the crashed car on the hairpin, the dead bodies inside, the bloodied windows. He covered his face with his hands trying to block it out. 'No!' he said. '*No!*'

Dvorak said, 'I forgive you, my little greylag, for all that you've done. But it's time to let go and come home.'

'Where am I?'

A voice said, 'Against the wall.'

Backing off, Lawrence said, 'What's going on?' He saw

a man in a balaclava pointing a gun at him. 'I thought you just wanted to speak to me.'

'There's been a change of plan.'

He thought he saw the flash from the end of the gun and felt the bullet smack him in the chest like he'd been hit by a club hammer. Finally, he saw himself on the floor, his hands full of blood, cold spreading over him, and the man in the balaclava standing in the doorway.

39

'THAT'S IT,' SEAN said, as they approached the turning, 'on the right.'

The gunman glanced over his shoulder to check there weren't any cars coming, then said, 'Okay. You know what to do.'

Sean slowed down and checked his mirrors, barely able to believe he was back here. The sight of the farmhouse in the distance made his stomach turn. He turned off the road and started down the rutted track.

The steering wheel juddered as the car headed along the rough terrain. He veered onto the verge to avoid the worst of the potholes. When he reached the gateway to the farmhouse, he stopped the car.

The gunman looked across at the farmhouse, then straight ahead up the track. 'Okay, keep going,' he said.

Sean continued up the track, the hedgerow now shielding them from the house, and could feel his heart beating hard and his stomach turning over like he was going to be sick again.

After going about thirty metres past the gateway, the gunman said, 'Okay, stop here.'

Sean pulled into a passing point in the track, leaving his hands on the steering wheel and the engine running.

The gunman said, 'Turn the engine off.'

Sean obeyed and saw the gunman check over his shoulder, then open the glove compartment and take out an ear piece and attach it to his ear. 'What's happening?' Sean said.

The gunman removed his cap and put on a balaclava, then checked the magazine of his gun and racked the slide. Checking his watch, he looked over his shoulder again.

There was the sound of a vehicle.

Sean looked up to the rear-view mirror and saw a black van approaching. It stopped on the track, just before reaching the gateway to the farmhouse.

The gunman, pocketing the gun, spoke into his headset, saying, 'In position. Let's move.'

In the rear-view mirror, Sean saw six balaclava-clad men, armed with semi-autos, get out from the back of the van. Two of them were also carrying battering rams, presumably to break down the door of the house. All six men moved along the line of the hedgerow in single file, then split up in different directions, with three men entering the field on one side of the house, and the other three spreading themselves around the courtyard.

The gunman said to Sean, 'Hold out your hands.'

Sean held them out and the gunman cuffed his wrists to the steering wheel, then got out of the car and closed the door.

Sean watched the gunman in the rear-view mirror, half-crouching, as he moved along the hedgerow towards the farmhouse. He stopped in the gateway where there was another guy waiting, backed up against the gatepost. Sean could feel his heart racing.

All the men settled into positions, behind hedges, against gateposts, or in the doorways to outbuildings. A minute or two passed like this, with no one moving or appearing to communicate.

Sean watched a sparrow bathe in the water of a pothole. The wind shook the hedge. Then the gunman and the other man at the gateway, using hand signals, moved off down the driveway towards the farmhouse.

They soon fell out of view, but after a few minutes, Sean heard banging and imagined they were bashing the farmhouse door down. Then there was quiet again. Another couple of minutes passed. Sean studied the handcuffs for a moment, slipping them down his wrists, moving his hands round the steering wheel, then pulling them up and feeling his skin pinch. The next time he looked up at the rear-view mirror, he saw the gunman coming back up the track towards him.

He got back into the car, removed his balaclava and put his cap back on. He then unlocked the cuffs and said, 'Drive to the house.'

Sean's hands were shaking as he turned the car round and started back down the track towards the farm. Nearing the van, he saw its driver smoking a cigarette. Sean turned up the driveway to the farmhouse; in his rearview, he saw the van follow on behind him. Sean could see the gunmen positioned around the courtyard and out in the field. The door to the house was open. There was a man in a balaclava standing in the doorway. He stepped out into the courtyard.

The gunman said to Sean, 'Stop here.'

Sean stopped the car and looked across at the house.

'Where is he?' he said, meaning the cargo.

The gunman took out his mobile, dialled a saved number, and put the phone to his ear.

Sean could hear it ringing. The gunman sniffed; then said, 'It's all clear.' Followed by, 'He's with me,' and ending with, 'Okay, understood.' He hung up.

Sean looked at the cottage, as the gunman pocketed his phone. All he could think about was whether the cargo was inside or not. Was he still alive? Had Terry done something to him? He couldn't hold back anymore and blurted out, 'Is he in there?'

The gunman scanned the courtyard, saying nothing. The breeze gusted dust off the concrete.

Sean said, 'Please. Is he dead?'

The gunman replied, 'This doesn't concern you now.'

Sean said, 'Fuck. He's dead, isn't he?' He held his head in his hands now, remembering how Terry had told him to wait in the van and then gone back into the cottage. What had happened in there?

Sean glanced at the gunman, then said, 'Who are we waiting for?

'Someone wants to speak to you.'

'But I don't know anything,' Sean said, shaking his head, and running his hand through his hair. 'Jesus, fuck!' He felt another wave of nausea and started taking sharp intakes of breath, his head spinning. He reached for the door handle to get out, but the gunman grasped his shoulder. Sean cried out, 'Please! I feel sick.'

The gunman let him go, saying, 'Open the window.'

Sean nodded, his lips sticking together, and opened the window. Sticking his head out, he sucked in the fresh air.

The gunman checked his watch.

Sean looked at the boarded-up windows of the farmhouse and imagined the cargo's dead body inside. On the floor? The bed? Against the wall? He remembered how the cargo had got him to write down what he said was his wife's phone number. Should he have rung it? Would it have changed anything?

As Sean thought about the cargo he realised he couldn't remember much about him. Was he tall? Short? What colour was his hair? How old was he? If he'd walked out of the house, Sean reckoned, he probably wouldn't recognise him. It was almost like he hadn't existed. Then he remembered the picture of the geese on the wall and wondered why it was he could remember that a lot more clearly than the cargo.

Sean saw the gunman check his watch again. 'Please,' he said. 'Is he dead?'

The gunman, without looking round, said, 'No more questions.'

Sean looked at the house and wondered why, if he was dead, they hadn't removed a body yet. Maybe they wanted the forensic crew to look at it first.

A gunman stood by the door. The breeze blew dust off the track. Sean tried to remember what the cargo looked like, but all he saw was the picture of the geese instead. It was then he remembered the children's home he'd been in as a kid and felt like the two were connected. Hadn't there been a picture of geese somewhere? It was the sort of picture they had there. He tried to recall the children's home, a detached house with large bay windows on the Sussex coast, but couldn't remember any of the pictures. But why would he remember the children's home now if there wasn't a connection? Or was his mind playing tricks on him again? He said, 'Did you see a picture in the house?'

The gunman said, 'What?'

'A picture. On the wall. Downstairs in the hallway. Did you see it?'

The gunman turned and looked at him. 'What about it?'

'I think I've seen it before.'

'Where?'

'At the children's home where I went as a kid.'

The gunman looked round at the sound of a vehicle. Sean glanced up to the rear-view and saw a black Range Rover with tinted windows and mud-splattered sides, coming up the farm track, leaving a trail of dust in its wake.

The gunman said, 'Wait there,' and opened his door and got out.

Sean watched the Range Rover approach at speed, as it rode out the ruts and potholes in the track. The other gunmen were taking up positions in the field, squatting on one knee and scanning the area like robots.

The Range Rover slowed up for the cattle grid in the farmhouse gateway, then accelerated again as it came up the driveway. The vehicle stopped beside them and two men got out of the back, one with a shaved head and goatee; the other a slim, smartly dressed, office type. The goatee guy removed a grey flat cap from his pocket and put it on; the colour matched his goatee. The gunman from Sean's car went over and spoke to the smartly dressed office guy. Then they both came over to the car, the gunman signalling for Sean to get out.

Sean did as he was instructed, got out and stood beside the car.

The office guy said, 'It's Sean, isn't it?' and held out his hand.

'Yeah,' Sean said, and shook his hand, feeling safe for the first time in ages, like no one had ever shaken his hand before.

'My name's Officer Collins,' the office guy said. 'I understand you remember something about a picture.'

Sean said, 'Yeah.'

'I would like to hear about that.'

Sean noticed the other guy with the goatee looking at him. Not in a bad way, just looking, like you would at a view. Sean suddenly remembered that Terry had described Mr Hayes as having a beard and wondered if it was him. And if it was, what he was doing here, and where Terry was. Sean looked back at Collins, and said, 'I just remember seeing it, that's all,' feeling safe again, like he could tell this guy anything. 'But I'm not sure.'

'And where do you think you saw it?' Collins said, giving a hand signal to one of the other gunmen who then set off in the direction of the farmhouse.

'I think it was in the children's home I was at. But I could be wrong.'

'In London, was it?'

'No, on the South Coast in Sussex. My mother left me at a hospital there – a week after I was born.' He felt tears come to his eyes; he couldn't remember this happening before, when telling this story. Sean said, 'It's a coincidence, right?'

Collins said, 'I'm sure it is. Take your time, Sean. Is there anything else you can remember?'

Sean glanced at the goatee guy again, and wondered if it really was Mr Hayes, and if he would know if Terry was all right. 'No. I don't think so,' he said.

Collins nodded at two of his gunmen and they headed towards the house.

Sean remained standing where he was, and they all stood there looking at the farmhouse waiting for Collins and his entourage to reappear. No one said anything. Sean glanced across at the goatee guy, wanting to ask him if he was Mr Hayes, and thinking he didn't look as mean as Terry had described him. The baseball cap dude surveyed the area, from left to right, like a CCTV camera. At one point, the breeze gusted a little stronger and you could hear the flapping of the polythene sheet snagged to a post. The sun appeared from behind the clouds and it felt warmer for a moment.

Collins and his entourage reappeared from the back door of the farmhouse. They stood outside talking for a moment. Collins then called over the gunman standing with Sean and they spoke to each other. The gunman was taller than Collins by several inches. When their conversation was over, the gunman signalled across the courtyard to one of the other men, while Collins came back towards Sean, and asked him, 'When were you last here, Sean?'

'Yesterday.'

'And you haven't been back since?'

'No. I swear.'

'That's all right.' He smiled.

The guy was nice; polite, Sean thought.

'And no one has been in contact with you since?'

'No... how do you mean?' Sean said.

'Have you received any phone calls? Or been approached in anyway?'

'No.' Sean looked at the house. 'Where is he? Is he not in there?'

Collins said, 'Sean, I need you to concentrate.'

'Jesus! I don't know anything. I swear.' He put his hands up to his head and ran them through his hair again.

'It's okay, Sean. I need you to think carefully. What happened before you left?'

'Nothing. We just left him here. That's it. Someone was meant to come and speak to him, weren't they? Jesus! He's not there, is he?' Sean glanced across at the goatee guy and wondered why he wasn't saying anything. Was he protecting Terry? Were they setting him up?

Collins said, 'No one passed you a note or said anything?'

'No.'

'Has anyone been following you?'

'No. I don't think so. Only you guys.'

Collins said, 'Cast your mind back, Sean.'

'Fuck!' Sean said. 'We just left him here, that's it.'

'And you've spoken to no one since then, Sean?'

'No. I mean, just to Terry. And my girlfriend. That's it.' He let Terry's name slip despite himself, but guessed it didn't make any difference now.

'All right, Sean. That's okay,' Collins said, nodding at the gunman. 'Do you want a drink?'

The gunman offered Sean the bottle of water. He took a swig and passed it back.

Collins said, 'Sean, did you speak to him before you left?'

'Who, the cargo? No…' He remembered the phone number again.

'What is it?'

'Nothing.'

'Sean, we don't have much time. What do you remember?'

Sean looked down at his feet. He heard the polythene

sheet flap behind him.

Collins said, 'You mustn't protect him, Sean. He is not who you think he is. He's very dangerous.'

Sean looked at Collins, then at the goatee guy, and said, 'Are you going to arrest me?'

'No, Sean.'

'Because I don't know anything about this. I just needed the money.' Sean felt tears come to his eyes again. 'I want to open a restaurant, you see. That's all.' Sean wiped his eyes with the back of his hand, and then said, 'He gave me his wife's phone number.'

Sean saw the gunman in the baseball cap move his hands towards his gun.

Collins said, 'It's all right, Sean,' shaking his head at the gunman. 'Go on.'

'It's in my wallet.'

'Let's see it.'

Sean, pointing at the gunman, said, 'He's got it,'

Collins nodded at the gunman, who gave Sean his wallet back.

Sean undid the Velcro pouch, took out the receipt, and handed it over. 'He wanted me to help him,' he said. 'But I didn't ring it. I swear.'

'That's all right, Sean,' Collins said, looking at the receipt and reading the number.

40

'SIT DOWN,' A voice said.

Terry felt a hand on his shoulder pushing him down into a chair. A sack covered his head so he couldn't see, and his hands were still tied behind his back. He sat down and someone pulled the sack off.

He squinted in the bright light. He saw a table in front of him and a man in a suit sitting behind it, looking through a folder. The man didn't look up. Terry said, 'Where the fuck am I?'

The man, reading from the folder, said, 'It says here: Terence. But I bet you prefer '"Terry"'… Is that right?' The suit looked up and smiled.

Terry said, 'Are you for fucking real?'

The man looked back at the folder again and, turning a page, said, 'I wonder if you're someone who thinks some people just deserve to die – that they have it coming. You know what I mean?'

Terry winced at him. 'This is a joke, right?' He took the opportunity to look round the room. It was empty except for a guard standing by the door.

The man opposite him said, 'I wouldn't blame you if you

were,' turning the page again. 'I'd understand. I sometimes feel a bit like that myself.' He looked up. 'They never found the body, did they?'

Terry waited, feeling his past close behind him now.

The man glanced at the folder again, and said, 'Gosh, it was nearly twenty years ago. Did you know that?' He looked up and stared at him and Terry knew then his past had arrived.

'What do you want?' Terry said.

The suit folded his hands on the table. 'How does it feel?'

'How does what feel?'

'To know you were responsible for someone's death and not say anything. Or maybe you just forget.'

Terry stared at the guy in the suit as he realised what he was talking about. Terry hadn't forgotten anything. What was twenty years when it came to memories like that? Terry remembered Mr Hayes had only sent him to pick the guy up. But when he got to the address, a house in Kilburn, the guy had legged it through the back garden, and scrambled over the fence onto a railway embankment. Terry remembered grabbing the back of the guy's jacket, the guy slipping, and rolling down the embankment. He broke his neck on the way down; you wouldn't think it possible. 'You're fucking kidding me,' Terry had said to himself, when he found him dead at the bottom. He rang Mr Hayes – on a pay phone in those days – to tell him what had happened. Once the initial shock had passed, Mr Hayes said, 'Well, we'd better get rid of him then.' It took them ages to drag the guy back up the embankment, what with trains going past. They dumped the body in the Thames.

The suit said, 'I thought you might remember something,'

looking into his eyes, not letting him go.

Yeah, Terry remembered. For years afterwards, he lived with the feeling that the guy's dead body would turn up someplace. Without warning, images of the guy's face would pop into his head: out fishing, he'd see it float up under the water. Lying in bed, he'd imagine a twisted arm hanging out of a cupboard. Terry often wondered if it was the same for Mr Hayes, if he was going through the same thing, waking up in the middle of the night, imagining stuff, or if he had managed to block it out. They never spoke about it. Certainly, Terry had never gone near a railway embankment again.

The suit said, 'They say it never leaves you.'

Terry shrugged and replied, 'Why don't you try it and find out?' wondering who the fuck these people were.

Ignoring him, the suit said, 'Tell me about Sean. You've looked after him over the years, haven't you?'

Terry hesitated, taken aback by the mention of Sean's name. 'What about him?' he said.

'You must feel like a father to him.'

'He's just a kid.'

'A damaged kid, though, wouldn't you say? But you've been there for him. You gave him a job, helped him out with his flat, looked after him along the way. That's beyond what a lot of fathers do.'

Terry said, 'You want to talk to me about Sean?'

'I don't know. You tell me.'

'Fuck this.' Terry tried to stand up but the guard behind him stepped forward and shoved him down in his seat again.

The suit said, 'I imagine having done it once, it's easier a second time around.'

Terry stared at him, getting the feeling there was more

to this than something that had happened twenty years ago.

The suit said, 'It's all right. I understand. You had a job to do.'

Terry looked over his shoulder and said to the guard, 'Did they bring my fishing gear back from the lake?'

The guard didn't reply.

Terry turned round and said, 'My fishing gear better be in one piece.'

The suit said, 'Don't worry. Everything will be handled with care.'

'I want to see it.'

'Terry,' the suit said, 'you need to understand. We're here to help you. But you need to help us in return.'

'How exactly?'

'We need to know where he is.'

'Where who is?'

'You last assignment, Terry.' The suit chucked some photos on the table.

Terry stared at the photos. They were of him and Sean at the golf club, parked up in the van, and of the cargo just before they took him.

The suit was saying, 'You were the last to see him, weren't you?'

'Was I? How should I know?'

'As I said, Terry, we want to help you. But you need to help us in return. Where is he?'

Terry paused; then said, 'He's at the farm. Where we left him.'

'And how did you leave him, Terry?'

Terry said, 'You're worse than my wife, you know that.' Terry was beginning to realise this guy must be Mr Hayes's contact in the security services. How else did he know so much about him and this job otherwise? But why were they interrogating him? Had someone crossed them behind the scenes?

'Answer the question Terry.'

'How the fuck do you think I left him?'

'I don't know. That's why I'm asking.'

Terry said, 'He was sitting there playing with himself.' Terry was conscious of acting a part in these situations. This wasn't really him, he thought. The real Terry was at home reading books about the D-Day landings or out fishing somewhere. However, he knew, if you wanted to get by in life, you needed a part to play. Without one, you were basically buggered. It was what he tried telling Sean, who was too soft in the head to realise, with all his talk of restaurants and women. Terry knew, until he'd spoken to Mr Hayes and established what was going on here, his part here was to say as little as possible.

The suit said, 'Terry, you're making it harder for me. I meant what I said about wanting to help you but I could just as easily not. And with your past, you need all the help on offer. How did you leave him?'

Terry shrugged. 'We just left him.'

'Be more specific, please.'

'He was sitting on the bed. How's that?'

'Were his hands tied?'

'Yeah.'

'And the doors were locked?'

'No, I left them open. *Yes*, the fucking doors were locked!'

'And you just left him there on his own?'

'That's what I said, didn't I?'

The suit held his chin in his hand for a moment, then said, 'He's not there, Terry.'

Terry hesitated for a second – was he bluffing? 'What do you mean?'

'I mean, he's not there.'

41

'GET ME A phone,' Collins said, gesturing to the driver of the Range Rover. He looked at the receipt with the number on again.

The driver walked round the side of the Range Rover and reached in through the door.

Sean said, 'He said it was his wife's. He just wanted me to ring her, to tell her he was all right. That's all.'

Collins, who was obviously the one in charge here, said, 'And you didn't attempt to ring it?'

Sean hesitated. 'No... I thought about it, but I was too scared.'

Collins said, 'That's okay,' still looking at the receipt.

The driver passed a phone to him and he started to punch in the number. But after hitting just a few digits, he stopped and looked up. 'What's that?' he said.

The driver turned to look at the field and said over his radio, 'What's going on out there?'

It was the sound of the quad bike.

Sean said, 'It's this farmer guy. He came to the house once.'

Collins said, 'Okay,' looking at the gunman in the baseball cap. 'You'd better go and have a chat with him.'

The baseball cap guy and the driver got into the Range Rover and they headed off up the track.

Collins looked at the phone again and entered the last couple of digits of the number.

Sean watched him put the phone to his ear and turn to face the house as he waited for an answer.

42

THE SUIT SAID, 'Did you kill him, Terry?'

Terry grimaced again. 'No.'

'Did you help him escape?'

'No.'

'What happened after you left the house?'

'I went home.'

'Did anyone make contact with you?'

'No.'

'We need to know where he is, Terry.'

'I told you. We left him at the farmhouse.'

'He's not there.'

'Then how the fuck should I know where he is?'

'We want to help you Terry. Just as we want to help Sean. So tell us where he is.'

'Fuck this.' Terry stood up again. This time the guard stuck a gun in the back of his head.

'Sit down, Terry.'

Terry sat down, feeling the gun follow him down.

The suit said, 'Where's the cargo?'

'I don't know. Tell him to put that fucking gun away.'

The suit nodded at the guard behind him, who removed

the gun.

'Whose orders are you following, Terry?'

'Sorry. I can't help you.'

'We're talking to Mr Hayes and Sean separately,' the suit said. 'So, you don't have to feel you need to protect anyone.'

Terry looked at the suit, wondering again if he was bluffing or not. Not that it mattered. He knew if they had what they were after they wouldn't be bothering him. He said, 'Thanks for the advice. Can I go now?'

The suit said, 'We found your gun, Terry.'

Terry hesitated. 'What gun?'

The suit looked up and nodded at the guard. 'It's been fired recently.'

The guard placed a sealed plastic bag on the table. Terry saw it contained his battered Ruger along with several empty .22 casings. He'd been reluctant about bringing the gun from the start. But Mr Hayes had said it was needed, so he fell in line.

The suit said, 'It's yours, isn't it?'

'Never seen it before,' Terry lied.

'We found it in the van.'

'Well done. So the fuck what?'

'There's trace evidence to suggest it's yours.'

Terry snorted in disdain. They'd have to do better than that, he thought… fucking 'trace evidence'!

The suit said, 'What was it doing in the van, Terry?'

Terry shrugged. 'Your guess is as good as mine.' Mr Hayes had told him to leave it there. It wasn't his place to ask why. He'd supposed the guy visiting the cargo was going to need it. It was far easier to have someone supply a gun than find your own.

The suit said, 'So you didn't leave it there?'

'Like I said, I've never seen it before.'

'I'm going to ask you again, Terry,' the suit said, looking up and giving the guard a signal, 'to give you another chance.'

Terry heard the guard's footsteps approach behind him.

The suit said, 'What was the gun for, Terry?'

'How the fuck should I know?'

'What was it doing in the van?'

'Maybe someone forgot it.'

'Why would someone do that?'

'People forget all sorts of things.'

'Were you asked to leave it there?'

Terry shrugged.

'Who was it for, Terry?'

Terry shrugged again.

'Did your client need a gun?'

Terry said nothing, getting the feeling they were just fishing.

The suit said, 'What did he need a gun for, I wonder? To get information out of this guy? To kill him?'

Terry shrugged. 'I wonder.'

'It'd make sense, wouldn't it? Get you and Sean to do all the leg work, take the risks – capture this guy, lock him up, supply the gun. You know what I mean?'

Terry didn't bite.

The suit went on, 'Even makes it look like you might have used the gun. Which is an added bonus, as far as they're concerned. Maybe it was another accident. Like before. He wasn't doing what he was told. You picked up the gun, threatened him, and the next thing you knew… bang… He's dead.'

Terry kept quiet, knowing it was all he could do until he spoke to Mr Hayes and found out what was really going on.

The suit continued, 'Only two people appeared to have handled that gun. One of them is you, and the other is Sean.' The suit paused, perhaps waiting to see his reaction. 'Perhaps you gave the gun to Sean to use. How about that?'

Terry wondered whether he was bluffing, pretty sure Sean didn't know anything about the gun – but then he suddenly remembered Sean being a bit off with him in the pub on the way back, and phoning him in a flap the next day. What was all that about? Sean hadn't done anything stupid, had he?

The suit said, 'Maybe it was Sean who had the accident, and you're covering for him.'

Somewhat feebly, Terry said, '*Sean* – you serious?' and for the first time wasn't able to convince himself of the part he was playing.

43

THE BLACK RANGE Rover kicked up a cloud of dust as it headed up the track away from the farmhouse.

Mark followed it through his binoculars. He was on his way home when he'd seen the Range Rover pull into Hillards Farm. Coming out of Sudley wood, he stopped the quad in a gateway for a closer look. It was early afternoon.

Scanning through the binoculars, he could see men dotted around the farmyard, like they were guarding the place, and a small group of people standing in front of the house.

Lowering the binoculars, Mark wondered what the hell was going on down there. He thought about phoning Simon or the estate office. But just then, he spotted a metallic glint up on the ridgeway. At first he thought it was something in the sky, a small aircraft, or hang glider.

He looked through the binoculars again, tracking along the fence to the corner of Sudley Wood, where tall beech trees stood against the horizon. There he saw a small car, like a Vauxhall Corsa, parked up in a clearing. He wasn't aware of there being a sight-seeing spot there. Then he saw a man appear from between the trees. The man stopped and looked back across the valley.

Mark played with the focus of his binoculars. The man just stood there, not moving. Then Mark heard the sound of the Range Rover getting closer. Lowering the binoculars, he turned round. The Range Rover had turned off the track and was cutting across the field in front of him, heading in his direction. He could see the guy in the passenger seat, his arm resting on the window ledge, was holding a walkie-talkie.

What the fuck?

Mark got out his mobile to let Simon know something was going on when – *boom!* A blast erupted from the farmhouse, blowing a hole through the roof.

Mark dived to the ground. The sound of the blast echoed through the valley. Dust pillared above the farmhouse. He heard the sound of debris – bits of brick, splintered wood and roof tiles – rain down over the rooftops of outbuildings. Looking up, he saw the people around the house lying on the ground, with their hands over their heads, covered in dust. Armed figures swarmed the building from all directions.

Mark stood up. He noticed the Range Rover had turned back. The people around the house were standing up, assisted by the armed men, who formed a circle around them, as if to shield them from any more danger. Mark froze for a moment, seeing everything as if in slow-motion. Smoke and dust hung above the house. There wasn't much left of the roof. He could see the exposed timber beams. A fire had caught inside the building. He saw the men in the farmyard getting into the vehicles.

Mark got back on his bike, thinking he should go down and check everyone was all right. As he started down the slope, he saw the car on the ridgeway pull away and he wondered if it was because the man had seen what he had and was coming down to help as well. Mark told the police later, 'I don't know how he couldn't have seen it.' But he never saw the man or his car again.

When Mark arrived at the cottage, most of the men had gone. He was just in time to see two men helping a grey-bearded man with a bleeding head into the side of a van. One of the men helping him appeared to be carrying the guy's cap, also covered in blood. They all got in, closed the van doors from the inside, and pulled away.

They drove past Mark as he came into the courtyard. There was just one car left and two men standing there. One of the men, the more smartly dressed of the two, wore chinos and V-neck pullover, while the other wore a baseball cap and jeans. The more smartly dressed man, who seemed to be the one in charge, came over and introduced himself, and said he was a surveyor, and that there'd been an accident but everything was okay; no one was seriously hurt. He apologised for causing him any alarm, reassuring him that everything was under control now. The man appeared not in the slightest bit panicked or worried by what had happened, which just wasn't normal. Mark asked the man more than once, 'Are you sure you don't want me to ring anyone?' but the man insisted, saying, 'No, no. It's all taken care of.'

The police and fire brigade arrived a little while later, and the surveyor guy spoke to them as well, giving them the same sort of assurances as he had to Mark earlier. The police took Mark's contact details and said they would be in touch. Then the smart guy, along with his companion, who hadn't said a word all this time, got in their car and drove off. It was all very odd. A surveyor, my arse, thought Mark.

But what could he do?

The police visited him at home a few days later, as did a reporter from the local newspaper, and he told them everything he'd seen, about the figures around the farmhouse, about the man he'd seen on the ridgeway, giving them details about his car, a Vauxhall Corsa, he'd thought. Then he'd told them about the explosion, about the possibility that the men he'd seen there were armed, and about the injured man he saw being whisked off in the van. The police wrote everything down but he never heard any more. The story went out that there had been a gas explosion. No mention of any injuries or calls for missing witnesses. There was no further investigation.

Mark even went up to the spot where he'd seen the man standing next to the parked car. Just to have a look. See what he could see. He stood in the exact spot where he reckoned the man had been. You could see the farmhouse clearly; there was no way he could have missed the explosion. Mark also noted that the man probably wouldn't have been able to see the spot where he'd been on his bike because of the undulations of the ground. He spent several minutes looking at the house with its blown-out roof and remembering the day of the explosion and wondering why the man hadn't come down to see if everyone was okay.

He asked both the police and the newspaper about it, trying to find out if anyone else had come forward to give statements. While the police couldn't comment on the matter, the guy from the local newspaper had hinted Mark was the only witness. He thought about posting something on Facebook, or running an advert in the paper, in an attempt to get in touch with the man in the Vauxhall Corsa, but decided not to in the end. Some people, he guessed, just chose not to get involved. You heard about it – passers-by who never stopped to help people in need lying on the pavement. It was probably more common than you realised. Or maybe this guy had his own problems. You never knew what was going on in someone else's head on any particular day. Maybe the man had gone up to the ridgeway to kill himself when the blast had interrupted him. Who knew?

For a while after the explosion, Mark often drove past the farm. On one occasion he drove into the courtyard, got off his bike and looked about inside the charred building. This was before they boarded up the door and windows again. It still smelt of fire. There was nothing much to see, apart from some burnt furniture, blackened bulbs and melted worktops. Nothing personal, nothing that seemed to belong to anyone, apart from a picture hanging on a downstairs wall, which he took down and had a look at. The glass was a little blackened, but you could make out the scene clearly enough: of some geese flying over a river.

The farm was eventually sold and the house completely gutted and rebuilt. The outbuildings were restored into immaculate-looking stable-blocks. They ripped down the corrugated barn and removed the silage press. The cracked concrete was transformed with pebbles and barrel planters. The driveway was tarmacked and lined with post and rail fencing and landscaped verges. Barely recognisable.

The new owners have just moved in, Simon reported to him by text one day. Mark had already moved to his new job by then; Clare was pregnant for a second time. *And guess what*, Simon told him in the text, *they have a chocolate lab*. That part made Mark smile.

When Mark got the message, he was sitting in his new

work vehicle, a 4x4 Hilux, a step up from a quad bike, and looking across a different valley. It felt like a while ago now all that business, but the text brought it all back – from his suspicions of criminals moving in, to the explosion, and the man on the ridgeway who'd never come to help. He remembered how afterwards life hadn't quite been the same for him again at Sudley. Nothing to do with work – in fact, he hadn't mentioned it to anyone, not even Clare – but after the explosion, he'd felt like he was always having to look over his shoulder. Something that day had spooked him – he just couldn't put his finger on it. So when another job came up, he didn't hesitate to take it.

44

'TELL ME ABOUT your father,' the therapist said.

'My father? Not much to tell, really,' Hayes said, scratching the mark on his forehead where he'd been hit by debris in the explosion. He'd been treated in a private clinic, courtesy of the government, but was home after a couple of days and told by the doctors to rest up. Hayes had taken them at their word. He'd been 'resting' for several months now and there was still no end in sight. 'I'm having a gap year,' he'd joked to his children. Taking his GP's advice, he'd started seeing a therapist, Dr Bryant, a few weeks ago.

'Well, then, how would you define your relationship?' Dr Bryant said.

'Our relationship?'

'Yes.'

Hayes dreaded such questions, but realised he was in the wrong place to avoid them.

Dr Bryant said, 'You said he died when you were still at school.'

'Yeah. Heart attack.' In his mind's eye, Hayes saw his father sitting in his armchair at home, the spilt cup of tea down his shirt, his arms twitching over the arm rests. 'It was just after the six o'clock news.' Hayes smiled.

Dr Bryant smiled back but in a different way to Hayes. 'It must have been a big shock,' he said.

'Yeah. But what can you do?'

'Did you get a chance to say goodbye?'

Hayes shrugged. He hadn't thought of it like that before. Was it as simple as that? He'd just needed to say goodbye and he would feel differently about everything now?

Dr Bryant said, 'It's always hard when someone close to you dies suddenly.'

'Yeah, well,' Hayes said. If he was being honest he wouldn't say his father and him had been that close. They hadn't talked much. 'As I said, that was that. What can you do?'

The doctor, seeming to ignore his attempt to bring the conversation to a conclusion, said, 'How does it make you feel now?'

'Don't know really. Old, I guess. I'm older now than he was when he died... just.' He'd finally had his fifty-third birthday.

'Does that bother you?'

Hayes considered this and guessed it did a bit. 'It made me think, I suppose.'

'What about?'

Hayes felt embarrassed to say the word 'death', and said instead, 'About getting old, I guess. I'm in uncharted territory.' He smiled again, trying to lighten the mood.

The doctor wasn't having any of it, obviously thinking he was onto something here. 'Did your father ever talk about getting old?'

Hayes chuckled at the thought of having such an intimate

conversation with his dad, but Dr Bryant looked back at him blankly, so he said, 'No. We didn't speak much. If that's what you mean. Don't get me wrong. Dad worked hard. Did his best.'

Dr Bryant said, 'It can't have been easy, growing up without him. You must have missed him.'

'Maybe. I think it was harder on Mum. There was less money. But, when you're a kid, you just get on with things, don't you?'

'I suppose. What about now?'

'What about it?

'Do you miss him now?'

Hayes hesitated. 'How do you mean?'

'It's a simple question, Graham. Do you think about your father sometimes?'

Hayes recalled imagining having a conversation with his father only the other night, in fact. It was late and he couldn't sleep and he'd imagined his father had walked into his bedroom. He hadn't actually seen him, just sort of felt his presence. It happened sometimes. They didn't speak about anything in particular, just routine stuff, telling him about how the kids were doing. But he remembered how good it felt to be speaking to his father like this and what a shame it was he wasn't still alive. But then he realised he'd never really spoken to his father like that when he was alive, so what difference would it make.

Dr Bryant said, 'What are you thinking Graham?'

'Nothing. Just when someone dies – what can you do?'

Dr Bryant raised his eyebrows. 'About what?'

'About – well – them not being here anymore.'

'Your dad, you mean?'

'Yeah – or anyone.'

'Do you wish he was here sometimes?'

Hayes shrugged. 'Maybe.'

'You don't seem so sure.'

He smiled. 'I'm fifty-three. It's a bit late now, don't you think?'

The doctor said, 'If you don't feel like talking about this now we can change the subject.'

Hayes looked at the doctor, wondering what sort of life he'd had, whether he was married, divorced, had kids or not. What his relationship was like with his own father. Hayes wanted to give him more information but didn't know what else to say. He said, 'My father was who he was. He did his best. None of us are perfect. No doubt my kids will say the same about me one day.' He chuckled, trying to make light of it again.

The doctor said, 'Have you spoken to your children about how you feel?'

Hayes smiled at the thought – was he taking the piss? Had he met Jamie? 'How do you mean?' he said.

'Do they know you're here for example?'

'No,' he replied, still smiling, 'why would they?'

'What about your wife, Pam?'

Hayes said, 'You're joking, right?'

The doctor looked at him carefully. 'You should speak to them. Tell them what's going on.'

Hayes remembered his ex-wife was always getting at him for not communicating. His usual retort to her had been, 'I don't want to bore you with the details.' Then Terry and him had disposed of that body in the Thames and he'd felt even less like speaking after that. It had become a habit with him, he guessed, ever since, keeping things close to his chest. What could he say? What was there *left* to say?

The session came to a close and Hayes thanked the doctor for his time, shaking his hand, but knowing he probably wouldn't come back. Therapy wasn't for everyone, he guessed.

When he got outside, he walked through the car park at the back of Dr Bryant's house, looking up at the trees swaying in the breeze. There was a small stream just the other side of the trees. He stood on the bank for a moment and looked along the stream's length. All the way up, insects danced over its glassy surface in patches of sunlight. He squatted down and dipped his hand into the water. It felt cool. Lifting his hand again, Hayes remained where he was for a while, feeling the water drying on his skin.

When he got home, he went to bed and slept for the rest of the afternoon. He couldn't think why he was so tired. In the evening, he sat outside on the patio with a glass of white wine, thinking about the lawn and when he was next going to cut it, and listening to Pam talking to Adam. Later, after Pam had gone to bed, he sat in the kitchen and watched TV, without really paying much attention to what was on. It was late when he went to bed.

He woke up around five and made a coffee and just sat in the kitchen, without putting the TV on. Later that day, without thinking about it, he picked up the phone and rang his two children – Chloe first – telling her he was sorry.

'For what?' she said.

'For everything that happened between me and your mum.'

'Dad! We're over that now, aren't we?' she said, half-joking and expecting him to be as well.

But he wasn't. Not this time. 'Yeah, well… And for not being around much when you were little.'

There was a pause. 'Dad, what's wrong?'

'Nothing. I just wanted to say it... I don't think I've said it before…' He knew he hadn't.

'Dad, what's going on?' Chloe sounded really concerned now.

'I'm sorry, that's all. You're a wonderful daughter.'

'Ah, Dad! That's so sweet.' She paused. 'Are you sure everything's all right?'

'Yeah, everything's fine. I promise.'

A moment later, he had Jamie on the line. Something about fathers and sons was always going to make this call the harder of the two.

Jamie answered with his customary, 'What is it, Dad?' like he had a hundred other things he'd rather be doing than speaking to him.

Hayes asked him, 'Why do you always answer the phone like that?'

'Because… ' he said.

'Because what?'

'Well, because you usually only ring when something's wrong.'

'Well, nothing's wrong, all right? I just rang because I'm your dad, okay? Don't be so rude.'

There was silence the other end. Hayes said, 'Jamie, are you still there?'

'Yeah, what is it?'

'I wanted to say I'm sorry.'

'*What?*'

'For letting you down.'

Jamie said, 'Is this about the curry again? I told you – forget it.'

Hayes had apologised several times for missing their curry after the explosion at the farm, although he knew Jamie had come to expect it from him, it not being the first time he'd let him down in his life.

'No, it's not about the curry. It's about being… ' Hayes hesitated, not sure where to go next, and then continued, 'well… not being there for you all the time… as a dad, I mean… in the past.'

'Dad, are you pissed?'

'No, not yet. And … it's about what happened between me and your mum.'

There was silence.

Hayes said, 'Jamie?'

'Yeah, what?'

'I'm sorry.'

'Dad, it's fine, really.'

'Yeah, well, I just wanted to tell you. You're doing well. I'm proud of you.'

When Hayes hung up, he imagined Jamie and Chloe texting each other, wondering if he was all right, Jamie saying, *'Chlo, I think Dad's lost it.'* They'd probably put it down to the injury on his head. He half-contemplated ringing their mother just to tell her he'd spoken to them and that everything was fine if they happened to call sounding concerned. Maybe, at the same time, it would be a good opportunity to say something to his ex-wife. But before he got a chance he heard Pam's voice in the kitchen and realised she was the one he really needed to speak to next.

His chance came later that evening. Pam had just gone upstairs to put Adam to bed. Hayes was sitting outside on the patio finishing his glass of wine. It was still warm, late spring, the smell of cut grass. He was admiring the garden – the one interest he had left, since his accident, which went well beyond just cutting the grass now. He'd got into gardening in a big way. He'd started watching that Monty guy on TV. He'd dug several borders, a kitchen garden, rose beds.

When Pam joined him and began telling him about Adam and how he'd been hard to settle tonight, Hayes interrupted her. 'Pam,' he said, deciding to come straight to the point. 'I'm not who you think I am.' He looked at her across the table, her dark eyes glistening in the half-light. 'I've done some bad things in my life.' He was trying to keep things as simple as he could, not wanting to have a communication problem at a moment like this.

Pam lowered her eyes.

Hayes said, 'My work. It's not quite what you think. I…' He stopped himself, wishing he'd thought more about how he was going to say this before he started. 'People have…'

Pam looked up. 'No. Please.'

'Pam, this is important.'

Pam said, 'I don't need to know.'

'But I want to tell you.'

'Why? You don't know everything about me, do you?'

Hayes looked at her in surprise, wondering what it was he didn't know about her. 'What do you mean?' he said.

'You see,' she replied. 'Sometimes it's best like that.'

'What is?'

'Not to know everything.'

'This is different.'

'Why is it different? You don't know.'

Hayes looked at Pam. He hadn't heard her speak like this before.

She said, 'I know you don't work in an office. That you're out late sometimes. But I don't need to know everything.'

'Someone died because of me,' Hayes said.

Pam froze to the spot and Hayes saw her blinking tears onto her cheeks.

Hayes said, 'It was a long time ago now. And he wasn't a good person. But still he died because of me.' He looked into his glass, then said, 'I either get people locked up, or killed, Pam. I do the dirty work that governments don't want to do. And I'm tired of it. Tired – you know.' He looked up and saw Pam wipe her cheek with the back of her hand. He thought she looked beautiful, and said, 'I'm sorry.' He reached out to touch her shoulder.

Pam pushed his arm away. 'You think I don't worry about you?' she said, looking up; there was fire in her eyes now. 'You think I don't know something's wrong? With you not sleeping, not working anymore, and going to doctors. You don't think I don't see all this?'

Hayes stared at Pam, completely astonished by her reaction. This wasn't what he was expecting. He'd never seen her like this.

Pam said, 'You can be so selfish.'

'Someone died, Pam.'

'But they were bad,' she said. 'And you were doing your job. You don't think bad things happen to us all?'

'But not this.'

'How do you know?'

Hayes doubted she could have experienced what he had.

She said, 'I know what it's like to be poor. To have no home. I've seen people die. Killed for no reason. Fighting about stupid things. And had bad men come to me. Do bad things. You don't think other people suffer as well?'

He watched Pam wipe her eyes with her hands. 'I'm sorry,' he said, reaching over and touching his wife's arm. 'I didn't know. You should have said something.'

'No. Why?' She pushed him away again. 'You don't need to know. To not always say is best sometimes,' she said, her English breaking down now.

Hayes lowered his head, feeling ashamed of himself for making Pam say these things. He looked into his glass again, then took a drink.

Pam said, 'I see you're a good man. Who loves his family. And we're happy, aren't we?'

'Yes,' he said, looking up. 'We're happy.' They held hands and smiled at each other and Hayes knew that it was true, and that this was enough for any man.

The months passed and Hayes's gap year continued. Then in the summer, Chloe and Jamie came down and quizzed him about the future, telling him, 'You can't just do nothing, Dad.' Smiling at his two children, his reply was, 'Why not?' Hayes realised for the first time in his life he had no immediate plans beyond the garden and life with Pam, and nor did he care. The things he feared most, not working, actually turned out to be fine. He had money to see they were all right for a while. If he'd finally lost it, as his children probably thought he had, the idea only made him smile.

He spent more and more time in the garden, cultivating borders, buying plants and specimen trees to create an arboretum. Three months ago he didn't even know what the word 'arboretum' meant, and now look at him, he thought. Before the summer was up, Hayes bought a rundown garden centre that had come up for sale in the area, despite nearly everyone, apart from Pam, advising him against making the purchase.

Within a month, he'd totally transformed the place, and was turning over a small profit. Terry and Sean came to work for him, though Sean left after a few weeks to set up his own restaurant. Hayes helped him with some of the finance on the condition he paid him back when he was up and running. And the kid did just that, making a real go of it. Now, every time Hayes went past his restaurant, the place was packed. Last thing he heard his girlfriend was pregnant and they were planning a wedding. Terry stayed on, though, and was in charge of the tree and large shrub section. They were also developing a four acre plot at the back where they were going to set up a small tree nursery.

Terry had taken to the new work well, becoming very knowledgeable about horticulture. They often walked around the garden centre together after closing, talking about nothing but plants. Terry was Terry. Loyal to a tee. Hayes wouldn't pretend he knew him well, his personal history and all that, but as Pam said, sometimes it was best not to know everything. They never talked about what they used to do, although sometimes they exchanged a passing glance – a look between them that seemed to say that while they shared a past, that past was no longer who they were now. Hayes thought of Terry as a friend these days.

45

IN THE PICTURE, streaky clouds tinged yellow and pink ran from the top corner of the frame and appeared to travel inwards, giving the picture a sense of depth. It was dusk in the image. There was a faint, inky blue-black horizon broken by two bare-limbed trees. Running through the centre of the picture was the wide bend of a river. It appeared to flow in the same direction as the clouds, travelling inward, away from the viewer, and it reflected the sky and all its colours. Above the river, again moving in the same direction, were about forty geese, curling in flight as they set up to land on the water.

The picture was on a large postcard. It had arrived a few days ago in an envelope. It was propped up against a window ledge above a small wooden desk.

When the man sitting at the desk looked at the picture he could remember the farmhouse and the events that had taken place them, except the scenes he recalled felt to have happened to someone else, that it was as if he was remembering someone else's memories.

There has been a change of plan.

He saw the balaclava-clad figure standing in the doorway, pointing a gun at him.

I thought you just wanted to speak to me.

He saw the figure shoot him in the chest and blood glug from the hole, and then the figure removed their balaclava.

The man standing there was him.

Both men looked at each other, one man thinking, *You shot me*, yet somehow watching himself on the floor, the man's eyes beginning to flicker, his chest rising and falling, blood soaking through his shirt and pooling on the floor.

Then he heard a voice beside him say, 'It's time to go,' and turning round saw Dvorak standing there, holding what looked like a small Ruger pistol. There was no longer a dead body of himself lying on the floor. It had been a hallucination, he realised, just as the shooting had been.

He followed Dvorak out of the room and down the stairs. Together, they wired some explosives to a mobile phone and strapped them under a chair. Then Dvorak led him out of the house, gave him a car key and pointed him up the slope through a wood. He hurried off, thinking Dvorak was behind him. But when he stopped and looked back he couldn't see Dvorak anywhere. For a second, it was like he'd imagined Dvorak as well.

He came to the top of the slope and walked along the track to where a Vauxhall Corsa was parked. In the valley below, he saw the guy on his quad bike drive across the fields towards the farmhouse, then stop. He saw what he thought must be government security officers arrive and watched the scene play out.

Was he dead now? Had he been dead all along? But then how had he escaped? And who was he now? Was he still Lawrence?

The man looked up from the picture with no answers

to these questions. In front of him was a window with its shutters pegged back. There was a view of mountains. The lower slopes were covered with conifers and the conifers were covered with snow. The first snow had come last week, early for the time of year. The man didn't yet know why he was there.

He remembered the sound of the explosion, getting into the Vauxhall Corsa and driving to London where he abandoned the car and spent a night on the streets before someone dropped a package at his feet as he dozed on a park bench. Soon afterwards, he found himself in Gatwick Airport making a pickup from a luggage locker where he received all the necessary documents and information to set up under a new alias. Then it was just a case of boarding a flight and memorising all the details.

He saw a buzzard turning above the trees half-way up the mountains. Dark clouds swelled in the distance. There was more snow on the way. He knew it would start with a scattering of flakes but within a short time become so heavy it would quickly fill his footprints when he set off up the mountains later that day.

He turned away from the window and looked round the rest of the chalet. There wasn't much in it – a fridge, a hotplate, a sink – the basics. A wood burner sat against one wall, which he lit every day.

In the room next door, he had a mattress on the floor, where he slept. He slept there alone but some nights dreamt Lucy was with him. Sometimes Amanda. Sometimes he dreamt about women whose names he couldn't remember. Maybe they were all the same in the end.

He'd been here over six months. But measurements of

time felt almost meaningless now. Sometimes it felt like it had been just a few weeks. While at other times it felt like he'd been here all along. He knew there were parts of his life he couldn't remember and parts he remembered in a different order from one day to the next.

There was a gun in the desk drawer. A SIG Sauer, compact model. There was also a sound moderator and box of 9mm ammunition. He was familiar with the gun. He didn't know why, but accepted he was. Occasionally he got the gun out, removed the magazine, the slide, the spring and inspected the chamber before putting it back together again.

The fridge he kept well-stocked with food. He cooked meals for himself that he ate alone. He lit the wood burner, emptied its ash and carried logs in from the stack under the building's eaves.

During the day, he worked on the chalet, which was part of his cover-story. A British expat, he'd supposedly grown disillusioned with the rat race back in London, left his job there and come here looking for a better quality of life. He was completing an extension on the rear of the property, which would provide him with a holiday-let, giving him the income and freedom to indulge in his passion for winter sports. Before the snow had arrived he'd been working on the roof. He'd finished it just in time and had moved on to the inside, bringing his work bench and power tools with him. He'd partitioned the area off with a sheet of tarpaulin to save the whole chalet from getting covered in dust.

The only time he really went out was to go to the supermarket in town, which was about a five-minute drive. He had the use of an old Toyota Hilux, which was parked outside the front of the chalet. If he needed to pick up building supplies, there was a timber yard and hardware shop nearby, but these trips were relatively infrequent.

His chalet was on the outskirts of a small Alpine village, which was situated at the head of a narrow valley. There were cattle on the lower slopes in summer, with a patchwork of fields, wooden outbuildings, farmsteads, and swathes of conifers. Depending on the time of day, angular shadows crept across the village from the snow-capped mountains. The village was 985 metres above sea level, with a population of just over two thousand. He was often surprised by what he knew.

He found he wasn't curious to go further afield. He presumed there were other villages and towns nearby and, if you kept going, no doubt cities and airports with flights to anywhere in the world.

He had everything he needed where he was, so didn't feel the urge to go any further. Apart from his shopping trips, when he interacted with shop assistants, he spoke to no one but himself. He did, though, feel he missed something or someone, and this feeling had been with him a long time. But at the same time he knew he wouldn't be able to compensate for this feeling by speaking to people. It was just something he knew he had to live with. Above all – and he wasn't sure exactly how he knew – he recognised the importance of keeping himself to himself.

And so the time passed.

Being that his knowledge about himself, his recollections and memories, were sketchy at best, he assumed no one else would know of his whereabouts or even his existence. If he wasn't sure himself, how could anyone else be?

He doubted anyone was looking for him, though. Only

now when he looked at the picture of the geese did he remember the men at the farmhouse. But were they really his memories? he wondered. Maybe it was just what the artist wanted him to remember. Maybe it was the artist's memories he was remembering. Who knew?

Some mornings, he woke up and it was as if nothing had ever happened to him. Getting up, he'd look at his surroundings with completely fresh eyes. While other mornings, he'd wake up and experience a series of memory flashes. Some of the memories he'd recognise, others he wouldn't.

He lived, it seemed, through periods of amnesia.

Sometimes he wondered if some of his memories, when he had them, weren't actually memories at all, but events that hadn't happened to him yet – premonitions of possible futures.

He tried not to think too much, in general. And mostly he was successful in this. He kept an empty mind. Work helped. There were occasional spikes of mental activity, and these could be quite distressing at times, and would wake him up at night and have him pacing around the room, but they were far from the norm.

Turning back round to the window again, he noticed how gloomy it had become outside. He tipped his head and looked through the glass. His view of the mountains was obscured by the falling snow. He looked at the picture of the geese again and remembered how the geese had got their name 'greylags' – being grey and lagging behind other geese when it came to migrating. Again, how he knew this he didn't know. But it made him think it would soon be time to go.

He picked up the card and turned it over now. Written

on the back were today's date and a telephone number. He'd known what it meant the day it had arrived and gone into town and purchased a phone. He took the phone out now, put in the SIM card and turned it on. Then, keying in the number, he put the phone to his ear. It rang twice, then a computer-generated message clicked in, telling him to leave a message. He read out a number he had memorised and hung up.

He sat there for about fifteen minutes before the phone buzzed with a message, giving him a time and location. Taking out a map, he checked the location. Then he removed the gun from the desk drawer along with the moderator and a box of ammunition. He filled the magazine and clipped it in place. He checked the time on his wristwatch and stood up.

He walked over to the door and took down a small rucksack hanging from the hook on the back. He slipped the gun, moderator and spare ammunition inside the rucksack. Then he put on a coat, a hat and laced up his hiking boots.

He looked round the chalet to check he hadn't left anything and opened the door. He felt the cold air on his face. He closed the door behind him and put on some gloves. Then shouldering the rucksack, he walked away from the chalet.

Reaching the conifers he looked back and saw how the snow had filled his footprints. He could no longer see his chalet or even the village. And for a moment, it felt like there'd never been a chalet or a village, but that he'd been here standing here in the snow all along.

Checking his wristwatch, he set off up the slope through the maze of conifers, crunching through the thick powdery snow.

After a while, he came to a clearing, the ground levelling off, where ski tracks marked the snow. Checking to make sure no one was coming, he jogged across the open ground, falling snow battering him in the face.

When he came to the trees the other side, he squatted down to catch his breath. Below him, he could see a road in the distance about five hundred metres away. He watched the road for a moment, then continued down the slope.

Coming to an animal shelter, he stopped and stood under its eaves. Removing the gun from the rucksack, he screwed the sound moderator in place. The snow fell silently around him. He knew that he was here for a reason and that in time he would know what it was.

46

AFTER ABOUT AN hour, the man heard the sound of an approaching car. It was still a long way off, traversing through the hairpins round the mountain, and it took a while to arrive. When it did, it pulled up into a lay-by just below him, the car's engine left running and exhaust fumes curling through the lower limbs of conifers. He noticed the car had snow chains on its tyres and ski racks on the roof.

He waited for a moment before stepping out from behind the animal shelter and walking down the slope. The snow was deep and he lost his footing a couple of times and slipped over on to his side.

When he stepped out onto the road clumps of snow were stuck to his trouser legs. He looked around himself, brushing the snow off with a gloved hand and walked over to the car. Stopping beside it, he looked back and noticed the snow he'd shed lying on the gritted tarmac. It would soon be gone, he thought, and he opened the passenger door of the car and got in.

The car was warm inside. The woman driving turned and looked at him as she shifted into first gear and they pulled away. She looked to be in her late-thirties, around his age;

she had short, spiky blonde hair with brown highlights in.

It took him a second to match up her face with the young woman on horseback in his memories, but when he did he smiled.

She smiled too when she saw the recognition in his eyes. 'How have you been, Lawrence?' she said, lifting a hand off the steering wheel and running it through her hair. 'I'm sorry it took so long.' As she spoke, she started to look more and more like the woman in his memories, and for a second, he pictured them lying on their backs in the churchyard, looking at the stars.

He said, 'I thought we were meant to be dead.'

Handing him a file, she smiled. 'Welcome back.'

He opened the file and began reading. The Greylag programme. The training regimes. The remote locations. The prescribed drugs. The hypnosis. Things he had always known about himself but kept buried all these years. It was an unsettling reminder. He came to a photo of Dvorak, their programme handler, smiling, younger-looking and experienced a flashback to the farmhouse, seeing himself lying on the bedroom floor covered in blood. He looked up from the file and turned to the window, observing jutting overhangs of black rock and snaking crash barriers.

Lucy said, 'The Greylag programme was shut down for good. We were all put to sleep in our different ways. We became their little secret. The sleeper agents put out to grass. And it was meant to stay that way.'

'What does he want?' Lawrence asked.

Lucy kept looking straight ahead. 'He wants to reactivate the programme.'

'Yeah?'

'He has a thing about selling secrets. And there are plenty of those.'

'Who's in control of it all?'

'We don't know. Access to the programme was limited. It was completely sectioned off, compartmentalised. No one knew more than they needed to. Dvorak was in charge of us, and that was it.'

'Someone must have headed the programme.'

'Yeah.' She lifted her eyes to check her rear-view mirror. 'He was known as Greylag.'

'Who's that?'

'We don't know. It's possible they don't even exist. Or they're a computer and algorithms are behind us all.' She changed down a gear as the car headed into a hairpin bend. 'Dvorak is hoping if he pulls enough of us out of retirement he'd be able to unlock the programme's code, so he can access the database where all the programme's information is stored?'

'What sort of information are we talking about here?'

'Whatever you care to imagine,' Lucy said, giving him a glance. 'These are secrets hidden away from all but a handful of individuals at the highest level of the intelligence community. The kind of stuff heads of governments don't get to hear about – let alone their citizens. Operations carried out by programmes like ours. Worth millions to the right buyer.'

'So, what's the code?'

Lucy smiled. 'All we know is that when the programme was set up agents were trained to memorise a series of numbers. We have no idea what they all mean. But each number, when employed, seems to trigger a response from the programme's network. Dvorak is hoping with all this activity he's going to be able to create a hack somehow.'

'How many of us are there?'

'We don't know. It makes you wonder, though.'

Lawrence understood the panic this must be causing the security services, with all that covertly-sourced information out there somewhere, not to be mention reactivated agents.

'How did you find me?' he said.

Lucy turned to him and smiled. 'You forget how good I am at this.'

'The phone call at the farmhouse?'

'That was the start of it. It must have triggered the system somehow, pulling you out of trouble and putting you into hibernation. You gave the number to someone there, didn't you?'

'Yeah, one of the guys in the house.'

'You thought he could help?'

'I suppose. Is he involved in this somehow?'

'We don't think so. It was an agency officer who rang the number in the end.'

Lawrence looked at the file again. He came to some photos of his wife and kids, taken on the day of his daughter's birthday and felt a rush of emotion.

Lucy said, 'We weren't meant to wake up again. We had our lives… Well, some of us did…' She glanced at him and smiled. 'I'm sorry. You always had the most to lose. But you can't go back. Not yet. It won't take Dvorak long to work out what's happened. He's been experimenting, seeing what would unfold all this time. He knew bringing you out of retirement would set off a chain of events. You've got to remember the programme has been shut down for years.

He had no idea if it all still worked.'

'How did the agency find out? They were there, weren't they?'

'As they normally do – they got a tip-off. Maybe from Dvorak – who knows? Dvorak wouldn't have known whether you'd rung yourself in or not. So, he wasn't taking any chances.'

'The explosion?'

'A distraction, a decoy. Maybe your number triggered it. Or Dvorak detonated it remotely. Either way, Dvorak got what he wanted and brought us all together.'

'He wanted to see who'd turn up?'

'Something like that.'

'But he let me go—'

Lucy smiled, and Lawrence realised he was looking at the reason why.

He said, 'He hasn't found you yet, has he?'

'Normal life didn't work out for me in quite the same way as it did for you.'

He knew that meant she was still working in the shadows, leading a life of dead doubles, as a lone contractor or agency insider now. He knew better than to ask for details.

She said, 'This fire needs putting out, Lawrence. Dvorak is dangerous. There is a whole lot of classified information out there. And no one knows where it is. Neither Dvorak nor the government agencies.'

'What about this Greylag figure?'

She smiled. 'There's a needle in a haystack you're never going to find.'

He smiled at the metaphor. It seemed strangely quaint given the circumstances.

'You know how this works,' she said, keeping her eyes on the road ahead.

Turning to the last page of the file, he saw a shadowy photo of Dvorak, older-looking, passing through a doorway of some building. Yeah – he knew how this worked.

'He'll find you,' Lucy said. 'You know that, don't you?'

Lawrence looked over his shoulder. There was a car behind them now.

Lucy glanced up to her rearview, and said, 'We're the agency's little secret. Who else were they going to ask to do their dirty work for them? They want this closed down for good.'

They crossed over a metal bridge; a steep-sided ravine plunged below them where a river crashed over grey rocks.

On the other side of the bridge, Lucy put on the indicator and pulled into a lay-by. The car that had been following them also slowed, pulling into the space in front.

Lucy held onto the steering wheel for a moment, and said. 'Well … I can't believe how the time flies… Look at us.' She glanced at him and smiled. 'Just do what he says. And leave the rest to me.' Then she leant over and kissed him on the cheek. 'Good luck.' She got out of the car, closed the door and walked over to the vehicle in front and got in.

Lawrence watched the car drive off, then looked down at the file again and the photos of Amanda and his children and of Dvorak and the farmhouse. He glanced over the information about Dvorak, his journey from government intelligence officer to rogue freelancer, the state-sponsored assassinations, the intelligence leaks and arms dealing. He needed no more than a few seconds to digest the information. It was what he did.

The engine was still running, the windscreen wipers clearing the falling snow. He could hear the sound of the river hitting the rocks below the bridge. He opened the door and got out. Putting his hand in his pocket, he took out the lighter he'd used for lighting fires at the chalet and set light to the folder. He dropped it on the ground and watched it burn on the snow, turning the papers over with his foot so it all burnt properly. Then he looked up and down the road, got back in the car and closed the door.

He sat for a second as he cleared his mind of the images of his wife and children, which he knew he would need to do to get through this, then released the handbrake and drove off.

47

IT WAS STARTING to get dark when Lawrence drove across a narrow stone bridge and came into a village where the houses and farm buildings were clustered together in a narrow valley and the last of the sunlight caught the upper slopes of the mountains, turning the snow a deep orange colour.

He drove past a line of shops; then, looking up to his rear-view mirror, he pulled into the side of the road, stopped the car and sat there for a moment. He left his hands on the steering wheel as he looked around at what was there: a cable car station, a scattering of shops, restaurants and hotels.

He looked up at his rearview mirror again. A car approached, its lights glimmering in the growing gloom. He watched it go past, then turned his ignition and set off again.

He drove to the end of the village and pulled into the car park of a hotel. An outside light flickered over a side door. He retrieved his rucksack from the passenger seat footwell and got out. Then, walking over to the entrance of the hotel, he went inside.

A woman with blonde hair was on the front desk looking at her phone. Seeing him come in she put it down, said hello and asked if she could help. He asked her for a room for three nights and she checked her computer and found one, saying, 'You're in luck. How would you like to pay?' She had a small tattoo on the inside of her wrist that the cuff of her uniform didn't quite cover.

He paid in cash and gave her a fake passport to photocopy for her records, then walked up three flights of stairs and along a corridor, counting down the numbers to his room near the end. He checked along the corridor, then went inside and shut the door behind him.

Once inside, he looked round the room and in the bathroom, getting a feel of the layout. Then he glanced at his watch and walked over to the window. The town's lights glimmered in the mountain darkness. He saw people getting off a bus back from skiing, carrying their skis on their shoulders.

Walking back across the room, he went into the bathroom and washed his face and looked at himself in the mirror; unshaven, chapped lips. Then he took out the SIG from his pocket, released the magazine, checked it, put it back, returned the gun to his pocket and looked at his watch again.

He left his room and came down the stairs. He could hear the woman at the desk talking to someone on the phone. He slipped past without her seeing him and walked out of the front door and headed into the village where he went into a small supermarket and bought some things to eat – bread and chocolate – and packed them into his rucksack before returning to the hotel.

Coming up the stairs to his room, he took out the SIG and held it inside the flap of his coat as he walked along the corridor.

He came to his door, stood outside for a second, looked

along the corridor in both directions, then went in. Closing the door behind him, he kept the lights off and looked round the room, then took off his coat and lay it down on the bed. He moved a chair next to the window and sat down with the SIG on his lap, looked outside, and waited.

The occasional car came and went. It wasn't exactly busy. He ate some bread and chocolate and sipped from a bottle of water. When he heard other guests returning to their rooms, he'd glanced towards the door.

He felt himself falling asleep in the early hours of the morning. He tried keeping himself awake by focusing on the street light opposite the hotel, but soon felt his eyes closing again. After a while, he got up and went to the bathroom to splash water onto his face. When he came back to the chair he saw a Mitsubishi SUV pull into the car park. Exhaust fumes rose over the rear of the vehicle. Lawrence picked up the SIG and watched the driver's side. A few minutes passed like this. Then the Mitsubishi pulled forward and drove out of the car park and off down the road.

It started getting light not long afterwards. Lawrence watched the sunlight seep into the valley, first catching the tops of the trees, then the steel cables of the gondola lift and rooftops of houses. A bus drove past. A man started clearing snow with a shovel at the front of his house. Putting the SIG in his pocket, Lawrence left his room and went downstairs, walking out the front of the hotel.

He found a café in the village and ordered a coffee and sat at a table by the window. He felt sleepy and his eyes kept closing on him even as he drank the coffee. He was there for about an hour when the waitress came over and asked if there was anything else he wanted. No, there wasn't, and he got up and walked out and off down the street. After a while, he noticed someone walking along beside him. He didn't have to turn round to know who it was. Lucy had said it wouldn't take him long.

'Hello Lawrence. It's good to see you.' It was Dvorak.

Lawrence kept looking straight ahead while trying to pick out faces in the crowd that didn't belong, wondering how many men Dvorak had with him, thinking it was unlikely he was alone. He closed his hand over the SIG in his pocket, playing through different scenarios in his mind. Was he being led into an ambush? Could he create some kind of diversion?

Dvorak said, 'Is this what you imagined?'

'Along these lines,' he said.

Dvorak smiled. 'I think deep down we all know how our lives are going to turn out. We just don't want to spoil the surprise. Only it's not a surprise. The future's with us all the time.' Then he said, 'You know what I want, don't you?'

Lawrence said, 'What you always want.'

'They're afraid we're going to tell the world their grubby secrets. And after all that we've done for them. She's turned on us, you know.'

Lawrence felt his eyes narrow as he gripped the SIG in his pocket.

'But they'll only protect her for so long,' Dvorak continued, 'then she'll become inconvenient to them as well. Like you will in the end.'

'I'll take that risk.'

Dvorak smiled again. 'She's got to you, hasn't she? Just as I was bringing you back to life as well. Oh, my little Greylags – how could you do this to me?'

'I'm not going to kill Lucy for you.'

Dvorak chuckled. 'Saying it like that makes it sound terrible. You know what I'm going to say to that, don't you?'

Lawrence remembered the photo of Amanda and his two children that he'd burnt at the side of the road, the image he'd fought to keep out of his head. He knew Dvorak would know about them and use them against him if needed.

Dvorak smiled, seeing him putting these things together in his head. 'There's only one way out of this, Lawrence – for you and your family.'

'It won't change anything,' Lawrence said.

'I know. The Earth will end as it began, with a bang, regardless of what any of us decides. But still...'

'You're full of shit.'

He smiled. 'Don't make that mistake, Lawrence.'

A car drew up alongside them. Its rear door opened and a man was sitting inside, pointing a gun at him, a man Lawrence thought looked familiar.

Dvorak said, 'You're caught in the middle, I'm afraid, Lawrence. You're here to bring us all together. But you know that already. Remove your hand from your pocket, please.' As he spoke, another man got out from the car and walked round behind Lawrence and waited for him to remove his hand. When he did the man slipped his own hand in Lawrence's coat pocket, removed the SIG and discreetly slipped it inside his own jacket.

Dvorak said, 'Please, get in the car, Lawrence.'

Lawrence got in and sat down next to the guy pointing the gun at him. Lawrence suspected the two men were the ones who'd fitted the camera in the farmhouse. They had that unmistakeable air of professionalism about them. No doubt, Lucy and her pals at the agency would find their faces on a database somewhere.

Dvorak and the other gunman got in the front and they drove away.

They headed up the slope to the hotel. No one said a word. Pulling into the car park, they stopped alongside Lawrence's car. The gunman next to Lawrence then got out and stood beside the car with the door open, waiting.

Dvorak looked out of the window up at the mountains in the other direction, and said, 'You remember the way, don't you?'

Lawrence then saw the gunman outside signal to him to get out of the car, his gun held inside the flap of his coat. Thin flakes of snow blew across the car park.

Lawrence climbed out and stood in front of him.

The gunman then signalled to him to get into his own car.

Lawrence did as he was instructed and, taking out a key fob, unlocked the car. He walked round to the driver's side and got in.

The gunman climbed into the passenger seat beside him and said, 'Let's go,' pointing his gun at him

Lawrence started the engine.

48

JUST AS DVORAK had found him Lawrence knew Lucy would as well. Dvorak was right about one thing: the future was already in motion and couldn't be stopped.

Lawrence led them up into the mountains, Dvorak's car never very far behind in his rear-view mirror. He remembered the way, saw it in his head, as clearly as if the images were being projected onto a screen. The hairpin turns, the valleys, the horizon of mountain peaks… where it all began and where it would all end…

When they reached the lay by where they had waited that summer Lawrence pulled up to the side of the road and stopped. Dvorak's car pulled in behind him.

They sat for a second, engines running, then the gunman next to Lawrence got a message on his earpiece and signalled for him to get out of the car.

Lawrence got out and the gunman did as well. Behind them, the other gunman got out of Dvorak's car and opened the boot and unloaded a stinger, a belt of spikes design to puncture vehicle tyres. The gunman next to Lawrence then signalled to him to cross the road and Lawrence started walking. Reaching the crash barrier the other side, Lawrence stopped and looked back. He saw the gunman push his car off the side of the road. It didn't need much help. It ran into the ditch and tipped up from where you would need a towrope to get it out. The gunman motioned with his gun for Lawrence to turn the other way.

Lawrence did as he was instructed and looked across the valley. Conifers ledged with snow, jutting outcrops, dark ravines and far below the silver strip of a river. He felt the breeze on his face. He heard the sound of the gunmen getting back into Dvorak's car, doors slamming, then reversing up the road. He didn't move. The car engine was turned off. There was just the sound of the breeze and the snow falling through the trees. Then came the sound of a motorbike far off in the distance.

When the first shots came Lawrence dived to the ground as bullets thwacked through trees and puffed into the snow around him. It was difficult to know where the shots were coming from to begin with. He lay very still, the sound of the bike getting closer all the time. Then he heard windscreen glass shattering and bullets clinking on metal. He crawled forward through the snow, then got up to swing himself over the crash barrier, to try and put something between him and the shooters, when he felt a hammer-like blow on his shoulder and his vision blurred. He fell forward, hitting his head on the way down and blacked out.

When he came round the shooting had stopped. He could have been out for a few seconds or several minutes; it was impossible to tell. But he suspected if it had been much longer he would have been dead.

Lying in the snow, he saw Dvorak's car parked at an angle across the road, windows shattered, bullet holes in the doors, one of the gunmen hanging out of an open door, dead, the other one slumped over the steering wheel in the same state. Then he saw Lucy lying in the middle of the road, her bike against the crash barrier on its side, steam rising from its engine, melting the snow around it.

He felt his heart beating hard. He told himself to get up and put out his hand, feeling the sharp metal edge of the crash barrier. He tried pulling himself up, his vision blurring with the effort. He noticed blood dripping off him from somewhere. He couldn't feel anything though, not yet. Then he heard heavy breathing behind him and footsteps on the tarmac. He turned his head and saw Dvorak staggering across the road, holding up his gun but unable to keep his arm steady. He fired twice in quick succession and Lawrence heard the crack of the passing bullets.

Dvorak then collapsed to his knees in the road, taking sharp and rapid breaths now, blood colouring the snow around him. He lifted his arm again and fired another shot, and this time the bullet nicked a tree branch just above Lawrence's head, showering him with snow.

Lawrence tried again to pull himself up, but his hands felt numb as he gripped the crash barrier and he didn't have the strength. Then out of the corner of his eye, he saw Lucy pull herself forward across the tarmac, her outstretched arm trying to reach for her gun. Her crash helmet was scratched up one side where she'd slid against the tarmac.

Dvorak said to him, 'Just like old times, isn't it?' And taking aim at him again, he glanced round, and said, 'Hey, Lucy. You're missing the best bit—' but she was already pointing her gun at him.

The bullet went through his throat, exposing his trachea,

and out the back of his neck. He collapsed onto the tarmac and lay there as steam pulsed out of the ragged hole in his throat and blood pooled round his head and shoulders.

49

LAWRENCE WOKE UP in hospital and felt pain again. He couldn't remember exactly how he'd got down the mountain or much about what had happened. He had memory flashes. A blood-soaked coat lying across his chest. Snow falling through headlights. Shadows of trees. IV bags.

There'd been an accident. It seemed he was the only survivor. A man came to see him called Collins. 'It's good to meet you after all this time,' he said. It was Collins who arranged his passage back to the UK.

Amanda and his children were waiting for him at the airport. Amanda smiled and did her best to look normal in front of the kids, then her eyes filled with tears and she threw her arms round him. The pain in his shoulder was much better than it was. They'd been told he'd suffered a breakdown and taken himself off before being involved in an accident. Collins visited him a couple of times at home and dealt with the police and media and told him not to hesitate to call him if anything was troubling him.

A few days after he got back, Lawrence read online about a car accident in the Alps near to where he'd been found. It was reported that three men had died in the accident when their car had skidded off the road. There were photos of their crashed car at the side of the mountain road. It was reported that the men were on a skiing holiday and two of them were brothers. Their names and ages were given but Lawrence didn't recognise them. There was no mention of anyone else involved.

After a while, Lawrence returned to work and life got back to normal. He and Amanda celebrated their tenth wedding anniversary that year and he took the family on holiday to the South of France where they hired a car and travelled along the coast for two weeks. He didn't recall much about his so-called breakdown, which, according to doctors, wasn't unusual in cases like his. But one evening in France something happened that jogged his memory.

They'd eaten at a restaurant in a harbour and Lawrence had waited behind to settle the bill while Amanda took the kids outside as they were getting restless. As he was leaving, he passed a woman on her way in and stopped, thinking he recognised her. She was about his age and her hair was blonde and cut short. He wanted to say something but just couldn't think where he'd seen her before. Seeing him looking at her, the woman smiled politely before carrying on inside. He thought he must have been mistaken. Then, as he was turning to go, Lawrence remembered her name – her real name that was. And just like that, he pictured a house with children sat round long dining room tables, with their names written on folded paper cards in front of them. The location of the house escaped him for a moment, but he was in no doubt the memory was real and it belonged to him.

Lucy was standing at the bar, ordering a drink, when Lawrence went over and stood beside her. He knew he didn't have long.

'Hello Milly,' he said, the name he'd remembered from all those years ago.

Picking up her drink, Lucy smiled. 'How much do you remember?'

'Not much.' He gave her a glance. 'You?'

'Same. Just the old snapshot here and there. It comes and goes, doesn't it?' She took a sip of her drink and looked at the glass, twisting it by its stem. She looked every bit as beautiful as she had that night in France when they'd laid down together in the churchyard.

'So you came back to check up on me?' he said.

'They said it wouldn't hurt.'

The barman looked at Lawrence, wondering if he wanted something to drink. Lawrence shook his head; then he said to Lucy, 'Did they find him?'

'Who? Greylag? Of course not.'

'Have they given up?'

'They think he'll either be dead or a very old man by now.'

'What do you think?'

She shrugged. 'Let sleeping dogs lie, I suppose.'

Lawrence smiled, reminded of her fondness for metaphors. 'What about his secrets?'

'They'll stay that way, I guess. Like us.' She smiled now, giving him a glance. Then, looking over her shoulder, she said, 'You'd better go.'

Lawrence looked round and saw Amanda and his kids had come to the entrance of the restaurant. Probably his son, William, had wanted to know where he'd got to and had dragged them over. Lawrence lifted his hand to signal he was coming. When he looked round again, Lucy had gone, only her half-drunk glass evidence that she'd been there at all, and picturing the house with long dining room tables one last time before that too faded away, Lawrence set off across the restaurant to rejoin his family.

50

It was on a warm, sunny day in the early part of summer that Sean found himself back at the house where he'd spent much of his childhood. He hadn't planned it like that. Not that he was aware of anyway. But, then, how much of our lives did we really plan? Sean wondered. We weren't able to control the thoughts that came into our head each second, what made us think we were able to plan our lives?

He had his son, Liam, with him. Tash worked at the saloon on Saturdays. It was good to get out the house and have something to do when it was just the two of them like this.

They drove down to the coast, parking up on the outskirts of town and walked along the beach, picking up pebbles. Liam ran down to the water, jumped up and down in the surf, then ran back again. Seagulls glided overhead. The sun shone.

Afterwards, they bought ice-creams and sat on a bench looking out to sea to eat them. Large tankers moved across a hazy horizon. The air was warm.

When they'd finished they headed back across town to where they'd parked the car. It was just after midday and people filed along the seafront. Sean chose backstreets to avoid the town centre. That's when he found himself a street or two away from the house.

Maybe it was having his son with him that had unconsciously led him this way. Did he want to show him where he'd grown up?

Sean stood on the pavement, looking up at a three-storey Victorian town house with large bay windows and a portico entrance covered in wisteria. The house stood in its own grounds at the top of a slope. There was a cedar tree in one corner of the garden and overgrown flowerbeds.

He noticed a 'For Sale' sign strapped to the fence with cable-ties. He pushed open the gate and started up the path towards the house.

'Where are we going, Daddy?'

'I just want to have a walk up here.'

'I want to go back now.'

'It won't take long.'

He could just make out the name of the house on a flaking wooden sign: 'Greylags House'. He wasn't aware of the name before, not that he would have been as a kid.

They came to the end of the path and stopped. Sean recognised the double bay windows of the dining room, picturing the long dining tables that had once been inside.

He said to Liam, 'This is where your dad grew up,' thinking he was probably about the same age as Liam when he first came here.

Liam didn't answer; ice-cream still covered his mouth.

Sean heard the footsteps of a woman's heeled shoes on the paving behind him and looked round.

A woman wearing a grey pin-striped suit and heeled ankle boots was walking towards them. She'd obviously just finished messaging someone on her phone when Sean turned round and was holding it in her hand like she was expecting a response any second.

'Can I help?' she said, pushing back some hair off her face. 'You'll need to make an appointment if you want to view the house.'

'What happened to the children's home that was here?' Sean asked.

'Gosh. It closed down quite a while ago, I think.'

'Do you know who owns it now?'

The woman hesitated. 'You'll need to make an appointment – I'm sorry. Do you want me to ring—?' She motioned to her phone.

'No, that's all right.' Sean looked at the house.

'It's a lovely property, isn't it?' The woman smiled.

'I used to live there.'

'Oh, right.'

'You don't know what happened to the guy who owned it, do you?'

'I'm sorry, I don't. The house has changed hands a couple of times in the last few years. It was a solicitors before.'

Sean held Liam's hand as they walked back down the path. 'Who was that woman you were speaking to?' Liam asked.

'I don't know,' Sean replied, pushing open the gate and ushering Liam through it, then closing it behind them.

Seagulls squawked overhead. A salty breeze blew across the street. The sun shone through gaps in the buildings, and Sean felt its warmth on his face.

Holding Liam's hand, Sean remembered the last contract he and Terry had done for Mr Hayes. In a flash, he pictured himself back at his old flat looking at the phone number written on the receipt. He reckoned he could remember all the numbers at a push, but then he'd always had a good memory. He recalled the farmhouse and everyone stood around as the explosion went off. He wondered what had happened to the man in the room. He remembered the picture of the geese on the wall and the one in the orphanage that had reminded him of it, then the name on the sign, 'Greylags House'. The guy who'd owned the place must have had a thing about geese, Sean thought. Or maybe it was just one of those random things. For a moment, Sean wondered if the picture was still there and thought about going back to have a look through one of the windows. But he knew Liam wanted to get back to the car and wasn't sure if he was that bothered anyway. What was it going to settle? Life was always going to have its loose ends.

They turned up the slope towards where they'd left the car. Liam wanted to be carried, so Sean lifted him up onto his shoulders and held onto his legs. He wondered what he would cook for supper tonight, his mind back in the present again. He wasn't going into the restaurant today and liked to cook at home when he could.

Liam covered Sean's eyes for a moment and giggled.

'Help! I can't see,' Sean said, making Liam giggle all the more.

An elderly man, walking a dog on a lead, smiled as he passed them on the pavement, and Sean returned his smile with what felt like a shared understanding of things. For it was that sort of day when the sun shone and people smiled at strangers like the oldest of relations.

ABOUT THE AUTHOR

PHILIP BENTALL IS a British novelist and poet. He holds a master's degree in Applied Linguistics from King's College London. A Japanese speaker, he conducted research into the use of loanwords in Japanese before going on to become an academic tutor. He is the author of the novels *Stray Dog* and *Wild Flower* and the collection of poetry, *Where cows are met*. He lives in Sussex, South-East England.

Printed in Great Britain
by Amazon